A GIRL, A GHOST,
AND THE
HOLLYWOOD HILLS

D0171048

Lizabeth Zindel

VIKING
An Imprint of Penguin Group (USA) Inc.

VIKING
Published by Penguin Group
Penguin Group (USA) Inc., 345 Hudson Street, New York, New York 10014, U.S.A.
Penguin Group (Canada), 90 Eglinton Avenue East, Suite 700, Toronto, Ontario,
Canada M4P 2Y3 (a division of Pearson Penguin Canada Inc.)
Penguin Books Ltd, 80 Strand, London WC2R 0RL, England
Penguin Ireland, 25 St Stephen's Green, Dublin 2, Ireland (a division of Penguin Books Ltd)
Penguin Group (Australia), 250 Camberwell Road, Camberwell, Victoria 3124, Australia
(a division of Pearson Australia Group Pty Ltd)
Penguin Books India Pvt Ltd, 11 Community Centre, Panchsheel Park,
New Delhi – 110 017, India
Penguin Group (NZ), 67 Apollo Drive, Rosedale, North Shore 0632, New Zealand
(a division of Pearson New Zealand Ltd)
Penguin Books (South Africa) (Pty) Ltd, 24 Sturdee Avenue,
Rosebank, Johannesburg 2196, South Africa

Penguin Books Ltd, Registered Offices: 80 Strand, London WC2R 0RL, England

First published in 2010 by Viking, a member of Penguin Group (USA) Inc.

1 3 5 7 9 10 8 6 4 2

LIBRARY OF CONGRESS CATALOGING-IN-PUBLICATION DATA
Zindel, Lizabeth.
A girl, a ghost, and the Hollywood Hills / by Lizabeth Zindel.
p. cm.
Summary: When the ghost of Holly's mother claims she was murdered by Holly's
aunt, Claudia, Holly must decide how far she will go to get revenge.
ISBN 978-0-670-01159-9 (hardcover)
[1. Death—Fiction. 2. Grief—Fiction. 3. Mothers and daughters—Fiction.
4. Aunts—Fiction. 5. Los Angeles (Calif.)—Fiction.] I. Title.
PZ7.Z646Gg 2010
[Fic]—dc22
2009049291

Printed in U.S.A.
Set in Palatino
Book design by Sam Kim

A GIRL, A GHOST,
AND THE
HOLLYWOOD HILLS

For my mom, with all my heart

A GIRL, A GHOST,
AND THE
HOLLYWOOD HILLS

WINCHESTER HALL: RESIDENTIAL HOUSING CLOSES AT NOON

Tuesday, December 15

It was ridiculously early as I sat on the steps of Reed Hill waiting for the cab to take me to the airport. I was bundled up in my favorite red peacoat and warm hat with earflaps that looked like some nice grandma had knitted it. There was no one in sight as my eyes scanned from the Humanities Center to the Memorial House and other brick buildings surrounding Ashford Field. It felt like everyone had already taken off for winter break except for me.

I was probably the only kid from my eighth-grade class at L.A.'s prestigious Brentwood School who had headed to the East Coast for high school. Most of the kids had stayed at Brentwood or gone to Harvard-Westlake, Beverly Hills High, Berkeley, or Crossroads. But I grew up knowing that I'd be following a family tradition. If you believe in those things. My dad and his father had both gone to Winchester Hall, a boarding school in Connecticut, and practically as soon as I was born, it was decided that I would go there, too. My parents were hard-core into education, and my dad, especially, was convinced I would have the top-of-the-line classes at his alma mater. He went to Yale, after all. And I had dreams of going to Brown and studying playwriting.

Finally, I spotted the taxi I had called turning onto the long driveway that ran from North Main Street into campus. It was about time, since my fingers were about to freeze into little Popsicles. I jumped up and grabbed my suitcase and my overstuffed, purple suede pocketbook. Then I raced down the hill to wave the cab down.

The sun was just starting to rise as the driver got out and helped me put my suitcase into the trunk.

"Mercy, it's early," he said, lowering a baseball cap over his gray hair. "I got the chilly willies."

"I'm not a morning person, either," I said. We had that in common.

As I climbed into the backseat, my purple bag exploded, dumping my things onto the sidewalk. I always over-packed, and this was total punishment for not being one of those superorganized people who somehow manages to bring only what they need. I thoroughly believed in traveling with options, and that meant tossing in twenty extra T-shirts and five pairs of jeans.

I scampered around the gutter, grabbing a loose silver flip-flop, a tube of peach lotion, and my lavender journal. I had left all my notebooks from school behind for winter break except this one, because it was for my favorite class, playwriting. I was hoping to write down some dialogue while I was home.

As the taxi drove away, I turned around and looked out the back window at the bare trees on campus. When I was a freshman, I'd been so excited to experience the changing seasons. Even though I was a senior now and had been through three years of East Coast weather, I still thought it was cool to watch the leaves turn fiery orange in the fall and to crunch across campus when the ground was covered in icy snow. Back in L.A., most days looked the same: sunshine and roses.

The cab sped away from campus toward the freeway. We passed my favorite thrift store, which sold the best vintage jeans; an abandoned convent that was rumored to be haunted; and the Dairy Queen in town, where my friends and I would go for ice-cream breaks while we were studying our butts off. When I spotted the first sign for Bradley Airport, I grabbed my phone and dialed my best friend Felicia's cell. We had met in kindergarten when I went up to her and said, "Girl in the blue shirt, will you be my friend?" And we'd been the closest of friends ever since. I knew she'd be fast asleep at her house in Brentwood. It was 7:23 A.M. in Connecticut, which made it 4:23 A.M. in California, but she wouldn't mind if I woke her up. Felicia and I had a pact that allowed us to call each other at all hours of the day; we were like each other's twenty-four-hour emergency hotline.

"I'm coming back," I said as soon as she picked up.

"For real?" she said. Her voice sounded groggy. "Thank God. I wasn't sure if you were gonna bail. I mean, especially after what you pulled at Thanksgiving."

Felicia was referring to the fact that I hadn't come home last month for Turkey Day. My dad had called me only a few weeks before to drop the bomb that he was dating my aunt Claudia. (Yes, you read that right. It's disgusting, I know. And, mind you, just because Jane Austen, one of my favorite writers, had a younger brother who dated and eventually married his dead wife's sister, too, that doesn't mean it's okay!) Needless to say, I made a change of plans and spent the holiday with my roommate at Winchester Hall, Lulu, and her family in Hartford, a thirty-minute car ride away from Winchester's campus. Plus, all my college applications had been due at the end of November and I had to focus on finishing them over Thanksgiving weekend. I was applying to Brown, of course, and a few safety schools, just in case. After pulling a few late-nighters, I was lucky to mail them in on time. Thanks, Dad, for distracting me with your torrid love affair.

There were more signs for Bradley Airport outside my window. "I'm definitely flying home. I woke up this morning and realized there's only so long I can run," I told Felicia. "Can you pick me up at LAX at noon?"

"I'll be there with my ankle bells on," Felicia said. She loved wearing this ankle bracelet she bought in a Himalayan store; it sounded like chimes every time she moved.

"You're the best," I said.

"I can't wait to see you," said Felicia. "We have so much to catch up on and—"

"Yeah, but," I cut her off, "I can't believe Claudia's actually dating my dad and I have to deal with her. I don't know if I'm gonna survive winter break, let alone the rest of my life."

"You can make it through this," Felicia said. "I'm there for you and we'll figure out a way."

"I pray it's just a phase and he'll dump her soon."

"A phase like you wearing a tie every day of fifth grade?" Felicia asked.

"Something like that," I said.

Just then the cab entered the airport and pulled into the far right lane. I talked faster into the receiver. "I mean, now that my dad's locking lips with that psycho, I'm like an orphan or a wandering hobo."

"You're too old to be an orphan," Felicia said. "And too well-off to be a hobo."

The cab drove around a bend and then pulled over outside the American Airlines terminal. I opened the door and got out. As I watched the taxi driver get my suitcase out of the trunk, my chest tightened. "Oh, no, I'm here. I, uh . . . maybe I should turn around."

"*No!*" Felicia said. "What shoes are you wearing?"

I looked down at my feet. "Black boots with a furry trim. Why?"

"Put one furry boot in front of the other until you get on the plane," she said.

I handed a wad of cash to the driver, then grabbed my suede pocketbook and wheeled carry-on suitcase. "One furry boot in front of the other." I repeated the words like a mantra.

"You got it," Felicia said, coaching me on. "Now, hurry or you'll miss the flight."

I headed through the automatic doors into the terminal. "All right, boots are moving," I said.

"Yeah, baby! Keep trucking!" she cheered.

"Okay, I'm getting my boarding pass, then it's off to security," I said as I dashed over to an automatic check-in machine. "See ya on the other side."

"See ya there, girl!"

BACK TO L.A.

Ismiled when I saw Felicia pull up to the curb at LAX, aka Los Angeles International Airport. She waved excitedly from her baby-blue Volkswagen Beetle, which she had nicknamed Smurfette.

Once the car stopped, I threw my luggage in the back and swung open the passenger-side door. I jumped inside and gave Felicia a huge hug. "It's so good to see you!" I said.

"Oh my God. You too!" she said. "It sucks when we're not on the same coast. Even after three and a half years, I still can't get used to it."

"Trust me, I know. I've been craving some Felicia time!" I pulled back and looked at my friend's familiar dimpled smile, sparkling blue eyes, and long, wavy blonde hair. She was wearing a pair of huge plastic earrings that were shaped like cherries. And she pointed out her silver ankle bracelet.

"Just like I promised," she said.

"Shake it, baby!" I teased, and she moved her foot so the bells went *ring-a-ding-ding*.

"All I can say is Cali ain't the same without ya," Felicia said as she pulled into the airport traffic.

"West Coast!" I said, and held up three fingers in the shape of a sideways *W*.

"That's right, girl!" She gave me the signal back. I noticed her fingernails were painted light blue and perfectly matched the color of her car.

"So? How did things go with that surfer last night?" I asked, settling into my seat. Even when we were three thousand miles apart, Felicia and I were in constant texting contact.

"Our date sucked," Felicia said, and then swerved in front of a hotel courtesy van. "He slobbered all over my face. Oh, and his tongue was bitter and had a bumpy texture!"

"Sounds like the worst kiss ever," I said.

"Yeah! It was like kissing a Sour Patch Kid," she said, rolling her eyes. "So what's the deal with you? Any new hookups at school?"

I shook my head. "Still totally single." There had been so much going on lately with my family that it had been hard to throw myself into the romance scene. I mean, there were a few cuties I had flirted with, but nothing actually panned out.

As Felicia followed signs for the 405 freeway, we drove past palm trees and the occasional taco stand and car-rental lot. Above us, the sky was bright blue and cloudless. Then I spotted a 7-Eleven on the right-hand side. "Ooh, quick pit stop for Slurpees?" I asked.

"Let's do it! I'm craving a Blue Raspberry Rush," Felicia said, and pulled into the convenience store's parking lot.

Inside, we filled up large cups. Felicia did a mix of blue raspberry and green apple. I went with wild cherry and watermelon. Then we grabbed long, neon pink straws and walked toward the cashier. On the way, I grabbed a bag of SunChips from the far left aisle, which had a rack endlessly filled with magazines. I flipped through some tabloids like *National Enquirer*, the *Sun*, and *Globe*, and a few headlines caught my eye:

ANGELINA JOLIE HAS BIGFOOT'S BABY

EXORCISM CURES MONSTROUS ZIT!

ELVIS SEEN SURFING IN HAWAII!

After I finished checking out the contents, I let out a sigh of relief. Nothing about my mom. In July, *Globe* had run a story on her; she had passed away a month before. It was a small piece—just a quarter of a page in the back of the issue—but word got around and I had to pick up a copy. There on page seventy-three was a small picture of my mom with her sweet smile and the words:

Ghost of producer Kate Goldmeyer
spotted dancing in Vegas!

Frankly, I was surprised *Globe* had bothered to make up such lies about her. They were usually interested in only big-time celebrities. But, you see, my mom was the daughter of one of the classic studio heads from the golden age of Hollywood. We're talking the end of black and white, the beginning of the talkies, and the launch of stars like Judy Garland, Katharine Hepburn, and Joan Crawford. Her dad was a big deal in this town, and my mom, a movie producer, was a pretty big deal, too.

When I saw that article, it had bummed me out because I wished it were actually true. I prayed there really was a ghost of my mom—that I could see it, that I could talk to her just one more time. It's funny, because I bet a lot of people who have family members show up in tabloids get angry and protective about what's being said about their loved ones. But this issue of *Globe* had left me with an intense desire to believe in spirits, which isn't as crazy as it sounds. Seventy-five percent of people believe in some sort of paranormal experience. It's a fact; I heard it on CNN. I was having lunch at Winchester in the Pinewood dining room and they always have the television on. While I was eating a plate of orange-glazed chicken with Lulu, Wolf Blitzer was interviewing the spiritual guru Deepak Chopra, and Mr. Chopra said that there was a survey done in a university and that three quarters of the students questioned held at least some belief in astrology, telepathy, and/or ghosts.

The way I see it is like this: The universe is beyond our

comprehension. Astronomers are constantly discovering new stars and black holes every year. I mean, Pluto isn't even a planet anymore! Plus, it's been proven that there are sounds and colors that we can't hear or see. Who knows what is really possible?

"Let's roll," Felicia said as she yanked me away from the magazine rack.

"I'm coming!" I said.

We paid for our frosty beverages and my chips and hurried back to Smurfette, who was waiting for us in the parking lot.

After exiting the freeway, Felicia took La Cienega up to Sunset Boulevard and then headed north on Laurel Canyon into the Hollywood Hills. I stuck my head out the window like a dog and inhaled the smell of fresh-mowed grass and jasmine bushes. We drove past tons of homes decked out for Christmas. One front yard had a life-size cutout of Santa Claus in a sled being pulled by eight reindeer. I looked at Saint Nick's huge smile and his wooden arm waving at me. It was like he was saying, "Ho, ho, ho, Holly! Merry Christmas! Hope you survive the holidays! You can do it!"

Felicia must have sensed that my mind was elsewhere. "You all right?" she asked.

"Just a little nervous to be coming home," I said. Then I took a huge sip of my frozen drink and got brain freeze.

"That's only natural," Felicia said. "I'd be totally freaking out, too, if I were you."

"Thanks for the pep talk," I said, and rolled my eyes.

As we turned onto Elsinore Drive, we passed the guarded gate that controlled entrance onto the private road where I lived. A lot of old movie stars lived here (including an actor who played one of the first James Bonds), and they didn't want paparazzi, stalkers, or sightseeing tourists with star maps anywhere near their multimillion-dollar homes. The guard recognized Felicia and me and waved us past.

We drove down the hill toward my house, passing one mansion after the next. As we rolled over a speed bump, I felt a lump in my throat. I tried my best to make it go away by taking deep breaths, but then my eyes started to water, too, so I blinked them tightly to fight back tears. Felicia reached over to hold my hand, and I got a grip by the time we reached the bottom of the incline, where the street opened up into a fork. My family's estate was perched right in the middle of the split in the road. It was a sprawling white two-story home with black shutters. Everything looked the same on the outside as it had when I left for school in September: the English boxwood hedges, the red rosebushes, and the cool small tree with a thick branch that bent down to the ground so you could sit on it. But I knew that inside the house everything would feel completely different. In the past, my mom had always been there to greet me when I came home from school. Now she was gone—forever.

"All right, I'll give you space to deal with the fam," Felicia said. "Pick you up at eight tonight? Two college guys from the Groundlings are throwing a house party."

Felicia had been acting since the fourth grade—she'd been in some commercials and she even got cast in a pilot for a sitcom once, but it was never picked up. Just recently she'd started studying sketch comedy after school with the Groundlings, a well-known acting program in L.A. where lots of people who would become cast members from *Saturday Night Live*, like Will Ferrell, Jimmy Fallon, and Maya Rudolph, had studied.

"Cool!" I said. "Where's the party at?"

"A house near the In-N-Out in Westwood," Felicia said.

"Sign me up. As long as I survive this," I said, nodding at my family's house.

"You're gonna do great," said Felicia. "It might be tense with your dad at first, but you'll work things out. And at least Claudia's only his girlfriend. There could be something permanent on her finger. Like a rock."

"If he ever married her . . ." I said, and shook my head. "Hopefully, he'll get zapped to his senses and dump her soon."

Just then the stained-glass front door to the estate swung open. I turned and saw Anna Maria, our housekeeper, hurrying out of the doorway dressed in light jeans, a black T-shirt, and sneakers. Our dog, a huge black Great Dane named Sampson, ran after her.

"I'll call you later," I told Felicia, and got out of the car, grabbing my suitcase and bag. "Thanks for the ride. You're the best!"

"Right back at you!" Felicia yelled as she drove away.

Anna Maria smiled as she and Sampson ran down the entranceway's steps, which were lined with Bishop's Castle roses and Augusta Beauty gardenia bushes. My mom had taught me the names of the flowers that grew on our property, and I was proud of my ability to identify all of them. But thinking of her made my chest hurt a little. I still couldn't believe she was gone.

"It's so good to see you," Anna Maria said in her Puerto Rican accent as she gave me a hug. She was short and a little heavy, and had a warm, kind face.

"You too!" I said as Sampson ran around me in circles, stopping to lick my hand.

"Finally, you come home," Anna Maria said.

"It doesn't really feel like home, without Mom," I said as Sampson jumped up on two legs and threw his front paws on me. He was the size of a small pony.

"Get down," Anna Maria said, patting Sampson firmly on the side.

Sampson obeyed and jumped off me. "Ah, he just wanted a hug, too," I said.

"Let me see you," Anna Maria said. She studied my eyes, looking deep into the pupils. "You look skinny and . . . your insides don't seem so good."

I shuffled my feet on the gravel driveway. She was right. Anna Maria had known me since I was a baby. Over the years, I had sometimes gone to her for advice about boys and friends. I'd usually gone to my mom first, but if she was feeling depressed or looked unhappy and preoccupied, I'd turned to Anna Maria.

"We talk more later," Anna Maria said, squeezing my arm. "Your dad's waiting to have lunch with you."

I looked at the clock on my cell phone. It was 12:25 P.M. Ordinarily my father would be at his office in the middle of the day, but I had sent him an e-mail telling him I was coming. My dad was a successful entertainment lawyer; his firm was located in Century City's MGM building. Growing up, it had felt like he lived at the office. He often didn't get back to the house until after I was in bed.

"He came home special for you," Anna Maria said.

"That's a first." And it would be a *special* visit—as in, *especially* weird.

"And Claudia's here, too," Anna Maria said. I could tell by her guarded tone that she hated dropping this news on me.

"Oh, fantastic! Can't wait!" I said, and plastered a big fake smile on my face.

Anna Maria reached out to help me with my suitcase. "Let me," she said.

"Thanks, I got it," I said, pulling back the handle. I didn't want her waiting on me like I was a spoiled kid. I successfully yanked my bag out of her grasp.

"*¡No seas testaruda!*" Anna Maria said. I wasn't 100 percent sure of the translation, but I guessed it meant something like, "Young lady, you are way too stubborn!"

As we walked into the house, I thought I heard voices

coming from the upstairs landing. Any minute now I would see my dad. I'd have to talk to him for the first time since he had phoned the week before Thanksgiving to tell me that his relationship with my aunt Claudia had "evolved." Since then he'd left messages, but I hadn't called back. And he'd sent e-mails, but I'd deleted most before reading them.

"I never predicted this would happen," my dad had said. "Both Claudia and I have been going through a hard time since your mother died. It started out as friendship, but we've been lonely. . . ."

Lonely? Ahem. *Or did you mean horny?* It was a big joke. And I bet everyone in this city was laughing at them. Except me. I didn't find this funny at all.

I dropped my luggage in the foyer, and Anna Maria and I walked toward the dining room. As we made our way down the hallway, I noticed a bunch of framed posters of flicks that Claudia had produced hung on the wall with crazy titles like *Gone with the Witches* and *Vampire Kings of England*. She was a movie producer, too, like my mom—but way different. My aunt liked to fancy herself the queen of cult horror films, but my mom and I had thought otherwise. The only thing regal about Claudia's flicks was that they were royally tacky. "I can't believe Claudia hung these up here," I said.

"She makes me dust them," said Anna Maria.

"What nerve. They belong in her house in Culver City," I said, looking around. "She still has her own place, right?"

"I think so," she said. "But she has been spending a lot of time here lately."

As we walked along the corridor, I noticed some of Claudia's horror-movie props mixed in with the antique decor my mom had so carefully purchased and arranged. There was a five-foot-tall statue of a zombie girl in hot pants, and a bunny head with antlers and bloody teeth suspended from the wall.

I had grown up hearing my aunt brag about her prized acquisitions, and the times I went with my mom to visit Claudia's place in Culver City she would show them off. My mom had done her best to spare me from hanging out with her nut-ball sister, but sometimes it couldn't be avoided.

As I looked around my family's living room, I also noticed something bizarre on the side table. It was a jar filled with formaldehyde and what looked like a fake alien baby floating inside it.

"What is that?" I asked.

"Not sure," Anna Maria explained. "Very strange creature." Did Anna Maria mean that the fake alien baby was a strange creature or did she mean Aunt Claudia? I couldn't tell, but it would have been a fair way to describe either of them.

"Apparently, she's been making herself quite comfortable here!" I said.

A few moments later, we arrived in the dining room.

"I'll make sure your father knows you're back," Anna Maria said.

"No need, no need. I heard the car pull up," my dad said as he walked into the room. He smiled warmly at me, oozing his usual charm and confidence. "There you are. It's so great to see you, honey," he said. Clearly, he was going to pretend that everything was normal between us.

"I'll get the food," Anna Maria said, conveniently ducking out of the room and into the kitchen.

"Give me a hug," my dad said. Then he hurried over and threw his arms around me. I went through the motions, but the embrace felt empty and cold, like my dad and I were players who were no longer on the same team.

"It's so wonderful to have you back. I've been looking forward to this all week," my dad said.

I have to say my dad looked really weird, like all put together and chiseled. His hair was cut shorter and his body looked buff like a lifeguard's. Well, like a fortyish lifeguard going through a midlife crisis.

"Dad, have you been pumping iron?" I asked, raising my eyebrows.

"Four times a week," he said proudly. Then he squeezed my arm. "This is going to be great. We'll have some real quality time together to catch up."

I shouldn't have been surprised that my dad was acting like everything was all right. He was an expert at grinning his way through difficult situations. This was so my typical dad.

He had been just like that after my mom died. He'd simply thrown himself back into his usual routine, like, a week after her funeral, and expected me to do the same.

"Dad, why are all those horror props in our house?" I asked.

"Oh, I'm just letting Claudia store a few things here," he said, his tone super casual. "She keeps most of the collection at her place."

"How 'bout keeping *all* of it there?" I asked.

But before he could answer, Claudia came into the room waving one hand in front of her face. My stomach got queasy as soon as I saw her statuesque body gliding toward me in snakeskin stilettos and a short black dress. Claudia's eyes were drowned in mascara and her over-plucked eyebrows looked like thin little worms. She had plump, collagen-filled lips and a pointy chin that you could balance a raisin on. And there was something about her cheeks that made them look like they had been yanked back too tight in a facelift.

"I'm terribly embarrassed to see you like this. I got a beard facial and it irritated my pores," Claudia said, flipping her hair, which was filled with gorgeous blonde highlights.

"A *what* facial?" I asked.

"It's the trend from Prague," she said. "A male beautician rubs his beard all over your face. It's great exfoliation."

"Whatever floats your boat," I said.

"You don't need to do all that stuff to look young," my father said, rubbing the back of Claudia's shoulders.

"Oh, that feels good, Gardner," Claudia said, smiling over her shoulder at my dad.

I turned away quickly. Seeing them standing side by side was hard enough; I couldn't bear to watch them touch.

"The treatment's supposed to flatten wrinkles," Claudia said. "But blah, blah, blah, you don't have to deal with this nonsense, Holly. You have such perfect skin." She gave me a peck on the cheek. I could smell her staple scent, an overpowering aroma of musk and cloves. She was like a bad sachet that you'd never want to stuff in your drawer.

"Shall we?" my aunt said, and gestured toward the dining table.

I looked over at the long antique farmhouse dining table. My mom had gotten it at an auction when I was in junior high. It had been one of her favorite pieces in the house. Now it was immaculately set for three with our expensive, hand-painted Italian plates. These were the same dishes we had been eating off of since I was a child. Claudia sat down in the seat traditionally saved for my mom. It made me want to pull the chair out from under her. But instead, I sat down, too, and balled up my linen napkin in my fist.

I noticed my dad look at Claudia and then back at me, biting his lip. I bet he was anxious to see how this would play out—all three of us together for the first time in this new dynamic, the latest example of a modern blended American family.

"It's your first meal back and I wanted to make it delicious," Claudia said, smiling at me sweetly.

"Uh, thanks," I mumbled.

"Anna Maria cooked up the salads and Patty picked up red-velvet cupcakes at Sprinkles," she said.

"Who's Patty?" I asked.

"My personal assistant," Claudia said, putting a single shrimp on her plate.

"You have a personal assistant now?"

"All CEOs need personal assistants. It comes with the territory," my dad said.

I gave my dad a stern look. "So it's official now?" I asked him.

"Holly, I e-mailed you all about it. This shouldn't be a surprise," he said, serving himself a plate of curried chicken with diced apples and raisins. This news must have been in one of the messages he had sent that I'd never read.

My mom had been the head of Goldmeyer Productions. She had inherited the company from my grandfather, who had willed it to her when he died. The legend goes that my mom was always his favorite daughter, while Claudia was their mother's favorite child.

When my mother passed away, my dad became executor of her estate and now it seemed like he'd made the stupid decision to pass the torch to my aunt. We had e-mailed back and forth about it when I was away at school in October—before I found out he was Claudia's boy toy and didn't want to talk to him anymore. He wrote: *I'm thinking of giving Claudia the reins of the production company. She wants it a lot.*

I wrote back: *That's a terrible idea. Like, the worst one ever.*

He responded: *It's practical for now. When you graduate from college one day, we can reassess the changes. Even put you in charge—if you want that responsibility.*

The truth was I didn't know if I ever wanted that responsibility. I didn't want to be a producer. I wanted to be a playwright.

"Claudia works out of the office in Burbank most days, but I offered her the home office upstairs in case she needs it, too," my dad said.

I was taking a sip from my water glass when he said that, and I totally snorted and liquid sprayed out of my mouth. "Here?!" I said, almost choking. "You mean Mom's old office?"

Claudia smiled and nodded, like, wasn't this the best news I'd ever heard? I can assure you, it was not.

"There was a lot of old paperwork in there that Claudia needed access to," my dad said. His tone was matter-of-fact, as if this made complete sense.

"So, you might see me bopping in and out," Claudia said. "And you'll really love Patty. I met her at Ralphs supermarket this past summer. She's a bit of a kook, but the price is right."

"Did you interview her by the watermelons?" I asked.

"No, the artichokes," Claudia answered. Her tone sounded serious.

Who finds their future employees in the aisles of a super-market? But then I remembered this was L.A. and that's how things worked. My mom had told me that since practically everyone in this town was in the entertainment industry, people networked wherever they could—lounging in Jacuzzis, surfing in Malibu, on treadmills at the gym, and even while stuck in traffic on the 405. Thinking of my mom again made me catch my breath. I was still kind of expecting her to come out of the kitchen, alive and well, as if her whole death had been a bad dream.

"Patty's a very nice lady," my dad said. "And she has a son at UCLA. He's about your age, I think." My dad raised his eyebrow at me as if he was trying to play matchmaker.

My aunt took a sip from her water glass and made a face. "Anna Maria!" she called out.

Anna Maria hurried back into the room and stopped in the doorway. "Is everything okay?"

"This *agua* is tasting *mucho* funky. Change the filter." Claudia grimaced as she licked her lips.

"So sorry. I will change it now." Anna Maria collected Claudia's water glass from the table.

"Also, bring in a bottle of Bordeaux. The Château Léoville," Claudia said.

As Anna Maria left the room, she and I exchanged glances. I couldn't get over how arrogantly Claudia talked to her, treating her like a servant. We had always embraced Anna Maria as one of the family.

"What a piece of work," Claudia said to my dad and me. "And I hate those shrines in the maid's room."

"She and my mom got along great," I said.

"Oh, your mom was nice to everyone," Claudia said, like it was a bad thing. "I'm scared Anna Maria's gonna do a voodoo curse and make our house slide down the hill. I love making horror films, but I don't want to star in one."

"It's her religion. And it's called Santeria," I said.

"Well, as long as she doesn't sacrifice a goat in her bedroom."

"She would never do that!" I said. "That's a complete stereotype! Not all people who practice Santeria sacrifice animals!"

My dad reached out and touched my arm. "Sweetie, relax. It's okay. We all love Anna Maria," he said.

"Yes! Of course, I love her. She's the best," Claudia said.

Could my aunt be any more hypocritical? And confusing! I breathed in deeply and dug my nails into my thigh.

Just then a woman appeared in the hallway. She looked to be in her mid-forties, with brassy, kinky hair to her shoulders. She wore black-rimmed eyeglasses attached to a green-and-white beaded chain. "'Scuse me. I don't mean to barge in," she said.

"We were just talking about you," Claudia said. "Holly, this is Patty."

"Oh, great to meet you! A thousand welcomes back home," Patty said, waving hello with both hands.

"Thanks, good to meet you, too," I said.

"As they say, home is where you hang your ten-gallon hat. Oh, and what's that other one?" Patty looked up at the ceiling as if searching the top of her brain. "Oh, yes. Good homes are still the best source of good humans!"

"Patty, did you pick up my bananas and Armani suit yet?" Claudia asked in an impatient tone.

"I had to leave my car in the shop this morning to get the battery changed so I took a cab here, but it's ready now and Oliver offered to drive me down the hill to pick it up right now. I'll be back in forty-five with the bananas and your suit."

Just then I noticed a really cute guy walk through the doorway. He looked to be about my age and had chin-length brown hair that was tucked behind his ears. He had on beat-up jeans and a worn-in light blue T-shirt. Around his neck was a small white seashell hanging off a thin piece of leather. I sat up straighter in my chair and tucked a strand of my long, light brown bangs behind one ear.

"Oliver, come on in and meet my daughter. She's fresh off the plane," my dad said, like I was a hot loaf of bread.

"Hey, what's up?" Oliver said to me as he walked into the room.

"Hi," I said, glancing at his bright blue eyes.

"Ollie's a marine-biology major at UCLA," Patty said, and then threw her arm over his shoulder. Oliver moved around awkwardly in his mother's grasp. "You better watch out, Jacques Cousteau. We're gonna have a new man taking care of the fishes!"

"Okay, that's enough, Mom," Oliver said, ducking out from under Patty's arm.

As Claudia dealt out orders to Patty—phone calls to make, lunches to set up—I stole glances at Oliver. He was seriously adorable. I liked how his hair was a little messy in the front. Plus his clothes looked worn in and soft, like you could curl up next to him and be completely comfortable.

But then quickly I pulled myself back. I couldn't forget, Oliver was the son of Claudia's assistant. And that meant I had to be careful. Who knew where his loyalties lay? Maybe he actually liked Claudia. Although, I found that hard to believe. Who, other than my crazy father, actually *liked* Claudia?

Patty turned to me. "So what do you have on tap for your first night back?" Her tone sounded super friendly, like she was already my good pal.

I glanced over at Oliver and then answered, "My best friend invited me to a house party in Westwood."

"A party?" my dad said, his eyes lighting up. "That's great. I'm happy you're going out on the town." Maybe he felt like me going out with my friends again meant things were back to normal, that I wasn't sad about my mom anymore—wrong—or that I wasn't upset about him dating Aunt Claudia—double wrong.

"Yeah, okay, thanks, Dad."

"Well, paint the town red," Patty said. "We're off like a herd of turtles!"

As Anna Maria came into the room with an open bottle

of wine and two glasses, Patty turned around and walked toward the door. Oliver followed behind his mother, but on the way out of the room, he looked back one last time. He smiled at me as he turned the corner out of view. And let me tell you, he had the best dimples that I'd ever seen.

HEART-TO-HEART

After lunch, my dad went back to his law firm in Century City. Claudia stayed behind and announced that she was going to work out of the home office today. So I headed upstairs to my bedroom to get far away from her.

My room looked the same, but it felt different—empty, somehow. Usually when I came home from Winchester, my mom would put a fresh bouquet of flowers from the garden on my dresser. But, of course, the dresser was empty now except for the silver-plated hairbrush and mirror I got for my tenth birthday and never used. There was my four-poster bed with a zillion pillows, a bookshelf filled with scented candles that smelled like vanilla and pomegranate, and a large, pale pink shag rug. And hanging above my bed was the framed black-and-white poster from *Breakfast at Tiffany's* of Audrey Hepburn in glamorous sunglasses. (My mom named me after

Audrey Hepburn's character in that movie, Holly Golightly, and she got me the framed picture as a birthday present when I turned twelve.)

Then there was the collage by my desk filled with pictures of my friends and family. I smiled at shots of Felicia and me stuffing our faces with chocolate-chip cookie dough. There were also photos of us with some of our other close friends from junior high dressed up as gang of girl pirates for Halloween.

One other picture caught my eye. It was of my mom and me during spring break last year, my junior year of high school. My mom was super pretty, a Cleopatra type with black hair to her shoulders that she often wore the same way—parted in the middle with one side pulled half up in a tortoiseshell barrette. Her nails were always painted ruby red, and she had loved wearing long skirts and pretty scarves in beautiful colors like aquamarine and dusty rose. In this picture—I think it is the last one taken of us together—my mom and I are hanging out in the Chinese garden in our backyard. I had held up the camera and snapped the picture with one hand as we walked in front of the gazebo. On a clear night, it was a great place to sit and watch the reflection of moonlight on the koi pond.

My mom had loved our Chinese garden, because my dad had proposed to her in a much bigger one located at the Huntington Botanical Gardens, just outside L.A. She always liked to go to our little garden to escape the distractions of the world, quietly read a book, and be introspective. The thought of going back out there now without her made my heart hurt.

Just then I was startled from my thoughts by a loud knock on my bedroom door.

"Can I come in?" I heard Claudia say. Without waiting for an answer, she pushed the door open. "This is for you," she said, holding out a red shopping bag.

"Thanks, but I don't need presents," I said.

"Everyone likes presents!" Claudia said, and strutted into the room in her snakeskin stilettos. I backed out of her way and leaned up against my desk. "When Elizabeth Taylor was a big star, she demanded two surprise gifts left in her movie trailer every morning. It was in her contracts."

"Is that even true?" I asked, looking at the gift bag. *Is she trying to bribe me into liking her? That's the oldest trick in the book.*

My aunt sat down on my bedspread, which was covered in a print of blue and white daisies, and her BlackBerry slipped out of her pocket. Then she looked up and smiled at me. "Listen, Holly, it's not a secret that your mom and I didn't always get along."

I nodded my head. She and my mom had always bickered. But my dad never took their tense relationship seriously. When my mom would complain to him about her sister, he'd say, "When are you two going to grow out of this rivalry?" And "I can't wrap my head around the petty things you two women argue about!" Or "Don't put me in the middle of your fights! I know underneath it all, you both love each other." I guess he thought he was an expert on the topic. See, my dad fought all the time with his older brother, who lived in Chicago, but he had still asked him to be the best man on his wedding day. To him, siblings just argued sometimes and it was no big deal. They still loved each other underneath. But I had known there was something darker between my mom and my aunt, something real under their seemingly silly arguments.

Claudia tapped her foot while sitting on my bed. "And I know you and I have never been very close."

That was an understatement. Claudia would drop by the house sometimes for a swim in our pool and we'd see her for the holidays, but I never felt connected to her. She never made an effort to do things with me on her own, like take me to the movies or shopping, the way Felicia's aunt sometimes did. I guess I had always felt that if my mom had a problem with Aunt Claudia, then I had a problem with her, too.

"But there's something you may not know about me," Claudia said. "The reason I've never had children of my own isn't because I didn't want them."

"Oh, yeah?" I asked.

"Even though I've never been married, I'm sure you remember the man I lived with in Canada. . . ." She played with the stack of gold and diamond bracelets on her left wrist.

"The special-effects guy?" I had a faint memory of Claudia running off to Montreal with some cheese dick with a bushy mustache who had chest hair so long you could French-braid it.

"Yes, Glenn. He and I tried to have a baby, but it just didn't work out. First I thought it was him, but then I had tests done and found out I was infertile. Whenever I saw you and your mother together, you always seemed so close. . . . And I knew that was something I could never have on my own."

"You could've adopted," I said.

"I suppose you're right. But maybe it was for the best that I didn't. I'm not sure I would've made the greatest mother." Claudia looked at me with big eyes that seemed to hope I'd refute this last point.

"You know your own limitations," I said.

My aunt's voice grew defensive. "Well, I certainly didn't learn from the warmest role model. Your poor grandmother was never the same after your mother was born."

"I don't want to hear about it," I said. I remembered my mom telling me stories about how her mother had had bipolar disorder—or manic depression, which is what they called it back in those days—but after she gave birth to my mom, she suffered from postpartum depression, and she never quite recovered. Claudia, older by four years, spent a lot of time caring for my mom, and I guess she always blamed my mother for being born.

When I was little, sometimes my mom would show me an old family album. I remember this faded picture of my grandma. She's wearing a long dress with a lace collar and floral print. And she has a round, pale face with huge eyes and her brown hair pulled back in a messy bun with loose strands falling down onto her face. I had thought she looked sad in the photo, but maybe that's just because I knew she was sad. I never got to know her myself because she died before I was born.

"The main thing I want to say," Claudia went on, "is I know you're going through a lot and I want to be here for you. As a mother figure." She smiled, flashing her bleached teeth.

What I thought was: *A mother figure! Are you serious?*

But what I said was: "Really?" And I put one hand on my hip. I couldn't believe the nerve. Had all the Botox injections gone to her brain? She couldn't waltz right in here and try and be my buddy. Not when she was sleeping with my dad.

"Yes, I think that would be nice!" Claudia said. Suddenly, her BlackBerry vibrated on the bed. She picked it up and checked the screen. "He can wait," she said, and clicked the side button.

"Please lean on me if you ever need anything," said Claudia. "And I think once you give me a chance, we're going to get along great. Now, take the gift already. What would Elizabeth Taylor do?"

I realized the sooner I grabbed the present, the quicker Claudia would get out of my room. I walked over and took the shopping bag. After throwing aside the tissue paper, I pulled out a dress that looked like a zebra's skin dipped in buffalo-wing sauce.

"Don't you adore it?" she asked.

"As of now, there's zero animal print in my closet," I said, and bit my lip.

"Trust me, I know." Claudia gazed at my worn-in purple suede bag. "The thrift-store look is cute for a while, but I thought you'd enjoy some adult clothes. That dress is an Emilio Pucci," she said, name-dropping a designer.

"I'm not into wearing labels."

"And I'm not into wearing someone else's pants," Claudia said, poking fun at my love of vintage clothes. "But you're such a pretty girl and I thought you could wear this to the Christmas Spectacular!"

"What? Oh, right." The memory popped into my mind like a horrible flashback. My father had e-mailed me about it before Thanksgiving—before he dropped the bomb about his new relationship—but I had successfully blocked it out of my head. "My dad mentioned you're planning a little shindig at our house."

"There's nothing *little* about it," said Claudia. "It's my coming-out party. If debutantes and gays do it, why can't I?"

"I don't really think gays throw a party when they come out," I said, and rolled my eyes.

"What I'm saying is I'm taking the company in a new direction. It's no secret your mom's movies weren't exactly *blockbusters*."

"They were art films," I said. My mom had spent her career producing quirky romantic comedies about neurotic intellectuals and biopics about famous artists like Gustav Klimt and Claude Monet. Sure, the movies had never made a whole lot of money, but they were meaningful. More meaningful than any of Aunt Claudia's zombie films.

"I plan on making bigger-budget, cult horror movies now. My fans haven't seen anything yet." Just then her BlackBerry vibrated again. Claudia grabbed it and read the screen. "Shit. I'm late for a call with a director."

"Yeah, better get on that," I said, hoping she would leave ASAP. I could only imagine what kind of sick auteur she had waiting in the wings. "I mean, you don't want to keep him waiting any longer."

"That's the truth. Tomoko Ishikawa is a brilliant Japanese director—I'm sure you've heard of him, everyone has—and we're going to collaborate on my next film, *Dead Bachelorette: The Musical*. Don't tell anyone the idea. This project is still completely top secret. It's gonna be like *The Rocky Horror Picture Show* meets *Night of the Living Dead*."

"Your secret's safe with me," I said. I wondered what my mom would think of Claudia using the studio my grandfather had worked so hard to build to make movies like this. I bet she wouldn't be too amused, and neither was I.

"This was fun hanging out," Claudia said, and jumped up from the bed. "Oh, and if you need anything, I'll be across the hall in your mom's old office till five tonight."

"Awesome! I'll come knocking if I need you." Which

translated to *never*. And I still couldn't believe she had the nerve to take over my mom's old home office. It was like she couldn't wait to stomp right in and snatch up everything she could lay her hands on.

"Ciao for now," Claudia said, blowing me a kiss good-bye.

"See ya," I said as she scampered out of the room.

SANTERIA

Later, after I had unpacked, I went downstairs and found Anna Maria in the laundry room folding clean clothes. She was the only person under this roof who still seemed to be in her right mind. In fact, if I created a pyramid right now charting the sanity of the other beings in this house (discounting me) from the most sane to the least, it would look like this:

Anna Maria

Sampson

My father

Aunt Claudia

I had grabbed a packet of Twizzlers from the pantry while I was on my way to the laundry room—I realized I had been too freaked out at lunch to eat, so now I was starving—and I held them in one hand as I jumped up and sat on top of the washing machine.

"It's like in mythology. My mom was Athena, full of love and wisdom, and Claudia's a Valkyrie."

"What's this Valkyrie?" Anna Maria asked.

I yanked out a Twizzler and bit the end of it. "They were these gorgeous maidens that were really spirits of slaughter." I remembered the image of one in a mythology book that my mom had read to me as I was growing up. There was an illustration of this Valkyrie wearing armor while riding a wolf. She had ravenlike wings, and her mouth was open wide, like she was shrieking into battle.

"They are scary, no?" Anna Maria asked.

"Extremely! I mean, if my dad needs to be with someone, why does it have to be my aunt? Any other relatives he wants to date? My cousins Rhylee and Ginger are cute. Oh, wait, they're barely twenty-one." I downed the rest of the piece of licorice.

"I understand. You don't like her much," Anna Maria said as she folded together a pair of my dad's argyle socks.

"I hate her," I said as I finished chewing. "Every time I hear the name *Claudia*, I want to cringe. It's like the C stands for . . . crass, cougar, crack face."

"You shouldn't say those things," Anna Maria said in a shocked tone. Then her voice softened. "But it's true. She isn't very nice."

"No, she isn't. And I miss my mom. I don't like it here without her." It had been hard when my mom was sad when I was growing up, when she was having one of her bouts of depression. I would come home from school and she'd still be in bed. But at least she had been there, in the house. Now she'd never be there again.

Anna Maria looked at me warmly. "I remember when your mom brought you home from the hospital. She was so happy. She told me that she always knew it was a girl because while she was pregnant, she felt the baby sucking in all her oils and beauty. Part of her is always here in you."

"I hope so." I smiled.

I watched Anna Maria fold one of my dad's undershirts, and my mind got rolling on a question I had wanted to ask her ever since I had gone back to school in September. You see, growing up, I was exposed to two religions. My mom was Jewish and my dad was Christian, and we celebrated all the Christian and Jewish holidays—Christmas, Hanukkah, Easter, Rosh Hashanah, you get the picture. But since I was a little girl, there had always been something about other, lesser known religions that intrigued me. I had fun playing with tarot cards and I'd always tried to read my friends' fortunes at sleepovers. But when I lost my mom, I started getting even more intrigued by mysteries of the unknown. And although I didn't know a ton about Santeria, the Afro-Caribbean religion Anna Maria practiced, I liked how it seemed tied into nature. Maybe there was even a way to use

Santeria to communicate with the dead. I know that sounds crazy, but when it came to my mother, I was open to anything that might reconnect me with her in some way.

I cleared my throat. "Is there a chance we could maybe do a ritual together in honor of my mom?" I said, my voice cracking a little.

"You know this isn't done," said Anna Maria. "It's important to protect the secrets of Santeria."

"I know, but I hoped . . ." I looked down at the yellow tiled floor. Anna Maria had told me many times before that people who believed in Santeria tried to keep the rituals very hush-hush. When I was growing up, she had divulged a few details (like that she wore a necklace of blue beads because it protected her from the evil eye, and sometimes left pineapples and muffins in her room as offerings to her patron saints), but she always said she could never do a ritual in front of me. Still, I was really praying she might make an exception for me today.

"Please, Anna Maria, I just feel so lost without my mom, and now that all this stuff is going on with my dad and Claudia . . ." I stared at the Twizzlers in my hand, but I didn't really feel like eating anymore.

Anna Maria must've taken pity on me, because she changed her tone. "Well, since I was close to your mother, too, I will do it this once."

"You will? What are we gonna do? Can we do it now?" I hopped down off the washing machine and jumped up and down.

Anna Maria stopped folding my dad's clothes. "Okay, come," she said, and waved for me to follow her.

I hurried after her toward the maid's room. Anna Maria slept there Monday through Friday. On the weekends she went to her own apartment, in El Segundo.

Her bedroom here was filled with a ton of plants and she had taught me the names of them over the years. There were braided ficus trees, dracaena, African violets, palms, philodendrons, ivy, and ferns. In fact, it was hard to reach the windows that lined one side of the room because you had to lean past so many pots of leaves.

I watched Anna Maria push aside a cascade of hanging ivy and pull back the curtains. "The *eggun* can only be contacted after sunset," she said as she peeked out the window.

"The *eggun*?" I asked, wrinkling my forehead.

"Spirits of the dead," Anna Maria said. Then she gestured to the little rug at the foot of her bed. "Okay, it's dark out. Go sit down."

I hurried and sat on the rug. Anna Maria grabbed a pen and paper from her nightstand and stuck them into her jeans pocket. Then she walked over to the altar she kept on the top of her dresser. This was my favorite part of her room—the *bóveda*, the magical altar where she kept herbs and offerings for the different spirits that she believed in. From left to right there were:

An incense burner
A vase with white daisies

A large bowl filled with water
A plate of fuzzy-looking rocks
A small plastic toy car
A pair of three-foot-tall statues made of plaster

One of the statues was beautiful. Anna Maria had told me about it when I was little. It depicted Yemaya, a pretty, dark-skinned female deity. She wore a flowing white dress, and it looked like seashells were falling from her palms into the sea.

The other statue had always freaked me out. Anna Maria had told me it was of Saint Lazarus; the statue showed him leaning on crutches while two dogs licked at his leprosy sores. It was seriously gross but Anna Maria had taught me it was meaningful because Saint Lazarus was a symbol of healing.

I watched as Anna Maria carefully took the big bowl filled with water from her dresser and walked over to me. Then she sat down on the floor and placed it between us.

"What's that for?" I asked.

"It's good to contact spirits this way. We have control because the water has strengths that the spirits don't. Now, let me see . . ." She took the paper and pen from her pocket. She focused on the basin of clear liquid and then without looking at her hand she began sketching on a piece of paper.

I wanted to know what Anna Maria was doing, but I decided it was best not to interrupt the energy, so I stayed quiet as her hand moved along the page. I tried to see what she saw in water, but all I made out were dust particles and a floating short black hair—I figured it was Sampson's.

Finally, after a few minutes, Anna Maria picked up the paper to look at what she'd drawn. I saw wild, messy strokes of ink, but she seemed to see more.

"Hmm," she said, and then shook her head.

I scrunched up my eyebrows. "Is everything okay?"

She turned the page around, reviewing it from a different angle. "Interesting . . . uh-huh."

"Please tell me," I said, rubbing my hands back and forth on the front of my jeans.

"You see there?" Anna Maria said, pointing to the drawing. "The Latino man in the bowler hat and black tuxedo? He's wearing dark glasses."

I tried with all my might, but I couldn't make out what Anna Maria was describing. It just looked like scribbles to me. "Who is that?" I asked.

"El Señor del Cementerio," she said. "The spirit that stands at the crossroads where human dead pass into spirit world."

"That doesn't sound good," I said, biting my lip. "Is that bad?"

"He's a wise judge and powerful magician. El Señor reminds us that death and life are beyond comprehension."

"Yeah, but what does this mean about my mom?" I asked.

"Usually he is good and protects cemeteries, but if he comes here"—she nodded toward the bowl—"it's not so good."

"Why?" I asked, and then held my breath as I waited for her answer.

"A spirit may not be at rest." Anna Maria played with the plastic tip of her sneaker's shoestring.

"Like my mom's spirit?" I asked.

Anna Maria nodded. "Maybe yes, maybe no."

"So because this Señor de Cemitar . . ." I said.

"Cementerio," Anna Maria said, correcting me.

"Because he showed up in that bowl of water, that means my mom's soul might not be at peace?"

"It is just what the water told me," she said. "But this is not your religion. You don't need to believe this."

"I know, but I can't help but worry. I mean . . ." I fidgeted with the seam of my jeans and then twisted the Twizzler packet. My hands just couldn't seem to stay still.

"You're getting upset. See, this is why I don't like to do this. It's not part of your beliefs. You don't need to worry. I'm sorry."

"It's not your fault," I said. "I just wish you could've seen something nicer. Like the pretty spirit with the seashells dripping from her hands." I glanced up at the beautiful statue of the Yemaya on the *bóveda*.

"I'd never lie to you," said Anna Maria. "I've always been honest since you were a little girl. Maybe I saw wrong."

I had thought doing this ritual with Anna Maria would make me feel better, but instead I only felt worse. "I really hope so," I said.

HOUSE PARTY

Felicia picked me up at nine that night and we drove down Laurel Canyon into Westwood Village, UCLA's college town. She was blasting Abba on Smurfette's speaker system and dancing around in her seat. As we drove, I tried to push Anna Maria's ritual out of my mind by filling Felicia in on the latest with Claudia.

"You have to check out the weird props she brought over!" I said. "There's a bunny head with red eyes and this jar filled with formaldehyde and a fake Martian baby."

"How bizarro!" Felicia said.

"Tell me about it. If my aunt has any more plastic surgery, she's gonna look like the alien's mother."

"Ooh, maybe she gave birth to it when it burst out of her chest," said Felicia.

"Yeah, like in that movie with Sigourney Weaver."

We turned off Laurel Canyon onto a tree-lined residential side street. Felicia parked Smurfette outside a two-story Spanish-adobe-style house. Through the front windows I could see a room packed with people laughing and drinking from red plastic cups.

"Come on, let's roll," I said, reaching to open my door.

"Wait one sec," Felicia said. She applied magenta lipstick while looking into the rearview mirror. "We like to joke around, but I know you're going through a lot right now."

"Yeah, okay," I said. "But I really want to take a break from all that stuff and have a good time tonight."

"Good call," Felicia said. "But if you decide you're not in the mood to party, just let me know and we can bail early, okay? I know you're not as tough as you pretend."

"That's sweet," I said as I looked down at my fingernails, which were painted ballet-slipper pink. For an instant, I could feel that deep, dark tightness wedged in the bottom of my rib cage. That feeling haunted me sometimes, ever since my mom had died. It lurked there like a goblin. I took a deep breath and shook the feeling off. This was my first night out with my best friend in the longest time and I wanted to have a blast.

"Look, we'll check out the scene for half an hour and if you're not into it, we can cruise," Felicia said.

"Deal," I said, and shook her hand, making a pact. Then we jumped out of the car and headed into the party.

But as I walked toward the front door, something very strange happened. I spotted movement out of the corner of my eye. And when I turned, I thought I saw my mother leaning out from behind a tall oak tree in the front yard.

"What the . . . ?" I whispered.

"Huh?" Felicia stopped.

I blinked my eyes hard and when I opened them, the apparition was gone. I took a few steps over to check behind the tree, but nothing was there.

"Yo, dudette. What's the problem?" Felicia asked.

"Uh, nothing, sorry," I said, and laughed at myself. "I think I'm suffering from major jet lag."

"Well, don't fade on me yet, girl. We're just revving our engines."

"Rrrr, rrrr!" I said, like I was stepping on the gas. "I'm ready to party."

The dimly lit living room was filled with mostly college kids, flirting and talking loudly over the blasting eighties music. Since Felicia studied acting with the hosts, I guess we made the cut and they didn't care that we were still in high school. I noticed that a lot of the guys were dressed up in over-the-top preppy clothes, like blue-and-white-striped seersucker pants and pastel-colored polos with the collars popped up.

"Oh my God," I said. "Why on earth are they dressed that way?"

A drunk-looking guy stumbled over to us. "It's a *Caddyshack*-themed party," he explained, and then burped softly.

Felicia giggled. "But Devin, I never saw that flick!"

Devin tucked his green golf shirt into his plaid madras pants. "It's the most badass golf movie ever. Chevy Chase, Rodney Dangerfield. The candy-bar-in-the-pool scene is classic."

"Maybe we can rent it sometime," Felicia said, batting her eyelashes.

"Certain-licious," he said, and playfully bumped his hip into hers.

Felicia turned to me and explained, "Devin's in my improv class at the Groundlings."

"Oh, cool." I turned to him. "What's up?"

But he didn't really answer. Clearly, he was way more into chatting up Felicia. As they talked about sketch comedy, my eyes wandered across the room. I recognized a guy in the corner sitting on a green La-Z-Boy chair. It was Oliver, Patty's son. Watching me, he held a bottle of beer up to the corner of his mouth and took a sip.

Felicia tapped me on the arm. "Hey, Devin and I are gonna grab cupcakes from the spread. Want one?"

"They're covered in Jujubes," Devin said, and raised one eyebrow as if to tempt me.

"No, thanks, I'm cool," I said. Then I quickly turned back to Oliver. He looked super cute in jeans and a white T-shirt with an unbuttoned green-and-blue plaid shirt over it. He smirked a little and then called me over to him by leaning his head to the right. My pulse quickened. I took a deep breath and walked toward him.

"Fancy meeting you here," he said.

"I should say the same thing to you," I said as I gathered my hair into a ponytail and then let it slip through my fingers.

"At your house today, you mentioned a party in Westwood, so I drove around with my buddy Spike until we heard music blasting."

"You followed me?"

"Is that creepy?" Oliver asked. He took another sip of his beer.

Oh man, I thought this guy was cute. But maybe he was just a stalker. "Um, yeah, extremely."

He scratched the back of his neck. "Mmm, I can see that. It's kinda stalkerish."

"Yep, that's just what I was thinking," I said.

"Well, relax. The guy throwing this party goes to UCLA with me. This is a purely accidental run-in, so thank your lucky stars that you get to spend a little more quality time with a nice young man like myself." He smiled at me confidently.

"Guess I forgot to read my horoscope today," I said, smiling back.

"Let's go and chat outside, where it's quieter," he said. Just then I noticed that the music was blasting and Oliver and I were practically yelling at each other just to be heard.

"I don't know," I said. "I mean, you *are* the son of the enemy's assistant." This was a test. I wanted to see how he felt about Claudia.

"Easy there," he said. "I think your aunt's a whack job. Is that okay for me to say?"

"The best!" I said, and burst into a smile. I wanted to stamp a big *A+* on his forehead. And maybe even a gold star sticker.

"So we can hit the backyard now?" he asked.

"Lead the way, mister," I teased.

Oliver grinned and then he jumped up from his seat. He took me through the crowd and into the packed kitchen. At one point, he reached back and loosely took my hand to help steer me through a bunch of kids devouring a tray of brownies with a spoon.

As we headed toward the backyard, Oliver playfully hit the back of a tall, lanky guy with a mop of curly brown hair who was chatting up some girl in the kitchen.

"That's Spike. He's who I came here with," Oliver explained.

Spike turned to Oliver and shot his hand in the air like a pistol. "This party's solid," he said.

Oliver laughed. Then he held the screen door open for me as we walked into the backyard. There was a small lawn with a well-used charcoal grill and a group of kids smoking cigarettes and chatting. Oliver and I grabbed seats away from the group at a rusty white patio table pushed back against the edge of the property. "So how long has your mom been working for

Claudia?" I asked, just to get the conversational ball rolling. I hadn't really meant to talk about Claudia tonight, or to think about her, but I hadn't thought I'd be seeing Oliver, either.

"For about three months now. She keeps my mom on a short leash."

"I can imagine," I said. "Booking her Botox injections and beard facials."

"Come again?"

"A man rubs his beard all over your face to get off the dead skin. She bragged to me about it earlier today."

"Weird," said Oliver. "What kind of guy wants that job?"

"Blows my mind!" I said.

We both laughed. He leaned one of his arms over the back of his chair. I couldn't help but notice the way his flannel shirt outlined his biceps. I mean, if there was a spectrum that ran from a bodybuilder on steroids to a lanky prepubescent, he was right in the middle: slender with the perfect amount of muscle.

"She has my mom do a lot of other stuff," Oliver said, "like make five hundred phone calls a day, keep track of her calendar, and make sure she buys bananas for the house with the perfect ratio of brown and yellow spots."

"Sounds mega high maintenance," I said.

"Tell me about it. And I don't think Claudia has many friends, because when she's not bossing my mom around, she opens up to her."

"What does she say?" I asked.

"Stuff like she was anxious for you to come home and that she really wants the two of you to be close."

"She should've thought about that sooner," I said. "Kinda made a wrong step when she hooked up with my dad. Don't ya think?"

"Listen . . ." Oliver said. He looked down at his hands. "Maybe it's not my place to say anything. . . ."

"Yeah, what is it?" I said, leaning closer to him.

"I'm sorry about what happened to your mom. I know I never met her, but I'm sure it must have been hard. I can't even imagine what you've been going through."

"Thanks," I said, then looked away. Most people seemed so awkward when they talked to me about my mom's death. They didn't look me in the eye when they talked about her, or they just said, "I offer you my condolences," which always sounded so impersonal. But Oliver didn't seem freaked out talking about my mom, and what he said seemed sincere.

"And I think it's royally messed up what happened." He picked at a brown rust spot on the patio table. "I mean, if my mom died and my dad hooked up with my mom's sister—she doesn't have one, and my dad's gay, but—"

"He is?" I asked, raising my eyebrows.

"Yeah, that's a whole other story. But I get a hundred percent why you didn't come back for Thanksgiving."

"I'm happy to hear you see it my way!" I said.

"I completely do," said Oliver. He moved in his seat and

looked at me with a mischievous smile, like he had a good secret. "Okay, please don't get weirded out. . . ."

"What is it? Tell me," I said. This sounded juicy!

"Before I met you today back at your house, I saw a picture of you."

Uh-oh. Maybe he was a stalker after all. "You did? Where?"

"About two months ago, I came over because Claudia wanted someone to repaint that office she uses sometimes at your house—"

I raised my hand to stop him. "Don't get me started. That was my mom's spot. My dad claims Claudia needs access to certain documents in it, but I know it's just an excuse for them to be close to each other."

"Yeah, I'm sorry. I only did it because I needed extra cash. You see, I'm living with my mom in her apartment in Los Feliz."

"I love that neighborhood," I said. "There are tons of great thrift stores and cafés. Have you been to Birds? They have the best grilled chicken!"

"Yeah, it's a cool area, but living with my mom blows. I'm just doing it because living in a UCLA dorm would be too expensive, but anyway, I spotted this framed photo of you in the living room. You looked so pretty."

"Ah, thanks." I could feel my face getting burning hot, as if the apples of my cheeks were getting baked into pies.

"And, even though we just met, I think we might have a lot in common. Is that silly? It's just an instinct, or an inkling."

"It can be both," I said. I wasn't really sure what to make of Oliver, but sitting there talking to him I felt happy, and given all the stuff I'd been going through, that was a pretty rare thing.

"Phew," he said, pretending to wipe beads of sweat off his forehead.

Just then Felicia ran out of the house. She hurried over to Oliver and me. "There you are. I've been looking for you. I wanted to make sure you're cool with staying longer."

I glanced over at Oliver. "This is my best friend, Felicia," I said.

Oliver introduced himself.

"He's Claudia's personal assistant's son," I told Felicia.

She raised her eyebrows like, *Huh?*

And I gave her a look back like, *Hey, it's cool. He thinks she's nuts, too.* When you've been friends for as long as Felicia and I have, sometimes you just don't need words to communicate.

"So do you wanna head out, or stay longer?" Felicia asked, fiddling with one of her plastic cherry earrings.

Then Oliver turned back to me. "Yeah, what's the deal? Do you have to go now?"

I bit my lip and looked up at Felicia. "Umm . . . I don't mind hanging out longer."

Felicia got the subtext: I had no desire to leave Oliver's side. "Okay, see ya inside," she said, and took off.

"So how long do you get for winter break?" Oliver picked up where we had left off.

"We get two and a half weeks off, so I'm heading back on January third," I said.

"I'm off from UCLA till January fourth. Let's hang. Give me your number," he said.

"Wow, no messing around, huh? Straight to the point," I teased him.

"I hope I'm not coming on too strong. I'm just not much of a game player. But I do hope to provide you with the proper courtship that you deserve."

"Oh, really?" I said, smiling. Then I took out my cell phone. He took out his, too, and we programmed in each other's digits. Oliver's number had a 503 area code. "Where's that from?" I asked.

"Oregon. Just moved here for college in August. I've had a hard time letting go of my old number."

"Wait. But your mom came, too?" I asked.

"Well, see, my sister left for college in San Francisco last year. And so when I came to L.A. this August, my mom kinda moved, too. There wasn't much left for her in Oregon."

I sensed that he was a little embarrassed about this, so I decided to save him from the hot seat by changing topics. "All right, I got your number programmed." I hit the SAVE button on my phone.

"And I got yours. Locked and loaded," Oliver said.

I smiled at him. "I'm glad I ran into you tonight."

"I'm glad you ran into me tonight, too," he said.

Then Spike came out and said he wanted to go to something

called "cosmic bowling" at this bowling alley in Santa Monica with disco lights, so the two of them took off and I went back inside the house and found Felicia.

"He's really Claudia's assistant's son?" Felicia asked me, playfully yanking my hair. "I want the details."

"Yup," I said. "She's pretty kooky, although not half as nuts as Claudia."

"Well, however crazy his mom might be, that lady's eggs worked magic," Felicia said. "He's adorable!"

"Yeah, and there's something different about him. In a good way," I said.

"Is he a college guy?" Felicia asked.

"He's a freshman at UCLA."

Felicia whistled at me. "Look at you with an older man."

"I think he's probably one year older than me. Big deal!" I said.

"I'm liking this," she said. "Hey, this party feels like it's winding down."

I looked around—she was right. A lot of people had left while I was outside talking to Oliver. The music was mellower and softer, and the remaining guests were sitting in groups of two or three chatting.

"Wanna go to Roscoe's Chicken and Waffles for late-night grub?" she asked.

"Sure," I said.

As we walked toward the front door, we spotted two

popular girls who had gone to junior high with us at the Brentwood School.

"Oh, shit, it's Melody and Bree," Felicia whispered.

"I thought we escaped those girls when they left for Harvard-Westlake," I said.

Melody twirled her platinum blonde hair around one finger while Bree chewed and snapped a big wad of purple bubble gum. They spotted us and ran over.

"Whoa, Holly and Felicia, what's up?" Bree asked, shaking her shiny brown hair so it fell perfectly around her shoulders.

"We heard a rumor that your dad's banging your mom's sister," Melody said. "That's so tragic."

"Is that like incest?" Bree asked, blinking her big brown eyes.

"No, actually incest is when two people come from the same gene pool," I said. I didn't know why I was bothering to answer her. "My dad and aunt aren't related by blood."

"Why don't you worry about your own messed-up lives?" Felicia said. Then she turned to Bree. "Holly still has the topless picture you e-mailed her dad in eighth grade."

"It was a dare. But so what? I looked great then and I still do now." Bree winked at me. "I'm sure your dad would agree."

I had never hit anyone before, but I was starting to wonder what it might feel like as I moved toward Bree. But Felicia grabbed my arm and pulled me back. "Come on, Holly, let's go," she said. "They're not worth it."

As Felicia pushed me out the front door, Bree hollered after us, "Tell your dad I wish him Happy Holidays!"

"Gross," I said as I stomped away from the party into the chilly night air. "Girls like that are what I did *not* miss about this town!"

"Bree has a serious Electra complex," Felicia said, shaking her head in disgust.

"But he's *my* dad. Can't she use her *own*?"

PRE-PARTY

Wednesday, December 16

The next day, preparations began for the following evening's Christmas Spectacular. Claudia was prancing around the place like she actually lived here, directing the party planner to do this and that as if he was her servant. I wanted to scream out, "No, *honey*, your two-bedroom in Culver City is waiting for you. Don't get too comfy at my family's *casa*!"

Over the years, my mom had thrown intimate holiday dinners for just her and my dad's closest friends, and she had always planned them herself. When I was little, I loved to sneak out of bed, sit at the top of the stairs, and listen to the adults laugh and tell stories down below. Everyone always seemed to have such a good time. But my aunt's stupid event seemed more about money and impressing people than creating an evening with substance and meaning.

I lay out in the backyard in a bikini, scribbling in my playwriting journal. I was jotting down some of the things Anna Maria had said to me during the ritual the day before, all the spooky stuff about El Señor del Cementerio. The French doors that led from the pool into the living room were wide open, so I could still overhear the pre-party frenzy.

First, a rental company dropped off huge crates filled with gold-rimmed wineglasses and plates, as well as big bags of red and green tablecloths and napkins. Then the decorator arrived and Claudia started bossing him around while the party planner screamed at the caterer over the phone. I couldn't tell exactly what had gone wrong, but it seemed to have something to do with domestic caviar being an unacceptable replacement for a lost shipment of Russian caviar.

The decorator had a bunch of sidekicks working for him and they started covering the estate in endless strands of rainbow-colored bulbs and those white icicle lights that dangle from the roof's edge. Then they began wrapping garlands of pine leaves covered in fake snow and gold ribbons around every banister in the house.

"More bows and berries! I want it to look like a magical holiday forest!" Claudia said to the decorator.

Out at the pool, I took a sip from my Diet Coke can and glared at her.

"Yes, anything you want," the decorator said. He was a tall

blond man with an effeminate voice. I felt bad for him, having to work for Claudia. Although I felt worse for me for having to be related to her. At least he'd be free of her when this job was over. I'd be stuck with her for the rest of my life.

"And put some Christmas garland on my props, like the zombie girl and the bunny head. I really shouldn't have to give you all of these creative ideas. Isn't that your job—to come up with this stuff yourself?"

I watched the decorator wrap pine needles around the zombie statue so that it looked like she was wearing a green feather boa.

Just then my cell phone rang. I saw Oliver's name on the caller ID.

"Oh, hey, what's up?" I said, acting casual.

"Just wanted you to know, Claudia hired me as an extra bartender for tomorrow night."

"Really? You're working for that tart?" I got up and walked toward the edge of the yard overlooking the panoramic view of L.A.

"I need the extra cash," Oliver said. "But I also get to see you."

I smiled. "All right, well, in that case . . . But I'm gonna put you to work, too—saving me from all the phonies."

"Maybe it won't be that bad."

"Oh, yes it will!" I said. "Tomorrow's gonna be a major kiss-ass fest. Just like that T. S. Eliot poem: 'The women come and go, talking of Leonardo DiCaprio.'"

"Wasn't it 'Michelangelo'?" Oliver asked.

"Yeah, in *the poem,* but not in *this town,*" I said. "So if you see anyone with fake boobs or leather pants cornering me, promise you'll come and save my soul?"

"I got your back," Oliver said.

"Okay, see ya soon."

"Hey, wait," he suddenly said before I could hang up.

"What's up?" I asked.

"There's something I need to tell you real quick," he said.

"Yeah, what is it?"

"It's weird to say, but . . . I guess, my mom said something to me yesterday. I feel like an idiot telling you. . . ." He laughed, embarrassed.

"Come on, spill the beans," I said.

"She saw the way I looked at you and said you were off-limits."

"But why? That doesn't make any sense," I said.

"She's worried if we got involved and something went wrong between us, it could jeopardize her job. Like if we got in a fight, you might tell Claudia to fire her."

"I would never do that. She has zip to worry about," I said as I paced back and forth.

"I know, but she's mega paranoid. I mean, she can't stop me from hanging with you. It's just for now, and, like, at the party tomorrow, can we keep this between us? I live with her and she'll nag me to death."

"Yeah, sure, no prob," I said. I understood because I knew firsthand how whacked out parents could be.

"Thanks. You're the best," he said.

"Me and you. We'll keep it on the down low. Like undercover agents."

Oliver laughed. "Copy that, Lady H," he said.

"See ya tomorrow, Ace-Man double-oh-seven."

CHRISTMAS SPECTACULAR

Thursday, December 17

By eight o'clock the following evening, the Christmas Spectacular was in full swing. Valet attendants in white shirts with black pants and vests sped off in luxury cars, parking them along the hillside's main road. Thousands of rainbow-colored lights were strung across the mansion's rooftop and there was a big fake stop sign by the front door that read, SANTA STOP HERE.

I was so over this party. Claudia stood in the foyer dressed in a long, shiny, red strapless dress—it looked cheap, but I guessed that it wasn't—greeting the guests as they arrived. She had hugs and kisses for everyone! And my dad was right by her side, oozing his usual charm. Was he even thinking that this time last year he'd been sitting beside my mom at a very different kind of holiday party? Was he even thinking about her at all?

The party was filled with an industry crowd. That meant directors, producers, executives, agents, and a few actors. There were, like, two A-minus-list actors on the scene; the rest of the actors were B-list, which means people care that they are at the party, but they don't jump up and down like when high-caliber people like Brad Pitt or Tom Cruise show up. This town had a strict power structure, kind of like high school, and somehow everyone knew their place. Claudia herself was probably on the B-minus list, but she was certainly looking to climb. I bet she hoped that after this big party she'd be at least a B-plus, and maybe even an A-minus. I doubted that would happen.

I heard Claudia introduce my dad to an Asian man and a statuesque blonde woman who had just walked through the door. "Gardner, meet Tomoko Ishikawa and his wife, Annie." I recognized the man's name from the call my aunt had run to take the day she gave me that *fabulous* zebra dress. What was the name of that horrible movie they were working on together? Oh yeah, *Dead Bachelorette: The Musical*.

I watched as Annie gave Claudia a gift wrapped in gold paper. "This is for you," Annie said.

Claudia opened the box and lifted out a tiara made of blue and white stones. "What on earth?"

"Costume jewelry," Tomoko said. "Next year, we'll bring the real diamonds."

Next year? I was hoping Claudia would be long gone from my house by that point.

"Put it on! Put it on!" Annie said.

Claudia gently lifted up the tiara and rested it on her head. Then she turned and checked out her reflection in the foyer mirror. "Wow, it's magnificent," she said.

Yeah, I thought, *magnificently tacky.*

"Wear it all night," Annie said. "You look just like a queen."

As Annie and Tomoko walked into the living room to eat some Russian caviar—the missing shipment had been found after all, thank God!—Claudia spotted me. She hurried over.

"Nice crown," I told her. "So I guess you're a queen now?"

"If the glove fits . . ." she said, grinning. Then she looked over my short, navy silk dress. "You didn't wear the Emilio Pucci."

"Sorry, it was too tight," I fibbed. The truth was the skinned-zebra fabric was now a ball in the back of my closet.

"Oh, that's too bad." She scrunched her nose. "What is this? Another one of your vintage numbers?"

"Yep, I found it at the Salvation Army in Connecticut. It's one of a kind."

"Interesting," Claudia said. "Well, enjoy yourself. I've got to go mingle. Merry, merry!" And she headed back over to my dad's side.

I walked toward the living room's entrance and peeked in at the hundred or so guests schmoozing in the shadow of a massive Christmas tree. Most of them had their BlackBerries out and were texting in the middle of their conversations.

Just then I heard a familiar voice and turned around.

"Hey, lady!" Felicia said, and ran over. She wore a silver dress and big earrings that looked like chandeliers made of magenta stars. I had invited her to the party over chicken and waffles at Roscoe's the other night. "Sorry I couldn't get here sooner. I just got off work." Felicia had been working part-time as a waitress at Geisha House, a trendy sushi restaurant, since September. They didn't usually hire high school students, but her uncle was a manager there, so he had pulled some strings.

"Can you believe this decor?" I said, pointing out the over-the-top rose-and-candy-cane bouquets, green balloon sculptures, and large piñata in the shape of Rudolph, the Red-Nosed Reindeer.

"Subtle," Felicia said. Then she squeezed my arm. "Ooh, someone's staring at you," she whispered.

I followed her gaze over to Oliver, dressed in a tuxedo and bow tie, at the side bar.

"Claudia put him to work," I said.

"Have you guys made out yet?" Felicia asked. "He's got nice lips."

"Trust me, I've noticed," I said. "But I haven't seen him since that house party."

"Uh-oh! Ring the alarm," she said. "Who's that girl moving in on your territory?"

I peered over and saw a girl about my age with auburn hair standing next to Oliver, chatting him up. She was wearing glasses and she looked really conservative in a sweater dress and pearl necklace. Not to brag, but she didn't seem like too much competition to me. "Never seen her before," I said.

"Go claim your territory," Felicia said, pushing me lightly on the back. "I'm gonna throw my coat in your room."

"Wish me luck," I said, and hurried over toward Oliver to say hello.

On my way, I spotted familiar faces of men and women my mom used to work with. It felt wrong having them here for a party hosted by Claudia instead of my mother, but no one seemed bothered. Did they think my mom and her sister were interchangeable? One of the men noticed me looking his way and hurried over. He was, like, fifty years old, with blond hair pulled back into a ponytail.

"Hi, Holly. It's nice to see you," he said. "Happy Holidays!"

"You too," I said politely. I recognized the man's tan, chiseled face but couldn't recall his name.

He must've picked up on that. "Do you remember me? My name's Kurt Rivers," he said. "I did wardrobe on two of your mother's films."

"Oh, yeah," I said.

"Listen, how are you doing?" he said, squinting at me intensely. "I'm sorry I couldn't make your mom's memorial service. I always meant to send a card."

"Yeah, thanks," I said, and looked away. I was so not in the mood to get into this.

"God, it was such a shock," he said. "Your mom seemed happy to me. I had no idea she was having such a hard time. We always used to laugh together when I ran into her on set at the crafts-service table."

He wasn't the first one to say something like this to me. Tons of people had told me how blown away they had been when they heard the news. My mom had been depressed on and off for many years, but when she was down, she just stayed in the house and hid. In front of most people she acted friendly, always making jokes and laughing. The only people who saw her real lows were the people closest to her, like my dad and me. And, I guess, Claudia.

But it's not like my mom was always down. She had bipolar disorder, just like her own mother, so sometimes she was super happy and filled with energy, vacuuming the whole house (even though Anna Maria had already done it the day before) and staying up all night working on the computer while listening to the Three Tenors. I had tried to enjoy her when she was like that, but I knew her highs would be followed by lows, and they always were. Whenever she finally crashed—after a few weeks or even months of being the life of the party—she crashed hard. She'd stay in bed all day. She wouldn't eat. And even though she would try to make her voice sound normal when she saw me, it would come out robotic and sad. She had tried different medications over the years, but she'd always go off them when she felt a happy phase coming on, because, she told me, she was her most creative and productive during those times. She and my dad had fought about her not taking her medication from time to time, but she always said it was her body, her choice. And I guess in the end my dad ran out of ways to argue with that.

The last couple of years, her films hadn't done as well and she had taken it to heart. She told me one time, "You can't separate yourself from your art. What you create is personal and connected to the deepest parts of your being. And when you put it out into the world, it feels extremely vulnerable."

This Kurt Rivers guy reached out and took one of my hands. "I offer my condolences," he said warmly.

"I really appreciate it," I said, planning an escape route. I glanced over at Oliver and saw that he was looking my way. "Sorry, gotta run. The bartender needs me. Nice seeing ya."

I hurried over to the bar, but the conversation I'd just had with Kurt stayed with me. I had never really understood that deep, dark place my mom would go to inside—but in those moments, when she couldn't get out of bed, when her voice didn't sound right, I had felt so powerless just standing by and watching her, like there was nothing I could do to make it better.

"Hi," I said when I reached Oliver.

"You look great," he said.

"Oh, this old thing?" I joked as I smoothed down my dress.

Oliver turned to the girl with auburn hair beside him. "Hey, this is my big sister, Lara."

Oh, they're related. . . .

"Super to meet you," Lara said coolly. I felt like she was looking down at me from the rim of her eyeglasses.

"Claudia invited her to the party. She's in town from up north," Oliver said.

"I study violin at the San Francisco Conservatory of Music," Lara said proudly, and then she reached up to touch her pearl necklace.

"Congratulations," I said. "That sounds so exciting!"

"Yep, it is. I've worked hard for the opportunity," Lara said. I noticed her eyes wander to a cater waiter carrying hors d'oeuvres through the party. "I mean, it wasn't handed to me on a silver platter."

Hmm. It seemed like she was trying to suggest that what I had *was* handed to me on a silver platter, but I decided to ignore her comment.

"I'm sure," I said. "I tried to play the violin in sixth grade, and was embarrassingly bad. Should've stuck with the recorder."

"Well, anyway." Lara broke into a small, forced smile. "It was a pleasure," she said, and then rushed off, making a beeline for that cater waiter's tray.

"She seemed to like me a whole lot," I said.

"Don't take it personally," Oliver said. "She's has a thing against L.A. girls."

"But she's never even lived here, right?"

"I know, but it's her San Francisco/L.A. rivalry," he said. "She thinks girls in L.A. act like it's permanent spring break and party all the time."

"Oh, come on. That's ridiculous," I said. I mean, sure, I did know girls like that. But there were girls like that everywhere, not only in L.A. I slipped behind the bar next to Oliver. "Psst, I think it's your break time."

"Claudia would shoot me. We got a pack of thirsty wolves." He scanned the roomful of networking guests.

"Come on, please? Save me from this shallow grave." I looked at him and batted my eyelashes. I couldn't take another talk like the one I'd just had with Kurt.

Oliver broke into a smile. He didn't take much convincing. "Where to?"

"The bathroom by the stairwell," I said.

"Meet you there in three minutes," he said. "Let me just find one of the caterers to cover for me behind the bar."

"It's a plan," I said, and playfully tapped the face of his army-green watch. "Countdown begins *now!*"

As I hurried to the bathroom, I cut along the edge of the dance floor Claudia had set up in the living room. The poor party planner guy had been there all night moving our regular furniture out of the way to make space for it and the small cocktail tables that surrounded it. There was a live band playing upbeat Christmas carols and right now they were banging out "Jingle Bell Rock." I watched as the guests

twined a little. "Welcome to my porcelain boat. We can sail away from here. Even for a few minutes."

"Hmm, that sounds nice," I said. My eyes wandered to his lips and I wanted to kiss them. A lot.

"Where can I take you to, m'lady?" he asked in a fake British accent.

I laughed and played along. "Captain, can you sail us to London, please?"

"Ahoy, check out the River Thames on the right," Oliver said.

"I think we fit in here pretty well," I said, leaning against the back of the tub.

"Me too," Oliver said, and then he put one hand on my silver shoe and played with the clasp. I could feel his fingers lightly tickling my ankle. Then he looked at me and cleared his throat.

"Hey, can I ask you a question?"

"Please do," I said.

"But you have to come closer."

We both leaned in toward the center of the bathtub. His face was only inches from mine. I got a close-up of his blue eyes and a few freckles on his nose.

"Are you a good kisser?" he asked.

I looked down and smiled. "I'll guess you'll have to find out," I teased.

My chest filled with warmth and I closed my eyes. Then I moved toward him slowly, waiting for our mouths to touch.

I could practically feel his lips on mine when suddenly, there was loud banging on the locked door.

Oliver and I pulled back from each other quickly and turned toward the sound.

"Ollie? Ollie, open up! I saw you go in there," a woman's voice yelled out from the hallway.

"Shit, it's my mom," Oliver whispered, and shook his head back and forth.

I could feel my lips wilting like an under-watered flower. They had been puckered and ready to go and now they felt so dry and alone.

"Ugh, I don't want to deal with her right now," said Oliver.

"Oliver, I can hear you. Open up! I need to use the throne!" Patty yelled.

I scrunched my face. "The throne?"

"That's what she calls the toilet. It's weird," he said.

The banging the door got louder. "I can hear you. Let me in!" Patty hollered.

"Can't she use another bathroom?" I whispered. "There are, like, nine."

"This is just her excuse to bother me," Oliver said. "But man, I can't take her finding us here together. She's worried enough about keeping her job already since Claudia is so demanding. This is going to push her over the edge."

"We need a plan." I focused on the large window. "I'll go that way." I nodded in its direction. There was more pounding on the door.

"Really? You don't mind?" he asked.

"I've always wanted to try this escape route," I said, and jumped out of the bathtub. Oliver followed and helped me push back the yellow satin curtains. Then I climbed up on the small wooden cabinet filled with extra towels and soaps. I felt my leg slipping, but Oliver grabbed on to my waist and helped me keep my balance.

"Be careful."

"I got it," I said. Then I turned up the latch and pushed the glass pane out into the night.

As Patty continued to beat her fist against the door, I stuck first one leg and then the other outside. Oliver helped me as I lowered myself down. Once safely on the ground, I peeked my head back through the opening.

"I'm sorry for making you do this," Oliver said. "It's kinda humiliating beyond belief."

"Don't worry. I get it," I said. "Parents can be insane."

"When can I see you again?" he asked. "I mean, after this party, when it can be just the two of us."

"The sooner the better," I said. Then I tried to give him my best "come hither" look before taking off along the side of the house.

As I made my way to the front entrance, I looked through one of the windows into the party. I could see my dad and Claudia schmoozing a group of guests. The last thing I wanted to do was go back inside there now, so I decided to walk along the front lawn, which was filled with orange trees. It was a warm night, and I spotted the full moon perched in the sky between the feather-shaped leaves of a palm tree. I headed along the driveway, my heels making a crunching sound as they pierced the gravel. As I got closer to the main road, I saw that it was filled with the guests' cars. There was the usual parade of Mercedeses, Lexuses, Porsches, and Lamborghinis parked one after the next. I was wondering which one belonged to that Kurt Rivers guy—was he the type to drive a Lexus or a Mercedes?—when I saw a woman walking toward me in the darkness.

THE WOMAN IN THE HILLS

A s the woman came closer to me, I noticed she was walking barefoot, and I took a few steps into the street to see her more clearly. She had big eyes, a heart-shaped face, and black, shoulder-length hair. Just like my mom. Then, out of nowhere, a white pickup truck sped around the bend, blasting rap music. The high beams blinded me for a second and I jumped back onto the lawn to avoid getting hit. As the truck zoomed past and disappeared from view, I blinked hard, trying to adjust my eyes back to the night. I glanced toward where the woman had been walking, but she was gone.

I looked every which way and finally I saw her again, closer this time, walking along the side of the road near a cluster of eucalyptus trees. She was looking directly at me with those familiar almond-shaped brown eyes. And I realized it was definitely her. My mother. I didn't know if I was dreaming or if I was crazy or what, but I was just so happy to see her again; it didn't matter what was going on. She wore a pale yellow skirt and a cream-colored top with pretty embroidery on it. It was the same outfit she had been wearing the last time I saw her.

She had been depressed ever since I got home from Winchester, but that day I thought she looked more cheerful. She had gotten out of bed, taken a shower, gotten dressed. I thought it was safe to leave her on her own—my dad was at the office, as usual, and Anna Maria had the day off—so I'd made plans to go to the beach with Felicia. As I left the house, my mom had stood at the door waving to me. "I love you, Holly. Forever and always," she had said. It wasn't a weird thing for her to say, "forever and always." That was how she had signed cards she wrote to me. My mom was kind of emotional like that. "Love you, too, Mom!" I'd called as I ran down the driveway and hopped into Smurfette. If I had known that was the last time I would ever see her alive, I'd have said so much more.

Now her dark hair was parted in the middle and one side was pulled back in a barrette, as usual—except I noticed she had strands of gray, which she'd never had before.

"Mom?" I took a few steps closer. "Is it really you?" I could feel my arm hairs standing on end.

I looked into my mother's eyes. They were harder than I remembered, and I didn't like how her lips were pursed tightly as if she was upset. Her skin looked pale, its once warm tones now bleached into a white canvas. Still, there was an energy about her that felt more charged than ever. I felt a little scared, but I wasn't going to turn my back on her. Not again. Because maybe if I hadn't left her that day to go to the beach with Felicia, she'd still be alive.

My mom waved me on, as if summoning me to follow her. I hurried after her in the direction of our house, weaving between tree trunks by the side of road. As my mom moved onto the property, she looked back over her shoulder.

"I'm following you," I said.

She nodded and kept going, moving quickly toward our house. The lights from the party made the house look like it was glowing, and I could hear faint sounds of the band playing and the murmur of guests talking to one another.

She was heading for the backyard, toward the entrance of the Chinese garden, with its overgrown pine and bamboo. I followed her and froze when I spotted her sitting in the gazebo. The koi pond lay between us and I could see the orange-and-white fish slipping through the water, unaware of the ghostly visitor in their midst. I moved my lips as if to speak—I had so much to say to her, so much to ask her—but she raised one hand to stop me.

"Shh, you can't let anyone know I'm here," she said.

Her voice sounded just like it had when she was alive.

"Don't be afraid. Come here, sweetheart, and sit with me." My mom touched the space on the bench beside her.

My body was shaking, but I managed to walk around the koi pond and sit down next to her.

"Look at your beautiful face," she said. My eyes started to tingle, and then I could feel the tears running down my cheeks.

"I never thought I'd see you again. I miss you so much," I said. I wanted to hug her. I wanted to cuddle in her lap like I had when I was little. But she looked almost translucent, like if I touched her my hand would slide right through her.

"This wasn't supposed to happen," she said. "My passing. I came back to tell you that."

"But how did you even come back?" I asked. "How are you here?" I thought of the ritual I had done with Anna Maria. Was my mother here because her spirit was restless? Was she upset with me for letting her go, for not taking better care of her?

"I only have a short time to visit and I can't linger," she said.

"I understand," I said—even though I didn't—and looked down at my hands. They were trembling. "Mom, I never got to say good-bye to you. And I just don't get it. . . . Why did you do it?" *And could I have stopped you? Should I have stopped you?* I wanted to ask that, too, but the words wouldn't come out.

"I want to answer your question, Holly. There's so much I want to say to you. So much I never got the chance to explain. But now, I need your help."

"What is it, Mom?" I asked. I was so glad she was going to ask me to do something. I would do anything for her—anything. I only wished she'd asked me for help before it was too late. I wished she had asked me not to leave her alone that morning. I would have stayed.

"I wouldn't ask you to do this unless I had to. You're the only one I can count on. I see other spirits resting peacefully. I want to be like them, but I'm tormented."

"Mom, what's the matter?" I asked through my tears. I hadn't cried this much since the week after she died, and it almost felt good to let it out. "Tell me what's bothering you."

"Claudia poisoned me."

"What?" Had I heard her correctly?

"She wanted what I had," my mom said.

"Mom, are you sure? I mean, I know you and Claudia didn't get along, but would she really . . . did she really do this to you?"

"She did," my mom said, and she sounded completely serious. "As your mother, I'm telling you, Holly. This is the absolute truth."

I was speechless. I hated Claudia for jumping on my dad the minute she'd had the chance, but I couldn't believe she could be responsible for my mom's death, too. All this time I had thought it was my fault.

"I keep thinking about what she did, and I can't sleep," my mom said.

Suddenly I stopped crying. My sadness was replaced by anger, by rage. I had always felt there was something wrong with Claudia, something wrong with this whole situation. Now I knew the truth. "I can't believe she hurt you! She needs to pay for taking you from me!"

"Yes, I think you're right, love," my mom said with an angry edge to her voice. "My soul won't rest until she's punished."

"But what should I do?" I asked. "Should I go to the police? Should I tell Dad?" I felt like I was little again and I was asking my mom whom I should invite over to play, or what I should wear for school-picture day.

"No, Holly, you can't do either of those things. Your father can't know what happened yet. I can see, from where I am now, what's going on between him and my sister. He's under her spell. And this isn't a matter for the police, trust me. This is between me and Claudia. And believe me, I hate to involve you. I *hate* to. But I could only come back to talk to the person I loved most in the world. And that person is you. So I have to ask you to take revenge on her, for what she did to me. For what she did to all of us."

I sat there silently, taking all of this in.

"Holly, sweetheart," my mom said. "I can't stay much longer. Can you do this for me? This one thing, so I can rest in peace?"

"I can do it, Mom. I'll do it," I said. And I wanted to do it, even though I didn't know how to begin. For my mom, I would figure it out.

"And promise me you won't tell anyone we spoke."

"I promise," I told her. My anger started to slip away and

I felt the tears prickling behind my eyes again. It was so good to be with her, even like this, even if she wasn't completely back. I couldn't let her go again. "Mom, I don't like being here without you."

She reached her hand toward my face. Her fingers moved slowly along the silhouette of my cheek without touching the skin. Or maybe she was touching me but I just couldn't feel her.

"I love you so much," I said. "More than anything."

"I love you, too. Forever and always," she said. I noticed tears in her eyes.

"Forever and always."

"I have to go now," said my mom. "But I'll be back."

"Wait! When?" I asked. "And how am I supposed to do this? I don't understand—"

But it was too late. She was gone. I was all alone again.

"Oh my God . . . oh my God," I said over and over. My shoulders started heaving, and my teeth were chattering even though I wasn't cold.

Just then I heard Felicia calling out my name in the distance. "Holly! Holly!" she shouted again.

I took deep breaths and wiped my face. "Over here!" I managed to yell out, and then I stumbled out of the Chinese garden. I leaned one arm against the entrance wall to balance myself. Felicia saw me and ran over.

"Where did you disappear to? You left me—" Felicia stopped talking. She dropped her head forward and inspected my face. "Oh my God, what's wrong with you? You're super pale. And your makeup is all streaked. Have you been crying? I can tell—you have been. What's wrong? What happened?"

I struggled to find the right words. "I feel kinda strange. . . ." I said. "Holy, man, oh, wow . . ."

Felicia rubbed my shoulder. "Are you okay? Did someone upset you? Was it Oliver? I'll go beat him up."

"No, this has nothing to do with Oliver. It's . . ." But I couldn't tell her; I couldn't tell anyone. This had to be a secret. It had to be just between my mom and me. "I feel sick," I said, leaning over to grab my stomach.

"Oh, no! I bet it was the lamb appetizer! Talk about rare. Let's hit the bathroom." Felicia grabbed my arm to lead me back to the house, but I wouldn't budge.

"No. I need to go as far away from here as possible!" I couldn't go back into the party. I couldn't face Claudia, not after what I knew. "My car. I need my car keys right now." I hurried quickly toward the back of the house.

"You're gonna leave the party? Where do you want to drive to?" Felicia asked, following after me.

"Away from here. Maybe the beach, the ocean. Somewhere that's peaceful where I can think." Yes, think. That's what I had to do. I had to make a plan. I had to avenge my mom's death. I went into the house through a door in the basement, then I ran up the second set of stairs, the one no one ever used, to my bedroom. Felicia followed close on my heels.

"Hey, you're not making any sense," she said after me. "What's the deal?"

"Just trust me on this one." I burst into my room, searching for my car keys.

"You have to tell me. We're BFFs!" Felicia said.

"I can't! This is something I have to do on my own." I spotted my keys on my desk. I grabbed them and tossed them into my purse. Then I threw the bag over my shoulder and moved toward the door.

"I need to know!" She stepped in my way. "Just give me a clue!"

"Fine! Something's twisted in the state of Cali!" I said, grabbing her by both shoulders.

"Is that like a riddle?"

"Just trust me. Everything's different now!" I let go of her. She looked so confused and I could tell she was hurt that I was yelling at her, so I took both her hands in mine and I looked her straight in the eye. "Felicia, I'm sorry. I know I'm acting crazy. But I'm fine, I promise. Or I'm not fine, but I will be soon. Anyway, don't worry. Please. I gotta go. Alone."

I ran out the door, down the back stairs, and to the garage. Then I jumped into my black Saab and turned the engine on. My parents had given it to me for my sixteenth birthday, but I kept it here when I went to Winchester because the campus was so small; I didn't need a car to get around. And I hadn't wanted to drive it cross-country. Before a valet attendant could run in front of me to fetch a Lexus, I zoomed out of the driveway.

Speeding down the canyon to Sunset Boulevard, I blasted the stereo. Had I really just seen a ghost? And had my aunt Claudia really killed my mother? Was this all a totally insane dream? Was I going to wake up in my bed and find out that none of this had ever happened, not even my mom's death? The thought was too sweet even to consider, because I knew it wasn't true. My mom was dead. But now I knew it wasn't my fault. It was Claudia's.

I found an entrance in Santa Monica to the Pacific Coast Highway, which ran along the coastline of Malibu. To my left was the ocean, lined with multimillion-dollar houses, and to my right were seemingly endless steep and rocky cliffs. As I drove, I grabbed on tight to the steering wheel. I lowered the windows and the wind blew hard into my face as I raced along the almost empty highway.

A cop car drove past me and I wondered if I should flag it down. Maybe I should go directly to the police department, even though my mom had told me not to. I mean, isn't that what they always told us in school when Officer Friendly came to do the annual presentation on school safety? If you're in trouble, tell a police officer? But no, I couldn't tell the police because they had already ruled my mom's death a suicide. And the LAPD would most likely laugh their heads off if I told them I had seen a ghost. Or they'd cart me off to the funny farm. I had to keep this to myself. My mom was right, no one could know. This was all on me.

Then suddenly, I swear I saw my mom again, driving the SUV beside me. I sped up to get a better look at the driver, but her face quickly dissolved from my mother's into a soccer mom's. Had it really been my mom? Was I completely cracking up? When I turned back to the road, I realized that my car had swerved over to the side; I was heading directly toward a cement barrier that was meant to protect the highway from potential landslides. "Nooo!" I yelled, and slammed on the brakes with all my might, but it was too late—the car smashed into the blockade. I felt my head snap forward and then backward, and the seat belt tensed up like a stiff arm, protecting me from flying through the windshield. Then it felt like I got smacked in the face by an inflatable punching bag, like the one I'd had when I was little, but much stronger and covered in some kind of weird powder. It was the air bag.

The crash had been so loud, like a crash scene in a movie, but then it was immediately silent.

I looked out the windshield at my poor car all banged up. The hood was smashed in and the lights were busted. Then I checked my face in the side mirror. I looked okay. Nothing was bleeding or crooked. I was in one piece.

I thought another driver might stop to help me, but the few other cars on the road just whizzed by. So much for fellow citizens looking out for each other. I pulled my cell phone out of my purse and debated whom to call for help. Felicia was probably already worried about me and I didn't want her to totally flip, so I crossed her off the list. There was Oliver, but I had just met him, and I didn't think calling from the scene of a car crash was the best way to make a good impression. Plus he was still working at the party. Ugh, the party. It was still going on. It felt like a million years ago that I'd been there; so much had happened. There was no way around it: I was going to have to call my dad. I would need a tow truck, and my father could help me get one. Plus, if I called him he'd be forced to leave in the middle of Claudia's party, which would be an added bonus.

"Hello?" My dad answered the phone. Thank God he always had his cell phone in his pocket, on vibrate. I heard music in the background.

"Dad, it's me," I said.

"Holly, where are you? I haven't seen you since the appetizers."

"I need your help. Come quick," I said.

"Oh, no. What's the matter? Are you okay?" he asked. His voice sounded super concerned.

"I'm on the Pacific Coast Highway near Moonshadows. I had an accident, Dad."

"*What?!*" he yelled into the phone. "Oh my goodness. Are you all right, honey?"

I told him I was fine but that the Saab seemed smashed to smithereens. He said to just sit tight and wait, that he'd be there right away. As I waited for my dad to show up, I put on the hazard lights, got out of the car, and paced along the edge of the road. I heard the waves crashing in the distance and smelled the salt in the air. A nice elderly couple in a hunter-green Volvo pulled over and asked me if I needed help. Finally! At least two fellow Los Angelenos had hearts. I told them I was fine and my father was on the way, so they took off.

Twenty minutes later, my dad rolled up in his silver Porsche. He ran over and threw his arms around me.

"Oh, God, Holly! I was so worried." He kept gushing about how happy he was that I was in one piece. My dad wasn't often that mushy, so it was weird to see him so affectionate with me.

"I called Triple A and they're on the way," he said, hugging me again. "Thank goodness you're all right. I don't know what I'd do if something happened to you."

About ten minutes later, a tow truck showed up and hauled off my smashed Saab. It was sad to watch my beat-up car being pulled down the road. It looked like an old friend being dragged away.

First my mom's ghost, then my car. Was this night ever going to end?

My dad and I hopped into his convertible. It seemed like a long ride home along the highway. He didn't say anything right away and neither did I. Finally, he spoke.

"You really scared me," he said in a small voice.

"Dad, I'm so sorry. It was an accident. One minute I was just driving along and the next I was crashing into a concrete barrier. I didn't see it. It was like it came out of nowhere."

"I understand, but you don't know what it's like getting that kind of call. Especially after losing your mother and . . . Why did you leave the party, anyway?"

"I overdosed on tinsel," I said. "The whole scene was giving me a headache."

My dad rubbed his hand up and down his leg, which he did sometimes when he was nervous. "I know this must be strange for you, but tonight was important."

"For Claudia it was," I said. I could hardly say her name without spitting. And now, after what my mom had told me . . . It took all of my self-control not to blurt the whole thing out to my dad. But I couldn't; I had promised my mom.

"And the company. I'm trying to balance things here. I want to be good to both of you so—"

"But I was your daughter before she was your . . . whatever she is."

My dad took his eyes off the road to look at me. "Right. You know, this isn't how I planned things. Claudia wants to reach out to you and she's been trying to connect. If you could make a little effort . . ."

"Dad, you're completely whipped," I said. "You realize that, right?"

"Excuse me?" He looked over at me, arching his eyebrows. "Great, thank you. Look, this isn't easy for me, either." His voice grew quieter. "I wish I could be better at talking with you about everything . . . and . . . I'm sorry. "

He stopped talking. Then he shifted around in his seat.

"You're sorry about what?" I asked.

"Every day I wonder if there was something I could've done," he said.

"Yeah, I think that, too," I said quietly. I guess my dad and I had that in common. But now I had a chance to make it up to her. And I wasn't going to screw it up.

As we headed back up Laurel Canyon, I found myself thinking about the night in early November when my dad had called me and broken the news about his relationship with Claudia. I was doing homework in my room at Winchester and Lulu was out at tennis practice when my cell rang. First my dad and I chatted about the usual stuff—my classes, how Sampson had chewed up some boots I had left at home, the weather. Then my dad cleared his throat like he had something important to say that he was working up to.

"I didn't want to talk to you about this on the phone, but . . ." he said.

"What is it?" I asked, and plopped down on my bed, clutching my favorite blue flannel pillow. I'd had it since I was a little kid.

"I didn't see this coming," my dad said. "If you asked me if I could ever in a million years imagine this happening . . ." His voice trailed off.

"What are you trying to say?" I said, nervously playing with the magnets on the miniature refrigerator pushed against my bed. Lulu's mom had just sent her one shaped like a tennis racket in a care package.

"It's just . . . you think you know how things will be, but then you realize that nothing is predictable. Even our own feelings. They can develop in new ways."

"Dad, you're rambling!" I said. "Please spit it out!"

"Sorry. You see, when your mom died, I . . . Well, you saw the way I couldn't sleep much," he said.

"I guess." Although, honestly, he had seemed just fine to me, much more fine than I had been.

"Well, Claudia's been there for me. She really helped me through this hard time. Especially after you went back to school and I've been alone here."

"Anna Maria and Sampson are still there," I said.

"You know what I mean," my dad said. "The grieving process connected both of us in a way neither of us imagined. There was this empty hole in me."

He stopped like he was waiting for me to say something, but I didn't know what to say.

"I'm so sorry to have to tell you like this. She and I have both been in a tough place, dealing with the loss of your mother in different ways. I suppose the grief has brought us together. And things have become romantic."

The first few weeks after my mom died, Claudia would come by the house and bring over snacks. Come to think of it, they were always my dad's favorite things, like mint Milano cookies, butter-pecan ice cream, and corned-beef sandwiches. How had I missed the signs? It was obvious now that she had been trying to sink her claws into him, but I never thought he'd actually let her!

I moved the phone to my other ear and then swallowed hard. "How long has this been going on?"

"I'm not sure . . . maybe a few months," my dad said.

"So, like, as soon as I left for senior year?"

"About then," he said.

And to think I had been kind of worried about leaving him alone when I went back to school. I had even asked if he wanted me to stay, but he'd assured me he'd be fine, that he had work to keep him busy. Now I knew he had something else to keep him busy: Claudia.

"Wow, Dad. I don't know what to say. I mean, I'm in complete shock."

"That's healthy," my dad said. "I know this isn't easy, but you're my daughter and I love you. I know we can work through this."

"Can I go now?" Then, without waiting for an answer, I hurled my cell phone against the wall and broke it. I had to buy a new one at the mall later that week. I bought the most expensive one I could find and charged it to the credit card my dad had given me "for necessities." Served him right.

I turned on my stereo and blasted White Stripes and chucked the See's Lollypops my dad had sent me in a care package across the room.

When Lulu came back from tennis practice later that night and saw our disheveled room, with lollipops all over the place and my bedspread thrown across the floor, she knew something was up. I was usually the neater one of the two of us, cleaning up after her.

"Wow. What happened?" she asked, putting down her racket and rushing over to me.

I told her the whole sordid, disgusting story. Then we sat down on the floor, picking up lollipops and eating them together one after the other until we were left with seven empty white sticks.

"Your dad's not the first man in history to hook up with his wife's sister," Lulu said. She told me about Jane Austen's younger brother. "Also," she continued, "Freud supposedly had an affair with his wife's sister, Minna, who lived with them."

"Sounds shady," I said. "Did Freud have any daughters?"

"Yep, the old man had three of them." Lulu was taking psychology this semester.

"I wonder how they took the news?" I asked. "Maybe they hated him and never spoke to him again." I was considering taking this approach with my own father.

"Not sure, but Freud appointed his daughter Anna to carry on his work after his death, so I guess they worked through it in the end."

"Well, that was a totally different era," I said.

"Yeah, you can say that again," Lulu replied. "It was filled with old-fashioned, crusty ideas. I mean, can everything really come down to the Oedipus complex? That's so simplistic."

Clearly we both had father issues—mine relating to my own dad, and hers relating to the father of psychology.

Finally my dad and I pulled past the guard gate and down Elsinore Drive. I looked at the other houses as we drove past and wondered if maybe the neighbor who used to play James Bond would want to adopt me. If only I belonged to another family, my life would be so much cooler.

As we pulled up to the fork in the road, I noticed that most of the guests' cars were still parked along the street. Was this party ever going to end? My dad stopped his Porsche outside the garage. He turned toward me and put his hand on my headrest.

"If anything happened to you, I would be devastated," he said. "Pay attention when you drive, okay?"

"I normally do," I said. "I have, like, no tickets."

He nodded, acknowledging that I had a point. "And while your Saab's in the shop, how 'bout using your mom's Prius? It's in great shape."

I looked over at the closed garage door. My dad and Claudia always parked in the driveway, but my mom's car had been in the garage since June. My dad told me in an e-mail when I was away at school—before I had stopped reading his e-mails—that he started the engine once a month and drove it around the block to make sure it stayed in good condition.

It would be kind of nice to be in my mom's old car, I decided. Maybe it would help me feel closer to her, until she came back. Her ghost had said she would be back, right? Now I just had to wait.

"Yep, fine, that works," I said. Then I opened my door and stepped out into the night.

As my dad and I walked back to the house, I glanced over at the Chinese garden.

I put one of my hands close to my heart. "Forever and always," I said aloud, as if my mother's ghost was still there.

My dad overheard me. "What?" he asked.

I shook my head. "Skip it," I said, and headed back into the house.

GAME PLAN

As soon as we walked into the living room, I noticed a commotion. The guests stood in a huge circle, hollering like they were at a boxing ring. I pushed forward past a man wearing a Christmas-themed tie with an image of Santa Claus golfing, and finally spotted what all the cheering was about. Claudia was in the center of the action, clunking around in her heels and red dress while wildly waving a baseball bat at the reindeer piñata. A black blindfold was over her eyes as she swung at the crepe-paper animal that had been lowered from the ceiling on a string. It looked like Rudolph the Red-Nosed Reindeer was about to be socked by the wicked witch of the West Hollywood Hills.

Patty spun the blindfolded Claudia in circles. Oliver's mom looked just as kooky as ever. Her kinky hair was pulled up in a messy bun and she was wearing a frumpy, long yellow dress and patent-leather black clogs. I could see Oliver stuck behind the bar, still mixing drinks for the guests. He waved at me and I waved back. He would never believe the night I'd had. I hardly believed it myself.

"Move to the right!" Patty yelled, pushing Claudia forward. "Cold! Cold! Hot!" she commented as Claudia moved farther from and then closer to the object.

"You got it!" a group of women screamed out. My aunt took a whack at the reindeer's eyes, but she undershot by a few inches. She swung a second time, but missed again. Then she ripped off her blindfold. Her eyes landed in my direction and she glared at me for a moment. Then she clenched the bat tighter in her fists and clobbered the piñata with all her might. I mean, she gave it a serious beat-down, and it was spooky because I kind of felt like she was imagining my face on that reindeer's head. Was she pissed that I had dragged her boyfriend away from her big party? Good. I hoped she was upset. I was pretty upset myself.

The bottom of the piñata burst open and the contents splattered across the floor. Instead of candy, the reindeer had been filled with Mac lipsticks, lip glosses, and samples of Bumble and Bumble shampoos, conditioners, and gels. It was like a celebrity gift bag stuffed into a piñata!

As the guests scrambled around grabbing the freebies, I cleared out of there in search of Anna Maria. I needed some serious advice. Plus, Claudia and me in the same room right then could equal serious trouble.

I found Anna Maria in the kitchen scrubbing a stack of dirty dishes. I ran over to her.

"Anna Maria, listen!" I said, practically out of breath.

"*Dios mío.* Are you okay?" She turned off the faucet and then wiped her wet hands on her red floral smock. "Your father said you crashed the car."

"Yeah, skip that. I'm fine," I said. There was no time to get into the details of my accident. I had more pressing things to talk about. "The Señor del Cementerio was right. Something happened!"

"Something what?" said Anna Maria.

"I can't tell you exactly 'cause I've been sworn to secrecy," I said. "But something came to me and it was amazing and frightening all at once. Is that possible, though? Or am I losing it?"

"Shh, shh," she said, running her hand over my back to try and calm me down.

"Help me make sense of this. Please! I don't know who to turn to!" I said.

"Listen to me." Anna Maria put both hands on my shoulders and looked at me intently. "Make sure you can see what's real and what's not."

"Like, how do you mean?"

"Test what you hear and what you see. Make sure you can trust it," she said. "Sometimes bad spirits come in the form of familiar faces. Maybe your friends are your enemies. Maybe your enemies are your friends."

"Okay, that makes sense," I said, nodding. Suddenly it was like my mind started spinning really fast and everything was coming together for me. Even though the spirit had come in the form of my mom, maybe it was a bad force trying to trick me. Or maybe it was my own mind trying to trick me. I had to be sure. And the only way to be sure was to find out if it was true that Claudia had poisoned my mom. If that was true, then the ghost had been real. Once I knew for sure, I could get revenge, like my mom had asked. And if it wasn't true, well, then I didn't know what I'd do.

"From here on in, don't take anything I do at face value," I said. I had a plan: I'd be nice to Claudia. I'd get close to her. I'd find out what really happened the day my mom died.

"How do you mean?" Anna Maria asked.

"If you see me acting sweet to Claudia, don't believe it," I said.

"I don't know exactly what you're doing," she said slowly. "*Pero ten cuidado.* Be careful."

"I will be," I assured her. "Thank you, Anna Maria. I don't know what I'd do without you."

I ran up to my bedroom and paced around, listening, until the party finally started dying down below. I swear, this had been the longest night of my entire life.

Then around two A.M., just as I was finally falling asleep, there was a knock on my door. I walked over in my tank top and pink-and-green plaid pajama bottoms and answered it.

Oliver stood in the doorway, his tuxedo jacket off and his bow tie loosened.

"Hey, I was about to take off. I heard you got into a car accident. You okay?"

"My *limbs* are fine," I said. I couldn't say the same about my heart or mind.

"Phew. I was worried." His kind eyes melted me a little, but I just couldn't deal with a guy right now. I had so much to worry about—my mom, Claudia. What was true and what wasn't?

"I didn't like Claudia's face when she looked at you and then smacked the reindeer," Oliver went on.

"Oh, you caught that?" I said. "They should arrest her for piñata cruelty."

Oliver laughed. "Listen, can I get you out of here this weekend? I have my job at Save the Harbor tomorrow in Long Beach—"

"Save the what?" I asked.

"It's this nonprofit I work at a few days a week—but how 'bout coming with me to the La Brea Tar Pits on Saturday?"

"The tar pits?" I asked. Maybe that was just what I needed, a date to distract me from the insanity of my life.

"I've been meaning to go for months," Oliver said as he pushed his hair back out of his eyes.

"I'm game," I said. "Haven't been there in years."

"Sweet!" Oliver broke into a grin, but then blushed. He

seemed embarrassed for acting so eager. "Oh, and my mom said she heard a girl's voice in the bathroom when she interrupted us earlier. I told her she was crazy. She *is* crazy."

"Happy you kept her at bay," I said.

"You can say that again." He softly pinched the side of my waist. His hands felt nice on me, but I pulled away.

"I'm completely beat," I said.

"That's cool, that's cool," he said. "Should I . . . ?" He gestured with both arms toward the door. "Head out?"

"Yeah, sorry. It's been an intense night."

"Got it. Rest up and see ya Saturday," he said, and then quickly took off.

I listened to his footsteps disappearing down the hallway. Then I walked over to my bed and crawled under the white and blue daisy-print comforter. Tomorrow, I'd begin testing what the ghost had said. I'd pretend I was sorry for being difficult lately and I'd tell Claudia I was finally ready to bond with her. It would be like the Trojan horse, which I had learned about in history class my freshman year at Winchester. The Greeks gave the Trojans a huge horse statue as a symbol of their defeat. The Trojans thought they had won the war. But at nighttime, when no one was expecting it, the Greek soldiers snuck out of the horse and destroyed the city, taking down their enemy.

APOLOGY

Friday, December 18

The next morning, I woke up and peeked outside my bedroom window. Claudia's white Mercedes was still parked in the driveway, but my dad's Porsche was gone. I assumed he had gone to the weekly Saturday basketball game he played with other middle-aged "suits" at some entertainment lawyer's plush estate in Bel Air.

I brushed my teeth and hurried downstairs. I guessed Claudia would still be angry with me for taking off during her party last night. But I'd be an actress like Felicia and I'd pretend nothing was wrong.

Downstairs, through the sliding-glass door of the sun-room, I spotted Claudia swimming the backstroke in the pool, her long, tan arms swinging over her head and then splashing into the turquoise water. Before I went outside, I repeated Anna Maria's advice in my head. *Test what you hear and what you see. There are good spirits and bad.* Then it was game time. I pushed open the sliding door and walked into the backyard.

As Claudia reached the deep end, she noticed me. She held on to the edge of the pool and looked my way through a pair of red goggles. Then she lifted them up and pushed them back over her hair like a headband.

"Mornin'," I said as cheerfully as possible, and walked over to the side of the pool.

"How're you feeling? I was really worried about you last night," Claudia said. Her tone sounded concerned, but I questioned the sincerity. Was she pretending to be nice to me, just like I was pretending to be nice to her?

"My neck's a little sore, but otherwise no bruises," I said, and sat down at the edge of the pool, dunking my feet into the cool water.

"Thank God. I mean, when your father told me you crashed, I couldn't think straight," she said.

Yeah, right. I knew she was pissed my dad had had to take off during her fiesta. But I brushed off her BS and stayed on the "nice" track.

"Hey, Claudia," I said. "I'm sorry about running out of your party last night, but all these changes have been overwhelming for me."

"I understand." She twisted her hair, and water dripped

from it. "I know it must be a lot to get used to, darling. But just know that I'm here for you."

Was she for real? What about the look she'd given me when she was destroying that poor piñata?

"Anyway, my dad thinks I should bond with you and I've decided he's right," I said. The goal was to sound apologetic, but not to lay it on so thick that she wouldn't believe my sudden change in attitude.

Claudia studied me for a moment. My pulse quickened as I waited for her reaction.

"So how about tonight?" I asked. "You and me."

"This evening?" She cocked her head to the side, surprised.

"Yeah, the Geisha House. My best friend waitresses there and I'm sure she can hook us up with a reservation. So what do ya say?"

Claudia looked down at the pool, scooping her hand through the water. I waited for her response. *Please say yes*, I prayed. Finally, she looked back up at me.

"Sure, that sounds great," she said with a smile, flashing her bleached teeth.

"Cool!" I said, jumping to my feet. "I'll make sure I get us a great table!"

Back inside, I ran upstairs to my bedroom and called Felicia. She picked up right away.

"First of all, sorry I acted a little nuts yesterday," I said.

"You were, like, possessed. I was really worried," Felicia said, her voice still groggy from waking up. "I mean, you could star in the next *Exorcist*."

"Can you blame me?" I asked. "The Christmas Spectacular was getting to me. And seeing my dad and Claudia all over each other pushed me over the edge. I think I had a panic attack." I felt bad keeping the truth from Felicia, but I had made a vow of secrecy to my mom's ghost, which I had to respect.

"Next time, talk to me about it, okay? Instead of acting like a raving lunatic."

"I will," I said. And I meant it. Mostly. Unless my mom's ghost asked me to make some more promises. "So, I have a big favor to ask. Could you get me a reservation for seven o'clock at Geisha tonight?"

"They're always packed on Friday nights," Felicia said. "But I guess I could talk to my uncle. He asked me to cover for some waitress who needs the night off, so maybe I can convince him that he owes me. . . ."

"Yes! Pretty please," I begged. "I want to come by with Claudia."

"Hold up," Felicia said. "You want to have dinner with your *aunt* tonight? I thought it was true hate."

"It is! But I want to get her trashed out of her mind and see if she talks to me about my mom," I said. "I need to learn more about their messed-up relationship."

"Hmm, all right," she said. "Anything to screw with your aunt. I'll make it happen."

"Has anyone told you today that you rock?" I asked.

"Dude, I just woke up," she said.

"Well, now they have!"

WILD, WILD WEST HOLLYWOOD

That night, as Claudia and I walked out to the driveway, the evening sky was filled with dark clouds and there was a chill in the air. I was wearing jeans, brown platform sandals, and this white and lavender peasant blouse that looked kind of seventies. Claudia was dressed up in a short dress that wrapped around her and tied at the waist. It was covered in a bright print of peacock feathers; she looked like a proud bird, parading over to her sparkling Mercedes.

"I'll drive," I said, and opened the garage to get my mom's Prius.

"No, I got it," Claudia said, taking out her keys.

"Come on, I want to see if this thing still works," I said. Then I hurried over and opened the Prius's door. Claudia shrugged her shoulders and walked over. The truth was I really didn't want her driving because I needed her to feel free to get totally sloshed.

Alone for a moment in my mom's old car, I looked around and spotted CDs thrown all over the place, along with my mom's favorite lavender hand lotion. Had the ghost smelled like lavender last night? I couldn't remember. Maybe that would have told me whether or not it was really my mom. In the future, I had to be more observant.

Claudia flung open the passenger-side door and climbed into the seat.

"Be careful!" I said, grabbing a loose Three Tenors CD from the floor mat before Claudia spiked it with her left heel. She was wearing these ridiculous pink patent-leather shoes with bows made of gold zippers on the toes. I'm sure they were expensive and made by some European designer, but they looked like something a stripper would wear.

"Oops." Claudia moved her foot away as she nestled into the passenger seat in her bird-feather print dress. Then she slammed her door shut, trapping me in a vapor of strong, musky perfume.

"This is fun! Just the girls!" she said as I drove down the twists and turns of Laurel Canyon.

"Yeah, we're gonna have a blast," I said. My mind was already filled with a bunch of questions I wanted to ask her. Like, "When was the last time you saw my mom? Did she seem upset about anything that day?"

On our way to Geisha House, I let Claudia prattle on and on about what a great success her party had been last night and all the people who had told her they'd had the time of their lives. Then we pulled up to the restaurant on Sunset

Boulevard and left the car with the valet. We walked through the orange-painted doorway and then the hostess led us into a red, neon-lit dining room that looked like a futuristic Tokyo nightclub. It was filled with beautiful twentysomething Hollywood types socializing over platters of artistically arranged sushi.

"This room has way too many perky tits and emaciated cheekbones," Claudia said as she looked around. "I feel like an old lady in this young crowd."

I bit my lip. "You fit right in here. Don't worry."

As soon as we sat at the table, Claudia excused herself to take a phone call. "Tomoko again," she said, looking down at her phone as it vibrated. "That man works twenty-four hours a day, every day. No Friday nights out for him. I wonder how Annie deals with it?" Once Claudia was out of sight, Felicia ran over to me. She was dressed in her waitress uniform, a turquoise kimono and a chopstick poking out of her ponytail.

"I owe you big-time for getting us this reservation. Thanks a million!" I said.

"Anything for my best friend," she said. "What can I get for you? I made sure to have you seated in my section."

"One iced tea for me and a super-strong cocktail for her. Please and thanks."

"What kind of cocktail?" Felicia asked.

"Just ask the bartender for his most potent drink that tastes sweet," I said. I saw Claudia heading back over to our table. "Quiet, she's coming."

I put on a fake smile as my aunt arrived back at the table. "Claudia, this is my best friend, Felicia," I said. I hadn't gotten to introduce them last night at the party.

"Hi, what's up?" Felicia said.

Claudia grinned. "Wow, what a pretty girl you are."

"Thanks," Felicia replied.

"She's an actress," I said. "Felicia's been in a bunch of commercials and guest-starred on one of those cop shows. Actually you've been on all of them, haven't you, Felish?"

"Shush, you're embarrassing me," she said with a smile. "I'll be right back." She turned around and headed in the direction of the bar.

Claudia sat back down at the table. "She's cute," she said. "But if she really wants to be a starlet, she should lose ten pounds."

"I think she looks great as she is," I said.

"I agree, she's adorable. But if she wants to work . . ." As Claudia put her napkin on her lap, I bit my tongue. *Be nice, be nice*, I reminded myself. It wasn't worth it to bicker with her over Felicia's weight. I had more important things to do tonight.

While we looked over the menu selections, Felicia came back with the drinks. She placed them on the table: an iced tea for me and a dark red liquid in a martini glass for Claudia.

My aunt raised one eyebrow at her glass. "What is this, monkey blood?"

"It's called the Geisha's Dream. I hope you enjoy it," Felicia said. She gave me a discreet wink as she left the table.

Claudia took a sip of the drink and then licked her lips. "I like this place. I think there could be a movie set here. Something about a geisha and a werewolf. Or a scene from *Dead Bachelorette*. Maybe this is where they go for the bachelorette party! Ooh, I'll have to mention that to Tomoko."

I played around with my appetizer fork. "I have to tell you, I'm not big into horror movies."

"Oh, honey, you're missing out!" She took another sip of her cocktail. "But I'm not talking slasher junk. What I love is pure cult horror. Have you ever seen any Lucio Fulci stuff?"

I shook my head.

"He was a brilliant Italian filmmaker. In *City of the Living Dead*," Claudia continued, "there's a scene where a girl gets a handful of worms and tomb rot thrown into her face. She starts foaming at the mouth and then vomits up her own organs."

I scrunched up my face. "Ew, gross. That sounds gnarly."

Claudia shook her finger in the air. "No, it's a masterpiece."

"I don't get why anyone would voluntarily want to scare the hell out of themselves," I said.

"Horror films are about much more than that. They fit a deeper purpose in this world," she said as she took another sip from her martini glass.

"Name one thing that's so good about them," I said.

"When you watch one, you get to experience the most primal of human instincts, the adrenaline rush. You're forced to confront your deepest, darkest fears. And, most importantly"—Claudia leaned in to me and lowered her voice dramatically—"horror movies remind us that we're not in control." She picked up her cocktail and took another big swig, finishing it. "Anyhoo, wanna split some appetizers? I think the tuna tataki looks delish. I love me my sushi."

"That sounds great," I lied. The truth was I had no appetite. I was completely focused on my task.

When Felicia came to take our order, I gestured to Claudia's almost-empty glass.

"Keep 'em coming," I whispered to Felicia after Claudia ordered her food.

Claudia was well into her third Geisha Dream by the time our entrées arrived. I noticed that her face was flushed and she kept running her fingers through her hair.

I rubbed my palms together and looked across the table. My aunt was busy mixing a bowl of soy sauce and wasabi. Then she dipped a piece of lobster sushi—the most expensive thing on the menu—into the sauce and popped it into her mouth.

"My mom was very allergic to crustaceans," I said.

Claudia glanced at me with her mouth full. Her cheeks swelled as she chewed. "Oh, yes, I'm well aware. Aren't you going to try any yellowtail?"

"Maybe in a moment," I said, biting on a fingernail. "So why do you think the two of you fought so much?"

Claudia took a sip of her drink and then put it down. "Growing up, I'm sure you only heard her point of view. But there's more than one side to the story, you know."

"Well, I'd really love to hear your side now," I said, all smiles.

"It's complicated," she said. She grabbed a piece of the yellowtail roll with her chopsticks.

"I'm sure. You guys were very different, right?" I said. "And maybe a little competitive with each other?"

"You can say that again," Claudia replied. "The relationship between two sisters is the most complicated one in the world."

"Well, what was your last memory of her?" I asked. "Like, the last time you saw her?"

"Let me think," Claudia said. "I came for a swim in your pool. She was going on and on about how she forgot to remind you to take your sunscreen. She was always very overprotective of you, if you want my opinion. You were at the beach, I guess."

Just then I remembered. I hadn't brought sunscreen with me to the beach the day my mom died. I had felt pale from a whole semester back East and I wanted to get a tan. But I'd gotten a terrible burn.

"I was at the beach the day she died. Were you with her then?" I asked.

"No, oh God no. I'm sure it must have been another day," Claudia said as she took another big bite of lobster sushi. She was looking right at me and I'd always heard that when someone lies, they look away. So was she lying or telling the truth? The police report had said that my mom was alone when she died. Did this mean Claudia had poisoned her and then left?

Before I could investigate further, Claudia pointed one of her chopsticks toward a table filled with three good-looking guys in their early twenties.

"How about one of those stallions for you?" she asked.

"Um, thanks, but they're not my type," I said. "So back to my mom . . . I want to hear more stories about her, like from when you guys were little. I think it helps me with the healing process and—"

Claudia cut me off. "Sorry, but these boys are too cute. You need to meet them." She smiled with her big bleached teeth and waved to their table.

"What are you doing?" I asked. "I don't want to hang out with them. I came here to spend the night with you."

"Come on, lighten up. We can chat anytime," Claudia said.

Just then one of the guys walked over to us. "I hope it's not too forward, but would you ladies care to join us for some sake bombs?" the guy said, running his fingers through his spiky hair. I thought I saw a glob of gel rub off on his thumb.

"No, thanks," I said.

"Yes! We'd love to," Claudia said. She jumped up from

her seat, stumbled, and then steadied herself on the chair.

"Great, we'll pull up extra seats," the guy said. "I'm Blake."

"I'm Claudia and this is Holly," my aunt said as she followed Blake, yanking me by the arm. She dragged me over to the other table, where Blake introduced his two friends, Drew and Jimmy.

I slid into a chair and scouted the room, looking for Felicia. When I caught her attention, she raised her eyebrows at me and mouthed, "Wow." Then Felicia came over and took the table's drink order.

"Hang in there," she whispered to me, and lightly punched me on the arm.

When the shot glasses and beer arrived, Jimmy moved closer to Claudia and taught her how to properly drink a sake bomb. "See, you cross a pair of chopsticks over the beer glass," he said loudly. "And you balance the shot on top. Then you do this. . . ." He led the table in pounding their fists and chanting "Sake bomb! Sake bomb!" until the shots dropped down into the cups.

"Now chug!" Drew yelled.

Everyone drank except for me. I watched Claudia chug her sake bomb like a pro and then slam the empty glass on the table.

"You, all of you!" Claudia said to us seriously, like she was giving a presidential address. "You can call me Saddlebags. You can call me Crow's-feet. But you can never, ever call me Old Fart."

The guys broke out laughing. I rolled my eyes.

"This lady's cool," Blake said to me.

I crossed my arms. "A delight."

He looked down at my full glasses. "Why didn't you take the shot?"

"I've got enough bombs exploding in my life," I said. "I don't need to drink one."

"Bombs? Are you, like, in the army or something?" Blake put his arm around my shoulder. I moved away. "I bet you make a slamming marine. Hot," he whispered close to the side of my face.

"I was being metaphorical, but forget it. I think we're on two different planes," I said.

"You fly a plane?" Blake said. "That is so sexy."

I shook my head and looked across the table at Claudia laughing with Jimmy and Drew on either side of her. Then Jimmy said, "Get out of town! You made the movie *Chainsaw Cheerleaders*? I saw that when I was in college."

I couldn't believe this guy had actually taken two hours of his life to watch one of Claudia's horror flicks.

"That's the one where the hot cheerleaders chuck their pom-poms into the bonfire and then steal chain saws from the local hardware store to kill the blood-sucking team of football players, right?" Jimmy asked.

Claudia nodded her head proudly. "Yes, you nailed it," she said.

"Man, that's so cool you're a producer," Drew said, and

then waved Felicia over and ordered another round of sake bombs. I looked up at her with "help me" eyes.

"I thought you wanted it like this," Felicia leaned down and whispered. "Drunk as a skunk."

"Yes and no," I said. I had wanted her drunk enough to spill some secrets, but not so drunk that she was incoherent, and that seemed to be where the night was headed.

"Over my head," Felicia said, and scrunched her eyebrows. Then she took off back to the bar.

"Whoa! You're her *aunt*? I thought you were sisters. I can't believe you're forty-six," Jimmy said as he checked Claudia out. I was surprised she had told him her age. She usually acted like it was strictly confidential. She was four years older than my mom but she had always tried to tell people they were really two years apart.

"You look, like, thirty-five tops," Drew said.

Blake leaned in to me one more time. "Hey, wanna, uh, go slow-dancing with me in my car?"

"Oh, thanks so much. But no chance in hell," I said.

"You're so uptight. Damn, girl, how old are you?" he asked.

"Too young for you," I said.

Felicia brought over the next round of drinks and everyone downed them again, except for me. I watched Claudia throw back the mug of beer and dribble some liquid down the front of her peacock dress.

"You don't want that one, either?" Blake said, eyeing my drink.

"You guessed right. I'm driving," I said. *And I'm seventeen,* I almost added. But I guessed these guys wouldn't have a problem with underage drinking.

"Oh, Holly." Claudia swayed back and forth in her seat. "Lighten up. It's girls' night out. This is fun."

"Is it?" I said.

"Whoa, that's the weirdest thing," Jimmy said, as if coming upon a sudden realization. "You're closer to our age and you're so serious, but your aunt is so much older and she's super cool."

"Usually it's the reverse," Drew said, slapping Jimmy on the arm.

"It's like that movie my little sister likes, *Freaky Friday,*" Blake chimed in.

"And today's Friday!" Drew said, as if this was the most amazing coincidence ever.

"What's it like having an old lady living in your body?" Blake asked me.

Then Jimmy winked at my aunt. "And what's it like being a hot teen?"

Claudia giggled and batted her eyelashes.

I clenched my fists and stood up from the table. "Okay, that's enough! We're going home!" I said.

The guys yelled out in protest.

"But, darling, it's still early." Claudia looked at her diamond-encrusted watch. "It's only nine thirty. We can stay a little longer."

"No! You're about to fall off your chair." I got up and walked over to her.

"I am not!" Claudia said. "I have been sitting on chairs for forty-six years and I'm very good at it." Then she laughed uproariously, like she'd just said the funniest thing.

"Come on, we need to go," I said, tugging at her arm.

"It's okay. You can stay. I'll take you home later," Jimmy said to Claudia. "The buzzkill can leave."

"No chance she's staying without me," I said. "Now, Aunt Claudia, get up." I helped her to her feet. Then I pushed her ahead of me toward the front door.

"'Scuse me, boys. The sheriff's in town," Claudia said teasingly over her shoulder as she stumbled away.

Before we left, I got the check from Felicia. Claudia mumbled that she wanted to pay, so I waited as she went through her large designer pocketbook. She kept digging in her purse and apparently couldn't find what she was looking for.

"Where's my wallet? There's too much junk in here!" she said, practically slurring.

"Want my help?" I offered.

"No, I can do it myself," she said. Then she turned to Felicia and gestured to a nearby side table that had a vase of fresh flowers and a bowl full of mints on it.

"Can I put my bag down here for a second?"

"Go right ahead," Felicia said.

Then in her drunken stupor, she dumped out her whole

purse onto the table. A bunch of customers were just leaving and I watched them stare as they walked by. Out of her bag flew a date book, a makeup case, her wallet, a ton of loose change, and four bottles of prescription pills. One of the brown pill containers fell to the floor. I reached down to pick it up, but Claudia beat me to it.

"I got that!" she said, and shoved the container, as well as the rest of her belongings, minus her wallet, back into her bag. I didn't have a chance to see the name of any of the drugs, but my curiosity was certainly piqued. Were these the pills—the poison—she had used to kill my mother?

"What are all those pills for?" I asked my aunt. Since she was sloshed, maybe she'd just come right out and tell me.

Instead, she turned to me and said, "You never ask a woman her age or her medication."

"But you already told those guys your age, so I think you can tell me about your medication," I said. "I mean, after all, I'm your niece." *And your boyfriend's daughter*, I could have added. But I didn't.

I thought it was pretty sound reasoning, but Claudia was busy paying the bill and I guess she didn't hear me. Or she just chose to ignore me. She handed over her credit card to Felicia. As we waited for the receipt, Claudia leaned one hand on the wall to balance herself. "I feel a little woozy," she told me. She stuck out her tongue a little bit and then made a face as if it tasted bad.

When Felicia came back with the receipt, Claudia told me

to sign it for her. I stepped away a few feet toward the bar and signed it on the counter. I made sure to give Felicia a great tip.

"Wow, thanks," Felicia said, looking at the check. "But are you okay?"

"I guess," I said. "I didn't get all the info I wanted, and now I'm left with this drunken mess." We both looked over at Claudia and watched her take a mint candy from a bowl on the hostess stand and then stick it in her mouth with the plastic wrapper still on.

"That can't taste good," Felicia said.

"I better get her home before we get kicked out and I'm never allowed back here to visit you," I said.

"All right, talk to you soon. Stay strong," she said. Then she validated my parking ticket using a stamp pad on the hostess stand.

Claudia threw her arm over my shoulder as we walked out onto the sidewalk, where I handed the valet my ticket. As we waited for the car, a group of young, pretty guys and girls stared at Claudia as she staggered around, and I tried to pretend I didn't know her. But when the attendant drove up with my car, everyone could see she was with me.

The valet left the door open and then walked around to open the passenger side.

"No, thank you," Claudia said to the attendant as he stood there waiting for her to get inside. "I want to go in back."

"What's the problem?" I asked.

"I don't feel well so I want to lie across the backseat."

The attendant opened the back door. Then Claudia dove in headfirst.

All along the way back home, I could hear Claudia licking her lips loudly in the backseat and occasionally saying things like, "What a great night! That was really super!"

Then when I stopped at a red light, she suddenly popped up from the backseat. Her head swayed back and forth. "This was so sweet of you to plan! Now I can see why you're so wonderful. Your dad always said you were."

I looked over my shoulder at Claudia and forced a closed smile. "Glad you had fun," I said.

"And the boys! They were so charming. I hope you gave them your number," she said, then slid back down into the seat.

"Keep hoping," I said under my breath. "So back at the dinner table . . . What were you gonna tell me about the last day you saw my mom, that day you went over to use the pool?" I asked.

"Oh, I forgot." Claudia started tracing circles with her fingertips on the headrest of the passenger seat. "It's horrible what happened to her, but your dad's so good to me. I've never been this happy. See, my whole life, I've had no luck with love. And it's been hard, but I feel so grateful to have your dad now. I've been attracted to him all these years and—"

This was the first time I had ever heard my aunt blatantly admit that she'd had her eye on my dad before my mom even

125

passed away. This, plus the fact that she'd been with my mom the day she died, plus the pills, seemed to prove that what I had seen the other night was really my mom's ghost, and that what she had told me was true.

Claudia kept blabbering in the backseat. "Your dad's so cute. He's like a sexy professor. He makes me want to dress up as a schoolgirl. And I can't wait to give him the Christmas gift I have for him. It's hidden away in my desk drawer. I mean, if he knew, it would knock his pants off."

"What is it?" I asked. I almost didn't want to know because I was so grossed out, but I had to ask. She didn't answer, though. And when I looked back to see what was up, she was fast asleep. I didn't need to hear another word. I had all the proof I needed.

The light changed to green and I stepped hard on the gas. As the car lurched forward, Claudia's body rolled off the seat and onto the floor.

"Oops, sorry," I said, and then raced the rest of the way home.

TAR PITS

Saturday, December 19

The next day, I met Oliver at the La Brea Tar Pits. He looked adorable. The pale blue shirt he was wearing was almost the exact color of his eyes.

As we walked toward the viewing platform, I told him about my night out with Claudia.

"She actually admitted she had her eye on my dad before my mom died," I said.

"That's really creepy," Oliver said.

"Tell me about it."

"What do you think your dad likes about Claudia?" he asked.

"He thinks she's really pretty. I can tell by the way he looks at her with this gleam in his eye, like he's checking out a hot mama. And I think he's one of those guys who always needs a girlfriend and can't be alone. My mom used to joke that he's had a girlfriend nonstop since second grade."

"So he's a serial monogamist?" Oliver said.

"Precisely," I answered. "And I bet Claudia's probably different when she's around him. Some girls' personalities change when they're around a guy they like."

"Oh, yeah. I've seen that before," said Oliver.

"Like there's this chick I went to junior high with named Melody. I actually ran into her the night of the *Caddyshack* party. Anyway, she's a huge snot face, but she had this serious boyfriend named Freddy D all senior year and whenever I saw her with him, she'd be acting sweet as pie."

"Buttering up her man," Oliver said. "So he doesn't see the real her."

"Exactly!" I said.

We reached the viewing platform and glanced down at what looked like a lake of liquefied tires. There was all this tar bubbling up from deep below the earth's surface and it somehow had gurgled up at this exact spot in Los Angeles. It had been doing so for tens of thousands of years, all the way back to the Ice Age. I had come here on a field trip in middle school, just like practically every other kid who grew up in L.A., and I learned that back in prehistoric times, all this tar was covered in water, so it looked like a lake. Woolly mammoths and saber-toothed tigers would come for a drink and then get stuck. Their legs got cemented in one place and they couldn't move, so they died. And today archaeologists were still pulling out the bones.

There were tons of tourists snapping pictures and parents with little kids running around, so we walked along the viewing platform to an empty area way down on one end.

We had this private oasis together in between a palm tree and a life-size replica of a wooly mammoth that looked like an elephant with long white tusks. As we checked out the lake of tar, Oliver reached over and grabbed my pinky and ring finger in his.

I told him what I remembered learning about this place on my school trip.

"So it's like the dinosaurs came here to drink and got stuck?" he asked.

"Yeah, plus, there's one other thing I remember hearing," I said.

"What?" Oliver pushed down the lid of his baseball cap and looked at me.

"They found a human skeleton here, too. It was of a woman dating back, like, nine thousand years."

"I wonder how she got in there?" he said.

"Maybe she was sacrificed in some old religious ritual," I said.

"I doubt it. If it was a ritual, there would've been a lot more human skeletons found," said Oliver. "Since she wouldn't have been the only one, right?"

"Then maybe she was murdered. Like, someone threw her in," I said, and cringed at the thought.

We both stared out at the bubbling tar for a few more moments.

"How did she die?" Oliver asked quietly.

"She probably drowned, or maybe she got eaten by a hungry T. rex," I said.

"That's not what I meant. . . ."

"Hmm?" I looked over at him and suddenly realized he was talking about my mother. "Oh." I looked down.

"Sorry, it's just no one talks about it," he said.

"Yeah, well . . ." I said, shuffling my feet. "This is like our first date—you really wanna talk about this now?"

"I can handle it," Oliver said. "But I don't want to pressure you."

I took a deep breath.

"I went to the beach with Felicia that day. It was June. I hadn't been back from school for that long, but from the second I got home, I knew something was wrong. The house would just get really quiet when my mom was sick, and it was quiet like that when I got home that first day. And of course it was a tip-off that my mom hadn't gone with my dad to the airport to pick me up like she usually did."

I looked at Oliver to see if this was too much for him, but he was looking right back at me like he could take whatever I had to say next.

"So I'd been home for, like, a week and I hadn't seen Felicia yet. I just hadn't wanted to leave my mom, in case she needed me. But that day she had seemed better, and Felicia had called, and my mom had been like, 'Go, I'll be fine!' I wasn't sure I should go, but . . . I did. And by the time I got home that afternoon, she was gone."

Oliver squinted his eyes a little, deep in thought. "Whoa, I can't imagine," he said.

"She had depression for many years. Bipolar disorder—that's what she was diagnosed with when I was little. The police said . . ." I hesitated. Part of me wanted to tell him about Claudia being involved, that it might not be true that my mom had really killed herself. But I knew I couldn't. One day, Oliver would know the truth. Everyone would. "The cops said she took her life. They said it made sense due to her history."

Oliver shook his head slowly back and forth. He looked down at his flip-flops.

"I always felt like it was my fault," I said in a small voice. "I felt like, if I had just stayed home that day. If I hadn't left her alone . . ." And now I knew there was another layer. If I hadn't left her alone that day, Claudia wouldn't have had the chance to do whatever she did.

"Man . . ." He stroked his hand across my cheek. "I wish I was . . ."

"What?" I asked.

"It's that I want to . . ." His voice trailed off.

"Yeah?"

"I want to, um, make you happy," he said.

I looked at him and our eyes met pupil to pupil, iris to iris. It was like we were really seeing into each other. And our eyes were pools, but not pools of tar, where parts of the past got stuck and died. These were pools that were warm, clear, and safe, the kind you'd want to jump into and swim in.

Oliver pulled me toward him and held me in his arms. I rested my head on his chest and he squeezed me tight. And for a few minutes, I just stayed there and breathed.

After Oliver and I finished looking around the tar pits and then the museum hall, we headed over to Swingers diner on Beverly Boulevard. We slid in next to each other across the vinyl seat of a semicircle booth below a framed picture of a cow. The restaurant was a quarter full of Hollywood hipster types in vintage jeans, tight old T-shirts, and purposely messy haircuts. We ordered hamburgers with extra-crispy fries and milk shakes.

Once the waitress brought over our food, Oliver opened up to me more about his own family life.

"My mom's like a dinosaur stuck in that tar pit. She tries to be my dad's buddy even though they've been divorced forever."

"Like, what does she do?" I asked, dipping a fry into a ton of ketchup.

"She sends presents to him every year and it's like, 'Happy

birthday, thanks for ruining my life, buy something nice with this Macy's gift card.'"

"But it's good she's trying to be his friend, right?" I asked.

"No." Oliver took a sip of his chocolate shake. "He didn't even love her."

"I'm sure that's not true."

"He told me," Oliver said. He took off his baseball cap and shook his hand through his hair, then he put the cap down on the table.

"What did he say?" I asked, keeping my eyes on him as I sipped from the straw of my milk shake.

"After he came out of the closet, he told me he never wanted to be with a woman or have kids, but he thought it was what was expected of him as a man, so he just pretended. Basically, I was born out of a twelve-year charade. Chew on that piece of fucked-up goodness." Oliver took a big bite of his hamburger and juice ran over his fingers. He wiped them clean on a napkin.

"Come on. How could someone not be jacked to have you show up as their baby?" I asked.

"He's kind of a huge asshole. Never calls me. Haven't seen him in years," Oliver said, crumpling his napkin in his fist.

"Well, he's missing out big-time," I said. Then I took the hat from where Oliver had rested it on the table and plopped it down on my head.

He looked at me and smiled. "You look cute," he said, and

touched my cheek with his finger. I thought he looked pretty cute, too.

Just then two teenage girls sat down at the booth next to us. One of the girls was complaining to the other in a loud valley-girl accent: "I texted Cliff and then he didn't text me back and, oh my God."

Oliver lowered his voice and put his arm up on the booth so it was around my shoulder. "I've been saving up money to move out one of these days so I don't have to live with my mom anymore."

"Where would you want to move to?" I asked.

"Venice Beach probably," he said. "Some of my friends from school have a place there and they've got an extra room opening up."

"That would rock," I said.

"Tell me about it," Oliver said, and then suddenly, out of nowhere, he leaned in to kiss me. It caught me by surprise as our lips touched, and suddenly I felt like I was the lead singer of a music video called "Ecstasy."

We made out for a few moments, and then I pulled back an inch.

"That's a French fry, hamburger, milk shake kiss," I said.

"Mmm, my favorite kind," he said, then leaned back in for more. As we made out in the booth, thoughts were running through my head like: *Holly, you're at a diner! This is major PDA! What are you thinking?*

But my body was like: *I want more of this! Bring it on!*

We kissed for a minute until one of the valley girls from the next booth made a fake coughing sound and then said under her breath, "Get a room."

Oliver heard it, too, and without flinching, he turned toward the girl. "Get a man."

Later that afternoon, it was starting to rain as Oliver stopped the car to drop me off at home. Actually he was letting me off down the street from my house so his mom wouldn't come out and see us. He still didn't want her to know he was dating me, since she was so paranoid about losing her job.

"I never know when she's working in the Burbank office or at your place," Oliver said.

"Totally. It's ridiculous the way Claudia comes and goes as if she belongs here," I said. "I don't get why she even has to work from my house. It's just an excuse to have her life more integrated with my dad's. I'm pretty sure she's staying over most nights, too."

"Anyway, sorry about the whole issue with my mom," said Oliver. "I feel like we're in middle school and sneaking around to avoid parents. And I'm the one who's older than you!"

"I kinda like it. It's so retro," I said.

Oliver laughed. "I'm gonna tell my mom about us soon, though."

"Whenever you're ready," I told him.

"I mean, it's ridiculous. I'm eighteen. I can hang out with whoever I want."

"Is that what we're doing? Hanging out?" I said, and tickled his arm.

"Well, if it's all right with you . . ." Oliver said. "I know it's fast, but I kinda know already. . . ."

"Know what?"

"That I want you to be my girlfriend," he said. "If you're cool with that."

As soon as I heard the G word, I smiled and my mouth probably looked like a huge uppercase U. "Sign me up," I said.

"Really?" Oliver said, confirming.

"Oh, yeah!" I said. And so it became official.

Just then I heard the sound of a car's engine. I looked over my shoulder and saw Claudia's Mercedes heading out from my family's estate onto Elsinore Drive. Claudia was driving and Patty was in the passenger seat. We could see their faces behind the moving windshield wipers.

"Oh, shit," Oliver said. "I hope my mom doesn't turn this way."

"She won't," I said. And I was right. "So they were at my house, after all. Glad I missed them!"

"I wonder where they're off to now?" Oliver said, watching the car pull away.

"Let me guess," I said. Then I pretended to be Claudia, saying in her voice, "Oh, get out of my way. I'm driving for a fake-bake and carp-sucking pedicure."

"A carp-sucking what?" Oliver asked.

"It's this treatment I read about in a magazine where fish suck dead skin off your feet."

"Sounds disgusting," he said.

"Yeah, that's why it'd be right up her alley. And oh, wait. Fish are involved, so you might like it, too, Mr. Marine Biologist," I joked.

Oliver laughed. "Thanks, but no thanks. I don't do pedicures," he said, and then he leaned over and kissed me. This was our second kiss (not like I was counting), and as we made out, he put his hand on the back of my neck and slid his hand into my hair. He moved his lips to my cheek and then he whispered in my ear, "Is that just like a normal, everyday kiss for you?"

I felt a little hot and dizzy. I shook my head. "No." There was nothing ordinary about that kiss. It was most definitely an unusual, one-of-a-kind, hard-to-find kiss.

"'Cause if you ask me," Oliver said, "that was metaphysical."

I felt this huge smile inside. I wasn't a hundred percent sure of the textbook definition of that word, but I was positive that I loved the sound of it.

WHAT I FOUND

Walking up the driveway under the now steadily falling rain, I daydreamed about my time with Oliver today and our different kisses. I replayed them in my head and tried to imagine that his mouth was still on mine. It was hard to think about his face without grinning nonstop. I felt like I had downed a chocolate lava cake in one bite and was riding a sugar high. I didn't even mind that I was getting wet.

As soon as I entered the house, I heard the roar of the vacuum and smelled the lemon powder that Anna Maria had been sprinkling on the carpets since I was a little kid. I tracked her down in the living room, where she was pushing the platinum Hoover in perfect lines up and down the length of the room.

"Hi, Anna Maria. Where's my dad?" I asked, breathing in the citrus scent.

She turned off the vacuum. "Still at the office," she said.

"I figured as much, but I wanted to confirm. Hooray! That means the house is all ours!" I cheered. Then I started singing. "It's your birthday! Get busy! Shake your hips and rock this way!"

Anna Maria moved her lips to one side, confused. "No, today's not my birthday."

"I know!" I said. "I'm just jazzed we have the place to ourselves." This abode was so much nicer to hang out in when my dad, Claudia, and Patty weren't in it. Plus, it was the perfect time to go through some of Claudia's things. Maybe I'd discover further proof of her guilt, like a packet of poison pills or demented doodles depicting her darkest thoughts. I wished I'd been able to see what types of pills were in her bag when it had spilled at Geisha House. Could she have used those to kill my mother?

"So tell me, you doing okay?" Anna Maria looked at me, her eyes squinting with concern. "We haven't talked much since the other night."

"I'm doing fine!" I said. "You'll be happy to know I've been following all your advice!"

"I hope so," she said. "Let me know if you need me, okay? I'm here for you."

"Yes, absolutely, but gotta run," I said. With my dad,

Claudia, and Patty out of the house, I wanted to start snooping right away.

I bolted up the stairs. The door to Claudia's home office was closed, so I turned the gold handle and pushed it open. This was my first time in here since my aunt had taken over the place. There were the same white desk and maroon couch that had always been here, but the rest of my mom's stuff had been packed up and stored in the hall closet. Now the space was filled with Claudia's eccentric knickknacks. On the desk sat a lifelike rubber bat with big black wings and painted-on white fangs, and a snow globe with a pair of vampire teeth inside. I shook it and then watched the white flakes fall down over Dracula's fangs. I bet if the Count magically could've gone to high school with Claudia, she would've had a major crush on him and hung pictures of his black, high-collared cape inside her locker door. And she'd have probably dreamed of him taking her to prom and after-partying in Castlevania.

Framed posters of Claudia's movies hung on the wall. One was called *The Clowns of Hell* and showed this scary image of a creepy jester with rainbow-colored curls and lips painted black.

Then there was this gray machine that looked like a projector plugged into the wall. I turned it on and a cloud of smoke rushed out of it. I couldn't believe Claudia had her own fog machine! I hadn't seen one of those since an eighth-grade dance!

Next, I opened the top two drawers in her desk. On the car ride back from Geisha House, Claudia had mentioned that there was something here that would surprise my dad. I dug through pens, Post-its, and other junk. She'd been using the office for only a little while, but she'd already managed to make quite a mess. My mom had always kept her desk so neat. Then I opened the bottom drawer and spotted a shiny red box. I grabbed it from the drawer and pulled the top off. My jaw dropped open like a cartoon character's as I stared at the contents: stacks of eight-by-ten color photographs of Claudia half-dressed in skimpy costumes. She was dolled up as a varsity cheerleader in some, her hair in pigtails, wearing a blue and yellow pleated skirt and holding matching pompoms. Then there were shots of her in a French maid ensemble, complete with the traditional black and white dress, knee-high fishnet tights, and a feather duster. Had Claudia taken these shots for my father as some sort of skanky Christmas present? I couldn't look at these photos for another moment or I'd suffer from post-traumatic stress disorder.

I bent down and put the box back exactly where I had found it. Then I decided to check out her computer. Maybe there'd be some Word document containing a deranged confession like:

Dear Diary,
I hate all animals and babies. And I killed my

sister, too. Don't tell anyone.
—*Claudia*

My finger plunked down on the space bar and the screen lit up. The calendar had been left open. I skimmed through the upcoming week's events, which consisted of meetings, lunches, and conference calls, and then my eyes landed on today's date. I noticed something unusual highlighted in blue:

4pm - Appointment at Bianca Couture Bridal,
234 Rodeo Drive

I had to read that entry three times to really believe it. A bridal salon? Was that where Patty and my aunt had been racing off to when I saw them drive away in the Mercedes just minutes ago? I had been holding on to the hope that this thing between my dad and Claudia was some kind of temporary insanity on his part. But if he was planning on marrying her, that was a whole different situation. It was bad enough to date your dead wife's sister, but to marry your dead wife's killer? That took it to a whole other level.

I paced back and forth and then looked at the clock. It was 3:40 P.M. If I bolted now, I could follow them. Then I'd see for myself what was going on. Yes, that's exactly what I should do! I grabbed my favorite blue-and-white-checked umbrella and ran out to the car. The sky was gray and it was dropping buckets, so I turned the windshield wipers on. As I drove down Laurel Canyon and into Beverly Hills, I was stuck cruising ten miles per hour behind an old lady in a Cadillac. Whenever it rained in L.A., everyone drove extra slowly because they weren't used to it.

Finally, I made it into Beverly Hills. It was 4:12 P.M. when I pulled into a parking lot on Camden Drive. Then I ducked under my umbrella and hurried past all the high-end designer shops on Rodeo Drive, including Valentino, Armani, and Versace, toward Bianca Couture. Since it was after four o'clock, I was pretty sure Claudia and Patty would already be there.

A few minutes later, I spotted the bridal boutique. The window was decorated with four mannequins dressed in elaborate white gowns made of silk and lace. I made my approach like a James Bond girl, quickly crossing the street and then slowly moving in toward the store. When I reached the shop's front window, I ducked down. Then I slowly raised my head back up so I could peek inside. And there was Claudia.

She was with Patty, talking to a sales associate, a man in perfectly tailored black slacks and a crisp white button-down shirt. I watched Claudia chat while she moved her hands around, posing them first by her neckline and then down by her waist. I guessed she was describing the wedding dress she wanted. I couldn't believe she'd actually want to wear white and not some horror-movie black-and-red getup.

Then, the salesman nodded and led Claudia and Patty behind a spiral staircase. Oh, damn! I couldn't see anymore. This vantage point wasn't going to cut it. I took two steps to the right and craned my neck over a mannequin's sparkling ivory veil to try and see what was happening, but no dice.

I realized there was only one thing to do—go inside and try and camouflage myself behind a rack of bridesmaid dresses that I had spotted. I closed my umbrella and then quickly slipped through the entrance. As I headed for the bridesmaid dresses, my wet umbrella dripped all over the marble floor. It was really uncool of me to mess up this fancy store, but I had to keep moving. There wasn't time to go back and put it in the umbrella stand beside the door. I couldn't risk anyone noticing me. I hurried until I was standing behind the lineup of colorful frocks. If Claudia or Patty came out from the dressing-room area, I could duck down behind them.

Just when I thought I had succeeded in my covert mission, a sales associate appeared out of nowhere and headed over toward me.

"Hi, I'm Katrina. Can I help you find something today?" She looked like she was in her late thirties. I took a quick glance at her left hand and didn't notice a wedding ring. Did it bother her to work in a bridal shop?

"I'm just looking. Thanks." I glanced at the back of the store. Claudia and Patty were still in the dressing room.

"Are you going to be a bridesmaid? We just got in Vera

Wang's new collection. Maybe you can recommend it to the bride." Katrina pulled out a pretty strapless number. "If you ask me, this cut is especially beautiful in fog blue."

"Thanks, but I'm fine looking around on my own. A-OK!" I said, and smiled extra big.

Just then Patty and the other sales associate hurried out of the dressing-room area and into the main store. I quickly dropped to the floor and out of view behind the rack of dresses.

"She wants the silver snakeskin with the four-inch heels and the rhinestones," I overheard Patty say.

Katrina raised her eyebrows and looked down at me crouching on the marble tile. "Is everything all right?" she asked.

"Yeah, I mean, no. I lost a ring," I said, pretending to look under the rack of dresses for it. "It just slipped off my finger."

"Oh, no. I'll help," Katrina said, leaning over. "What did it look like?"

"Silver, round, you know . . ." Could I be more vague? That sounded like half the rings on the planet.

Suddenly the male associate hurried over to us. "Katrina, could you do a quick stock check for me? We need a size thirty-eight in the Chloe T-strap."

"Sure, I'm on it," Katrina said.

"And size forty, too. Just in case," I heard Patty say, followed by the sound of her clogs hurrying over to us.

I bit my lip as I glanced up and saw Patty looking down at me. She cocked her head to the side and squinted her eyes like she was confused.

"Holly?" she asked.

"Shh, I'm not really here," I whispered, waving my hands in front of me like two stop signs.

"You're *not*?" Patty asked.

"Yes, you didn't see me!" I quickly got up off the floor. "And I'm leaving now, so no need to tell my aunt. Please." I don't know why I thought Patty would be an ally for me in my moment of need, but I was desperate. I turned and ran for the door, and before I knew it, I was sliding on the wet marble. It was my own fault for dripping my wet umbrella through the store. It felt like slow motion as I fell backward and landed flat on my backside. Katrina rushed over to me.

"Oh, no! Are you okay?" she asked, her eyes bulging with concern.

Then I noticed the male sales associate standing with a phone up to his ear. "Just stay still. Don't move. We're calling for help."

And next I saw Patty kneeling beside me and snapping her fingers in front of my face. "Stay with us. Holly, tell me your name! And what day is it?"

"You just said my name. And it's Saturday," I said. "I fell on my butt, not my head." My back did hurt, though, right at the base of my spine. Damn marble floors. Couldn't they use carpet?

"Keep her down on the floor!" the male sales associate yelled. "The ambulance will be here in a minute."

"Ambulance?" I asked as Katrina gently lowered me down so I was lying flat on the ground. "Hey, I don't need an ambulance. Cancel the order!" Claudia was still in the dressing room and I was hoping against hope that there was still some way for me to get out of the store without her seeing me.

"We have to call for one. It's our policy," Katrina said. "We're liable for accidents happening on store property. There was a bad situation last summer. This bride-to-be slipped and fell and she had to walk down the aisle in a cast."

"Oh, but I promise I won't sue or anything. Cross my heart!" I glanced back at the dressing room.

But it was no use. They wouldn't let me leave, and a few minutes later, two paramedics showed up on the scene. I wanted to vanish from this earth when I saw one male and a female EMT rush into the store with a stretcher.

The female paramedic asked a bunch of questions. She wanted to know exactly what had happened; Katrina explained it all. Then the male paramedic asked me if anything hurt. I told him about my back but that I was sure I'd be fine.

"Can't I just walk it out?" I asked. "Pretty please?"

"From the sound of it, you fell pretty hard. It's best to be as still as possible till we get you checked out," he said.

The two EMTs got me onto the stretcher and buckled me into place. I had seen rolling stretchers like this before in movies and newscasts, but never thought I'd actually be the person taken for the ride.

The paramedics pushed me toward the door. We were almost outside, where I noticed a crowd of Beverly Hills shoppers had stopped on the sidewalk to see what was going on, when suddenly I heard Claudia's voice from the back of the store. "What's all the commotion out here?" she asked. "Patty, I really need your opinion on these shoes." Then she noticed me on the stretcher.

"Holly? What happened? Are you okay?" she asked.

Claudia appeared above me in a white strapless gown with a veil cascading down her long blonde hair. I know brides are supposed to be angelic, and usually they are, but she looked like a monster in lace.

"Darling, what happened to you? Are you all right?" my aunt asked, leaning over me. She reached out and gently touched my hand. Her eyes were wide open, filled with concern that seemed completely fake to me. "Oh, sweetheart, poor thing. Talk to me." Nice how she was pouring on the distress in front of all these people. As if she really cared about me. As if she cared about anything other than marrying my dad and stealing the rest of my mother's life.

As I looked at her, my eyes filled with tears and the crystals embroidered on her gown began to shimmer. "I can't believe it's true," I said. "You're getting married."

☠ ☠ ☠

At the hospital, they ran all sorts of tests, like X-rays of my vertebrae. Then they wheeled me into my room. I was lucky to be put in a single, because I wouldn't want to have to hang out next to a loud moaner or heavy breather. My dad was waiting there when I arrived, with a plastic bag from Jerry's Famous Deli, this well-known chain of restaurants in L.A. that serves up yummy corned-beef sandwiches, cheesecake, and tons of other down-home comfort foods.

"Honey, how are you feeling?" he asked.

"They gave me a painkiller, so that softened the blow," I said.

My dad nodded. "The doctor told me. And he said nothing's broken. You whacked your lower back pretty badly, and it'll be tender and bruised for a little while, but you're going to be fine."

I nodded. Stupid sales associates. I knew I was fine. They should have just let me go.

"Here," my dad said. "I brought you Chicken in a Pot." He opened up the plastic bag and pulled out a big container of chicken soup.

"Thanks, Dad," I said. "But I don't have the flu; I banged my rear end."

My dad pushed a side table over to me and handed me a plastic spoon. "But you're in the hospital, and I used to always get this for you when you were sick."

"I remember," I said. Then I dipped the spoon into the

warm container filled with broth, matzo balls, noodles, carrots, and chicken.

He watched me slurp down a sip. Some egg noodles dropped down on my blue hospital gown. "Oops," I said.

"Tasty?" he asked, smiling.

I nodded and kept eating. The liquid felt warm and comforting as it slid down my throat and into my stomach.

"So," my dad began. "Quite a bit of trouble you caused in Beverly Hills today, huh?"

The vision of Claudia dressed in that white gown was seared into my memory. "I don't know if I was really the one causing the trouble. I think I was just reacting to it. I mean, is there something, like, really huge you forgot to tell me?" I asked.

"Listen, I'm sorry this played out the way it did. I feel horrible," he said, and ran his finger along the metal railing on my bed.

"How could you?" I asked, propping myself up higher on my pillow. A dull ache went through my lower back. I wanted to tell him right then about what my mom's ghost had said. Then he'd rethink this whole crazy idea about marrying Claudia. But then he'd think I had hit my head, not my back, on that floor. He would never believe me.

"You need to know that Claudia and I have been bouncing the idea around, but by no means have we arrived at any decisions yet and—"

"Hello?! She's already trying on dresses!" I accentuated

what I said by waving my plastic spoon in the air.

"I didn't know that till today," my dad said as he cracked his knuckles. "I guess she's excited by the idea."

"You can say that again. More like chomping at the bit." I flicked around a piece of matzo ball in my soup.

"We're still talking it over. No decisions have been made yet," my dad said. "I want to be clear about that and—"

"But, Dad, this is so fast. I mean, what about Mom? Don't you think it would hurt her feelings if she knew?"

He looked down at the floor. "Honey, I don't know how to explain this to you, but as you get older, you'll learn things."

"Like what?" I blurted out.

"Sometimes people grow apart. I loved your mother and will always love her, but you should know, we weren't perfect."

My dad was talking to me like I didn't know anything about their marriage. But I knew they hadn't been a perfect couple. Sometimes I'd hear them arguing, and there had been a couple of days when my mom said things to me like, "Your dad talks on and on about his work; it drives me crazy." Or "Your father is so introverted and cold sometimes." And "I wish he was more affectionate. I can't remember the last time he held my hand."

But it sort of seemed like he was getting at something different, something deeper. "What are you trying to say?" I asked.

"It's just when she was going through her depressions, she was hard to be around. You know, there were times when she didn't like to talk that much and she was sleeping all the time. It was hard to connect with her when she was off in another zone."

"She was always loving to me," I said. I mean, yeah, sometimes she had been quiet and tired, but she'd always let me curl up next to her and watch a movie. And she'd give me a kiss on the cheek and tell me she loved me, and she'd thank me for being patient with her.

"I know that. But you had a different relationship. You were her daughter," my dad said as he rubbed his hand back and forth on his thigh. "Listen, honey. Let's save this for another time. I want to focus on helping you feel better now."

"But it just seems so fast. I mean, is Mom that easily replaceable?"

My dad shook his head. "She will always be a part of me. That will never go away. We spent a huge part of our lives together."

"But then how can you—"

"Shh," he said, resting his hand on my arm. "Now, lie back and relax. And don't worry about anything."

Easy for him to say, I thought. My dad didn't have the ghost of my mom talking to him. His life was so simple. He just went to work and did whatever lawyers do and then he came home and laughed and cuddled up with Claudia while drinking wine from his vintage collection.

I rested my soup container on the side table. "So you're not getting married?" I asked one last time. "Nothing's official?"

"That's right. Nothing has been decided," he said. "And I will certainly let you know if anything changes."

"Yeah, just loop me in," I said sarcastically.

"Of course I will," my dad said, and squeezed my arm.

Luckily, I didn't have to stay in the hospital that night. The doctor came in to discharge me after I finished the soup. During the car ride home with my dad, I texted Oliver and Felicia about what had happened. They both were concerned, but I told them I was doing fine and the champ was back up for another round.

When we got back, Claudia stopped by my bedroom and gave me a "get well" goody bag filled with a ton of fashion magazines, including *Vogue, Glamour,* and *In Style,* as well as a pair of fluffy hot-pink slippers.

"Don't worry about today," she said, and gave me a big kiss on the forehead.

I pulled away from her and said, "Yep, thanks." I didn't have much to say because it was hard-core mortifying that I had been caught spying on her. Did she wonder how I had found out about her appointment? Should I play it off like I was just walking by the store and stopped in to browse?

But how would I explain that? It had been such a long day; I was too tired to lie. If she was willing to let it go, that was fine by me.

I glared at the back of her turquoise pantsuit as she walked out of the room, wondering how she always seemed to find the cheapest-looking expensive clothes. Then I eased myself out of bed—my lower back really did hurt—and checked out my reflection in the mirror. There was a huge red lipstick mark on my forehead. I had been struck by a murderer's kiss, branded by her venomous lips! I went into the bathroom and scrubbed off all traces of her makeup, using a ton of rose-scented soap and water. Then I threw the ugly slippers in the back of my closet with the zebra-print Kool-Aid-red dress. And I would've tossed the magazines away just because she had given them to me, except an article on the cover of *Vogue* caught my eye. It was called "The Frail Nature of Men," and I decided to read it before I went to bed. Maybe it would give me insight into how my father could forget about my mom so quickly.

The author of the piece wrote that we can't forget that human beings are still animals, and most species are not genetically programmed to mate for life. She said that a man isn't wired to be with only one woman, but some species are, like gibbons, termites, coyotes, barn owls, beavers, bald eagles, condors, swans, pigeons, and black vultures.

The author, some sort of sociobiologist, even claimed that

black vultures discourage infidelity. If one is caught philandering, all nearby vultures attack that cheating member of their posse. *Whoop! Whoop! A shout-out to all vultures! Way to keep up a moral code, my feathered friends!* Who knew vultures could be so virtuous? These scavenging creatures that feed mostly on the carcasses of dead animals are more loyal than my own father.

TIDE POOLS

Sunday, December 20

The next morning I was feeling fine, except for some pain in my lower back. Oliver called me around ten A.M. and asked me if I wanted to go to Malibu with him.

"The fresh salt breeze will be good for you," he joked.

"Hell yeah!" I said.

A couple of hours later, he picked me up. Per usual, his old green Toyota was waiting for me down the street from my house so his mom wouldn't see us. As I walked toward him, he smiled at me and pushed his hair out of his eyes. I got into the car gently so I wouldn't hurt myself, and gave him a kiss on the cheek. He was wearing this cool red T-shirt that read, PENGUIN SPICY CHILI SAUCE, with an illustration of the Antarctic bird on it.

The sun was shining as we drove along the Pacific Coast Highway to a beach called Point Dume. Oliver said he had picked the area because he wanted to show me the awesome tide pools. I had been to this beach a ton growing up, but I had never gotten a personal tour by a marine biologist in training. And ever since I was a kid, Point Dume had held a special place in my heart because the beginning of *Grease*—a movie my mom and I had both loved, no matter how cheesy it was or how many times we watched it—had been shot on its sands. In the opening scene, Danny and Sandy are frolicking near the crashing waves on their summer vacation. And I always thought it looked so romantic and heavenly. Now here I was with my very own honey potpie. I wished my mom could have seen this moment. And I wished she could have met Oliver.

Oliver parked the car in an area called Cliffside Drive, which was set aside for a wildlife preserve. It was located on the top of these huge, gorgeous bluffs that ran along the coastline of the Pacific Ocean. As we started hiking down a path that led to the sand, thoughts of my mom kept nagging at me.

"Has anything mysterious and unexplainable ever happened to you?" I asked.

"Hmm, I'm sure," he said. "I mean, this whole universe feels that way sometimes."

We got to an extra-steep part of the cliff and Oliver held his hand out to help me down. "Thanks," I said. "Let me put it this way. Has anyone close to you ever passed away?"

I watched the back of Oliver's red T-shirt as he walked down the incline. "My mom's father, my grandpa William, died a few years ago. He lived down in Florida. He was a total octogenarian playboy with a boat."

"Do you think about him sometimes?" I asked.

"Once in a while," he said. "We were pretty close. He took me out on his catamaran when I went to visit him. He had this great laugh. And he made these unusual sculptures out of driftwood."

"But since he passed away, has he ever tried to communicate with you?" I cleared my throat and hoped the question didn't sound too bizarre.

Oliver glanced back at me and then kept walking. "No, but I guess something weird happened when he was dying."

My ears perked up. "What?" I asked, hurrying so I was walking closer to him.

"He was in his hospital bed with a bad case of pneumonia and all of a sudden, he said, 'I have to get ready. They're coming for me.'"

"Who was he talking about?" I asked.

"I had no idea," said Oliver. "He got out of bed in his hospital gown, grabbed this bag that was on a chair next to him, and started walking toward the door. And then suddenly he stopped and turned back around and said, 'They said it's not my time yet,' and got back into bed."

"Wow," I said. "That's pretty deep. I mean, I wonder who 'they' were?"

"If anyone," he said. "I mean, it could've all been in his head. I guess we'll never know. And you?"

My mind was still absorbing Oliver's story. Could his grandfather have been seeing spirits or ghosts of people that had passed away before him?

"Have you ever had a strange experience like that?" he asked.

I looked at him and bit my lip. "Not exactly."

"What is it?"

"Nothing." I wished I could tell him the truth. But of course I couldn't.

"Come on. You can tell me," he said.

"Really. I promise. It's nothing. But if anything mysterious like that ever did happen to me . . . I bet it would change my life forever."

He searched my eyes for more of an answer.

By then we had reached the bottom of the path. "Wow, we made it! Check out how pretty it is!" I exclaimed. The sand felt powdery soft and the ocean was beautiful despite the cloud of L.A. smog, which always hung like a gray vapor along the horizon.

"Yahoo! It's low tide! I'm gonna give you the VIP tour," Oliver said.

He led me over to the clusters of rocks and tide pools. I loved how he got really into pointing out the sea anemones, sea urchins, and crabs. Then he held my hand and helped me across a group of slippery rocks covered in green algae. But suddenly, I lost my footing and almost fell into the tide pool.

"Oh, no!" I yelled.

Oliver grabbed me by my waist and steadied me. "Nice move," he teased.

"Yeah, I'm pretty smooth," I said, laughing.

I was in his arms now and he started to kiss my neck. "God, you're so attractive. There's, like, a magnet pulling you to me," he said.

"Really?" I said with a shy smile. I'd had a boyfriend my freshman year at Winchester. His name was Zack and he played guitar and was on the soccer team. We'd dated for six months until he dumped me to get back together with his ex-girlfriend. It had really stung and I'd cried a ton. I remembered thinking that I would never feel about anyone else the way I'd felt about Zack. But now I realized that what Zack and I had shared had never felt as amazing as this.

"Man, oh, yes," Oliver said, and nibbled on my earlobe. "You are really driving me crazy. Your body is some sort of genetic miracle."

His lips felt warm on my neck and they tickled. But then this terrible thought came into my mind: Had my parents felt this way about each other at some point, too? And where had it gotten them? My mom was dead and my dad was hooking up with her sister. I pulled away from Oliver and looked up at him.

"Do you believe in monogamy?" I asked.

"Yeah, completely." He leaned in to kiss me again.

"You don't worry it's impossible to really be with just one person? I read this article in *Vogue* last night about the frail nature of men. It said guys are constantly having to battle between their desire to spread seed and society's pressure to commit."

"Holly, what are you talking about?" he asked, pulling back from me.

"Sorry." I realized that I must be putting a serious damper on our make-out session. "It's just maybe everyone is replaceable. I mean, look at what's going on with my dad and my aunt."

"Oh, I get it—that's what this is all about. Well, all I know is I want to be with someone forever," Oliver said. "Get old with them, die in each other's arms, be with them when our souls move on."

"You do?" I asked, a surge of hope rising inside me.

"With most other girls I've gone out with the whole thing's felt mechanical. But with you, it's different. I haven't felt unhinged in a long time," he said. "Unhinged in a good way, I mean."

No guy had ever been this honest with me before. And it meant a lot to me. In all the pain I had been in since my mom died, meeting Oliver was the one great thing that had happened to me. And I felt a part of me starting to open up, a piece that had been shut down since I had lost my mom. Oliver seemed so fearless about sharing his feelings and I wondered why.

"Have you ever had a girlfriend before?" I asked.

"Yeah. I mean, not a serious one, but there were a few girls back in Oregon."

"Did one of them ever dump you, or hurt you?"

"Not really," he said. "I was never that into any of them and I either ended things or they just sort of faded."

I thought over his answer and then nodded my head knowingly. "I figured it out," I said. "You're like those animals I learned about on the Discovery Channel. These adventurers found this hidden part of the rain forest in the Amazon that had never been seen before by humans. And the animals there came right up to them, not worried at all that they would be hurt or killed. They never had anything to fear, so they put themselves right out there."

"Are you comparing me to an undiscovered species?"

"Yeah," I said. "You're, like, the only pure thing I know."

HANKY-PANKY

O liver showed me around the tide pools for a few more hours and taught me some cool facts he had learned in his marine biology classes at UCLA. I tried to really listen so I could remember what he was saying and how he was saying it. I thought I might write down some of what he said in my playwriting journal.

My three favorite things he told me were:

1. There's evidence to suggest that gray whales have dreams.

2. Many fish can change gender during the course of their lives. Others, especially rare deep-sea fish, have both male and female sex organs.

3. French angelfish mate for life.

As he drove me back home, I thought about those angel-fish. It sounded like they had real dedication and loyalty. I could add them to the good company of vultures. I was starting to realize that loyalty might be one of the most important qualities a person could have. It was vital to try to find at least a couple of people in this world that you knew would be there for you. My mother was that way. Even when she was down, she would always listen to me and show up if I needed her. Felicia was that way, also. And now I was thinking I might have that with Oliver, too.

After getting back to the Hollywood Hills, Oliver pulled over to our usual pickup/drop-off point down the street from my house. We sat there in the car, talking and stalling our good-bye.

"So I got a text from my buddy Spike while we were in Malibu," he said. "It looks like he and his roommates would be game for me moving in."

"Sweet. That'd be awesome," I said.

"Yeah, this guy who was living there is taking off to teach snowboarding in Tahoe. So the room is mine as soon as I want it."

"Nice. But how are you going to break it to your mom?" I asked.

"Looking for the right moment. But it's happening. We're moving forward," he said, and then leaned in to kiss me good-bye.

I opened the door to the car but stopped before I got out. "You're the coolest," I said. "In case you didn't know."

Oliver smiled. "Me and you equals all good things."

As I walked up the driveway, I noticed that my father's Porsche was parked next to Claudia's Mercedes. I looked at the clock on my cell phone. It was only four o'clock—this was super early for him to be back from the office, even on a Sunday.

Sampson ran over to me as soon as I got inside. After I patted his back, he ran off to play with a carrot-shaped squeaky toy. I headed upstairs to my room, but as I reached the landing I heard a strange noise, followed by silence. It seemed like the sound was coming from the master bedroom. I paused and waited for it to happen again. Then I heard deep grunting, followed by Claudia saying, "Yesssssssss!" and then my father's name over and over again.

I scrunched up my face. There was no denying it: these were the sounds of lovemaking. I hurried to my room and called Felicia right away. I couldn't believe I had to listen to my dad hooking up with his wife's killer. The whole thing was twisted and dark on so many levels.

"Oh my God! She's boinking him," I said as soon as Felicia picked up.

"Come again?" she asked.

"My dad and Claudia are doing it! Right now in my parents' bedroom!"

"With you home? How vulgar!" Felicia said.

"I was out with Oliver. They must've not heard me come back."

"Blast some music. It'll announce your arrival and hopefully they'll cut it out," she said.

I walked over to my stereo and turned on Bright Eyes. "Can we have a sleepover tonight at your place? I can't take her much longer!" I said loudly over the music.

"Yeah, totally. I'm down with that," said Felicia.

"You get the cookie dough. I'll get the movies."

"Done and done," she said.

Just then there was a knock on my door. "Come in!" I yelled, and then turned down the music.

My father walked in dressed in his work slacks with his button-down shirt messily tucked in. "Hi, sweetie," he said, standing just inside the doorway.

I quickly talked into the phone. "Felish, my dad is here. See you tonight, seven o'clock?"

"Cool, and good luck," she said, and hung up.

"How long have you been home?" my dad asked. "And how are you feeling today? Is your back okay?"

"Five minutes," I said. "And it's fine." The truth was I hadn't thought about my back all day, but now that my dad mentioned it, I still felt sore. I guess being with Oliver had taken my mind off it.

"I didn't hear you come in," he said. The back of his hair

was standing up. I could imagine Claudia running her French-manicured claws through it.

"Yeah, I was *quiet*," I said. Unlike some people in this house.

Just then Claudia appeared in the doorway wearing a short skirt and tank top. She draped one hand over my dad's shoulder. "Hi, Holly," she said. "I told your dad about how much fun we had at Geisha House the other night. It was great of you to plan that. You're just delicious!"

"Oh, great, thanks," I said, putting on a fake smile. *And why are you talking about me like I'm a doughnut?*

"Well, I'm happy you've been enjoying each other," my dad said. He sounded so corny. "Maybe you'll have time for another night on the town before you go back to school. Anyway, I gotta get back to the office. See you both later."

He took off down the hallway, but Claudia lingered behind a moment. "Oh, and just between girls . . ." She nodded in the direction of the master bedroom and then lowered her voice to a whisper. "Hope I wasn't too loud." Then she winked at me and quickly walked away.

"Hoochie," I said under my breath as I watched her leave.

SLEEPOVER

Felicia lived in Brentwood just north of Sunset Boulevard. Her dad owned a recording studio and her mom produced movie trailers. I had grown up playing at her huge house since I was five years old, so it was very familiar to me.

We took over the living room, which had a flat-screen TV. Her two cats, Dreamer and Fancy, curled up with us on the L-shaped couch. We took the tube of cookie dough and dug into it with two spoons.

"Call me a horrible person, but I don't care about the risk of salmonella when I'm eating this stuff," I said.

"Are you kidding? It's orgasmically delicious," Felicia said, pulling her hair up into a ponytail. "Oh my God, so I didn't tell you? Devin asked me out."

"The guy who bumped butts with you at that house party?"

"Yep. We're going hiking in Runyon Canyon tomorrow," she said. "With his dog."

"Ooh, sounds like a hot date," I said.

"Devin's got washboard abs. He pulled up his shirt during an improv and I saw them."

"Nice! Nothing wrong with that!" I said.

Then we got the first movie started. I had brought over flicks with female avengers: *Kill Bill, Volume 1*; *Mr. & Mrs. Smith*; and *La Femme Nikita*. I thought this would be a good chance to do some research on how to make Claudia pay. Now that I was pretty sure what my mom's ghost had told me was true, I had to figure out how to get revenge.

The first movie we watched was *Kill Bill, Volume 1*. After one of the scenes in the movie in which the bride character, played by Uma Thurman, displays martial-arts prowess while dressed in an amazing yellow jumpsuit, I hit the Pause button on the remote.

"Can I ask you a serious question?" I asked, turning to Felicia.

"Sure, shoot."

"What happened to good old revenge? Do you think it's gone out of style?"

"Like fanny packs and acid wash? Uh, yeah," Felicia said. "I mean, now people go to prison."

"But do you remember in kindergarten when that girl Amy used to pull our hair? We'd yank hers right back."

"We were five years old," Felicia said.

"But it was instinctual, like a gut response."

"Where is this coming from?" she asked. "Or let me guess—your dad and Claudia."

I ground my teeth. "I wish I could make Claudia pay."

"For shacking up with your dad?"

"Yeah, for starters," I said.

"What would you do if you could?" Felicia asked, and playfully tossed a pillow at me.

I caught it and gave her a devilish smile. "I would take all her designer clothes and throw them away!" I said. "And pour Nair in her mascara. And—"

"Put a nest of cockroaches in her pillowcase!" she said, jumping in.

"Do roaches even have nests?" I asked.

"Hmm, maybe not."

"We could take out a billboard ad on the Sunset Strip and put an embarrassing picture of her on it!" I said.

"And give her a Mohawk while she's sleeping."

"Or make her drink a cocktail made with that liquid from the formaldehyde jar with the fake alien baby," I suggested.

"Love that!" said Felicia. "Like a piña colada, E.T.-style!"

And then I came up with the best idea ever. "I could put a Santeria spell on her!" I couldn't believe I hadn't thought of it before. Santeria had helped me reconnect with my mom's ghost. Maybe it could help me avenge her death, too.

"Ooh, I dig it. But how would you know how to do that?" Felicia asked.

"I could borrow one of Anna Maria's books," I said. "I bet they're filled with a ton of great ideas."

"I dare you," she said with a wicked smile.

"I'm gonna do it!"

"I wouldn't be surprised," she said. "You're my little fire-cracker."

"Crack, crack, bang, bang!" I said, and it was decided. I knew Anna Maria would never help me with this, but that was fine—I'd delve into some of this magical stuff on my own.

I hit the Play button on the DVD remote and the film started up again. But my mind was running a movie of its own. Something about a ritual and an aunt.

THE SPELL

Monday, December 21

The next day, I found Anna Maria kicking a coconut around the house.

"It's the winter solstice," she told me when I saw her.

She had taught me years ago that on all the solstices, she kicked a coconut from room to room because she believed it absorbed any evil energy lurking in the house. This year the custom seemed especially appropriate.

"Thank you so much for doing that!" I said.

While Anna Maria was dribbling the coconut like a soccer ball through the upstairs hallway and the master bedroom, I quickly hurried down to her bedroom. I looked both ways to make sure no one was watching, even though that was pretty unlikely since my dad was at work and, shockingly, Claudia and Patty were out, too. Then I pushed the door open. There were a bunch of books stacked by the nightstand; I hurried over to them. I would normally never go through Anna Maria's stuff, and I felt kind of guilty, but this was an exceptional situation, and it called for special measures.

After I skimmed through a bunch of the books, I discovered they were all in Spanish. Damn! The only language I knew other than English was some French from my classes at Winchester. Still, I wasn't going to give up.

I hurried outside. My Saab was still at the shop, and I knew with the holidays coming up, there was no way it'd be repaired while I was home from school. Besides, I was getting used to zipping about in my mom's old car. And I loved how, everywhere I drove, it felt like a part of her was cruising around with me.

I jumped inside the Prius and drove to the Beverly Hills library. I went through the stacks of books and found one on Santeria spells. I checked it out and then hurried to my car to read it more carefully in private. I skimmed the table of contents until I found a chapter called "Hexes and Curses." In that chapter, I focused on a spell that sounded like it might be right up my alley. It was called "Destruction of an Enemy."

I read over the instructions and the things needed for the spell. The list looked like a recipe:

A piece of paper
A pen

A spoon

Scissors

Matches

A chicken heart

What?! I had to reread the last item twice. Gross! How on earth was I going to get that? I needed some advice, so I called the BFF.

"Can't talk! I'm getting my hair done," Felicia said when she picked up the phone. "Big date tonight with Devin."

"Oh, sorry, but I have a quick question. This may sound weird, but where can I find a chicken heart?" I asked.

"Dude, the guy's cutting off my dead ends! Can't this wait?"

"Nope. Operation: Santeria," I said. "I need a chicken heart. Where am I supposed to get one?"

"Look, just ask the butcher," Felicia said. "Go to the closest Ralphs and chat up one of the guys walking around wearing an apron covered in blood."

"Ah, thanks," I said. "Makes total sense."

"I gotta go! Scissors by my ear," she said. "Good luck!"

As soon as I hung up the phone, I jetted over to Ralphs. In the back of the store was a glass case filled with fresh sausages, chopped meat, and steaks. I searched for an employee working behind the counter and spotted a woman in a red apron slicing a chunk of ham for a customer. As soon as she finished with the other customer, she turned to me.

"Yes, what can I get you?" she asked. She was wearing pink lipstick, which seemed a very cheerful choice for a butcher.

"Hi, I was looking to buy the insides of a chicken," I said.

"The giblets," she said, correcting my lingo.

"Yeah, but I don't see any in the case," I said.

"We don't put them out, but I can sell a giblet pack to you special. It includes the neck, liver, and heart."

"I don't need the neck and the liver," I said. "If you could wrap up just the heart, that'd be great."

"Sure thing," said the butcher.

I watched as she went over to a white tub and pulled out a delicate piece of red meat. She had reached right in there with her hands! She was wearing gloves, but still, it was pretty gross. Anticipating a bad smell, I scrunched my nose up as I watched her wrap the small heart in white paper. Then she handed me the parcel.

"Thanks," I said, and headed to the checkout line. I wondered if the butcher was suspicious about what I was going to do with my purchase, but then I remembered that sometimes animal organs are considered delicacies. So maybe she thought I was cooking up some fancy dinner, like grilled partial giblets with mushroom sauce.

As I watched the white package move down the conveyor belt, I thought about the chicken that heart had once belonged to. And now here was the organ that used to keep it alive chugging along the conveyer belt of Ralphs supermarket, exposed, without a body to keep it warm.

☠ ☠ ☠

On the ride home, I put the chicken heart in the trunk so I wouldn't have to smell it. Then I walked quickly up to my room so Anna Maria wouldn't see me and ask what I was doing. My hands were shaking as I stored the package carefully outside my window between the screen and the glass. Then I closed my pale pink drapes. This way no one could see it from my bedroom and the organ would be safe from Sampson, who might smell it and want to gobble it up.

I waited anxiously for the sun to fall, because the book specifically said this spell had to be done after dark. I wrote in my playwriting journal for a while, trying to remember some of my conversations with Oliver. I also lounged around by the pool, working on my tan. Finally nighttime came, and my dad and Claudia came home, had dinner, and went to bed. But then I had to wait for Anna Maria to finish mopping the kitchen floor. I couldn't risk her seeing what I was up to. Finally at around eleven o'clock she went to her room and shut the door.

In my bedroom, I grabbed a pen, paper, a book of matches, scissors, and the Santeria library book and threw them into my purple suede bag. Then I carefully got the chicken heart from the window.

I could feel my own heart beating fast as I tiptoed downstairs. When I opened the sliding door to the backyard, it made a swooshing sound and I heard Sampson barking. I froze as I listened to the dog coming down the stairs, hoping the noise he was making wouldn't wake up the whole house. A moment later, he was right beside me, licking my hand.

"Hey, boy, it's okay," I whispered, patting his side. He started sniffing my purse and I knew he must be dying for what was inside. I pulled my bag up higher on my arm.

"Now just be good and stay quiet," I said, and kissed the top of his head.

Then I held Sampson back by the collar as I headed outside and closed the door behind me. I could see him inside through the glass, begging me with his eyes to let him outside to play.

"I can't," I whispered. "I'm really sorry, but I promise to take you for a long walk soon. All through the canyon." Ever since we had gotten him when I was in seventh grade, I liked to take Sampson on long hikes through the canyon near our house. It was so cute to see how excited he'd get, parading around with his huge pink tongue sticking out of his mouth.

I turned around and headed out into the darkness. As I walked to the Chinese garden, I could feel my knees start to wobble. The night I had seen my mom's ghost here flashed through my mind. I wished she'd come back now and talk to me again. But if she didn't, I hoped at least she'd be watching and proud of what I was doing here tonight. *I'm doing what you asked, Mom,* I thought, hoping she was listening.

I picked an area on the ground near the wooden pavilion and began to dig a hole with my spoon. I chose an area covered with dirt, not grass, near some of my mother's favorite flowers. Then I opened the white package the butcher had given me and lowered the chicken heart into the ground. I almost gagged when I got a whiff of its putrid smell. My window faced south and it must've baked in the sun all day. I followed the directions in the book step-by-step. First, I drew a female figure on the piece of paper and wrote Claudia's name in the center of it. Next, I cut out the figure, struck a match, and held it up to the cutout. As the paper burned, I read aloud an incantation from the book. The words felt warm as they fell from my lips.

> *Darksome powers of the night*
> *Gather round my match's flame*
> *Send my enemy in shaded flight*
> *Send my enemy away in shame*

After I said the last words, I put the ashes from the paper in the hole and started to cover them and the chicken heart with dirt. But then I heard a noise. It was the swooshing sound of the sliding door. There was my father standing at the entrance to the garden. He was dressed in his pajamas, rubbing the corners of his eyes.

"Holly?" he asked. "What are you doing out here?"

"Nothing. I couldn't sleep so I thought I'd get some fresh air," I said, still filling the hole with soil. Maybe it was so dark that he wouldn't notice what I was doing.

"But it's almost midnight," my dad said.

"Yep, well, I'm fine. You can go back to sleep. Good night." I stood up and tried to block his view of the hole behind me.

"Come on, now. Why are you acting so strange?" he asked, taking a few steps toward me.

"I'm not! You're the one acting strange. And nosy! I mean, can't a girl go for a walk in the moonlight? Without her dad getting all up in her business?"

"Of course, but—" My dad stepped to the left, like he was trying to look behind me.

"Yes?" I said, and mirrored his movement so I was blocking his line of sight. "That's the whole point of a Chinese garden, right? To seek quiet reflection. *Alone!*"

He squinted his eyes. "Is there something behind you?"

"Yeah, a koi fishpond. Duh," I said.

"Something's going on here, Holly," he said, then quickly jerked to the left so he could see around me. "Were you digging?"

"No. Why would I be doing that?" I said, dropping the spoon.

He crouched down on his knees and looked into the hole. "What is that?" he asked, peering at the half-covered heart inside.

"Get away from there! It's nothing!" I said, pushing back on his shoulder, but he wouldn't budge.

"Ew. Is something dead?" He curled his upper lip as he poked inside the hole with the spoon.

"Dad, stop!" I said, trying to grab the spoon from him. "Please."

He turned to me and raised his voice. "Holly, you have to tell me what this is! Is it an animal?"

"Dad, chill out!"

"Did something die? Tell me right now!" Now my dad was practically yelling. "What the hell is this?"

"It's just a chicken heart!" I blurted out.

"What on earth are you doing with a chicken heart? Where'd you get it?"

"At Ralphs. Leave me alone!"

"Honey, relax," my dad said. "I'm not mad. More concerned and . . ." Just then he noticed the Santeria book. "Is this something to do with Anna Maria?"

"No! Dad, you're messing everything up!" I yelled. He was screwing up my hex. It would never work now. I was letting my mother down—again. First I couldn't save her life, and then I couldn't avenge her death. I felt like the most useless daughter ever.

"I don't even understand what you're doing," he said. He had been crouching on the ground, but now he sat down and sighed. I sat down, too. "I'm just worried about you, honey. And I'm sorry, but I don't want this thing buried out here. It's gonna decay and attract raccoons." My dad scooped the heart out of the hole with the spoon and put it back in the white wrapping paper that still rested nearby.

"Dad, this was my private business and now it's ruined. Now everything is ruined." And I meant not just the spell but also our family.

My dad picked up the package with the dirty heart and held it away from him. Then he stood up. "Man, oh, man, oh, man . . ." he said.

"You don't understand what you're doing to me," I said.

"Maybe I don't. I wish I did." He looked up at the sky and shook his head.

After I gathered up the rest of my stuff and put it back in my bag, we walked back into the house. My dad turned on a side light in the kitchen. Then he poured us each a glass of water as we sat together at the table. He looked as serious as he had the day my mother died.

"I'm worried about you," he said. "And I really want to help. There's someone I'd like you to go see."

"Who?" I asked.

"Her name's Dr. Arbuckle. She's a highly recommended psychiatrist who specializes in working with teenagers."

"I should've known. It was only a matter of time before you sent me to a shrink," I said. My father had suggested I "talk to someone" after my mom's death, but I had never wanted to. I hadn't known what anyone could say to make me feel better. My mother had died. She had taken her own life. Maybe some part of it had been my fault, for leaving her on her own. Those were the facts, and there wasn't a thing any sort of teen expert could tell me to change any of it.

"She'll be good for you. I think she can help you deal with all of these recent changes," my dad said.

"How do you even know about her?"

"She was referred to me by Linda." He ran his finger over the rim of his glass.

"Oh, Linda," I said. Linda was the psychoanalyst that my dad had gone to a few times after my mom died. I guess because she was a psychologist he got to call her by her first name, but because this Arbuckle lady was a psychiatrist who could prescribe medicine, she was called "Doctor."

"It really helped having someone for me to talk to," my dad said. "I wish you'd done it, too, at the time. Maybe I should have insisted. . . ."

Maybe it helped too much, I thought to myself. Apparently he had packed up all his emotional baggage with no trouble at all and moved right on with his life.

"So can I go ahead and make an appointment?" he asked. "She might be in the office tomorrow. Otherwise, we'll have to wait till after Christmas."

I thought it over. Most of me didn't want to give in to my dad. I still didn't know how just sitting in some office talking about my feelings was going to do any good. But this little part of me felt like I didn't really know what else to do or who else to turn to. It wasn't like I could tell this doctor about my mom's ghost—the last thing I needed was a real-life psychiatrist thinking I was insane—but maybe I could hint a little, feel her out, see if she thought what I had seen was even possible. Plus, I remembered that, like, half of the students at Winchester were rumored to have been in counseling at one time or another, so I was just joining the flock.

"Okay, sign me up," I said. "I'll go."

LOOK INTO MY MIND

Tuesday, December 22

My dad drove me down Olympic Boulevard into Beverly Hills. Today was the beginning of his holiday vacation—he'd be off work from now until the beginning of the new year. And I bet he was psyched to be taking me to get my head checked. He was drinking an iced coffee and playing a classic-rock station on the car stereo. I told him I could've driven myself, but he had insisted on taking me. I guessed he was worried that I'd skip the appointment unless he escorted me right to the building's front door.

"I think you're gonna really like this woman," he said.

"Hope so," I said.

He pulled the car over next to a parking meter outside an office building. "She's just going to talk to you, ask you some questions, and get to know you. You'll be in and out in forty-five."

"Whoopee. See ya then," I said, and jumped out of the car.

"I'll be out front waiting for you," he hollered after me.

I hurried inside the tinted-glass doors. "Dr. Arbuckle's office?" I asked a heavyset female security officer sitting behind a desk.

"Second floor," she said. "Go on up." As I headed toward the elevator banks, I glanced back and could see my dad watching me from the car.

A few minutes later, I was sitting on a couch across from Dr. Arbuckle. She was a petite woman—her feet barely touched the floor—with her hair in a loose side ponytail. She was wearing a baggy white cotton dress. I guessed she was in her mid-fifties.

"So Holly, what brought you here today?" she asked.

"A Porsche Carrera with vanity plates," I said.

Dr. Arbuckle smiled. "I want to be sure you know that everything you say to me is confidential. It's important you feel safe."

"Yeah, I'm familiar with the protocol," I said, fidgeting with the armrest of the couch. "I've seen *The Sopranos*. Hey, do you know what's funny about this arrangement?"

"Tell me," said Dr. Arbuckle.

"If I walked by you on the street, you wouldn't care about me at all, but for two hundred and fifty dollars for forty-five minutes, you suddenly do. Don't you think that's a form of emotional prostitution?"

I thought she might've gotten offended by what I said, but instead she smiled again and I could see the smallest gap between her two front teeth.

"Sometimes we laugh about that amongst ourselves—that we get paid by the hour." She played with her long necklace made of orange beads the size of ping-pong balls. "Yes, money is part of the arrangement. It's how I earn my living, but that doesn't take away from me truly caring about my patients."

I guessed her tone sounded pretty sincere. I took a pillow from the couch and clutched it in my lap. We sat there for a minute and I settled into my seat.

"So tell me, Holly, what's on your mind?"

She didn't seem affected by my attitude so I decided to drop it. Maybe now was a good time to see what she thought about everything that had been going on with me and the recent visit from my mom—in a covert way.

"I have a friend who talks to me about seeing ghosts. Do you think she's crazy?" I asked.

"What has your friend seen, specifically?" Dr. Arbuckle asked.

"My friend's mother died a long time ago—like, many, many years." I accentuated that part so that, in case my dad had told this doctor about my own mom's passing, she wouldn't think the friend I was talking about was really me.

"And she tells me that she sometimes sees her mother's ghost. Do you even think ghosts exist?"

"Extrasensory stuff isn't my forte," she said. "But I do believe some people have a great sense of intuition."

"So you're open to it?"

"Yes, I'm open to anything you want to tell me," Dr. Arbuckle said. She just won favor with me. Plus, I looked around her office and there were all these cool things on her bookcase, like a huge white conch shell, a chunk of white crystal, and a framed photograph of Egyptian hieroglyphics; this made me think she might be at least a little New Agey, and not a square like my dad.

"So about your friend . . ." Dr. Arbuckle went on. "I wonder how she feels? Does she like seeing the ghost? Or does she get scared?"

"She mostly likes seeing the ghost. Except . . ." My voice trailed off.

"Yes? You can tell me."

"It's just that the ghost recently said something terrible to her," I said.

Dr. Arbuckle nodded her head as she listened. I clenched my hands together. I wanted so badly to tell her everything about what had happened and get her opinion, but I couldn't. I had given my mom a vow of secrecy.

"Do you feel okay telling me this?" She must've sensed my hesitation.

"Well, see, the ghost wants my friend to . . . Um, it's just that the ghost told my friend that her mom didn't die by accident."

Dr. Arbuckle crossed her legs. "What does the ghost think happened?"

"Well, the ghost said she, uh, was poisoned," I said. Then I bit my lip as I studied Dr. Arbuckle's face for a reaction.

I watched her look out the window for a moment and nod her head, as if deep in thought. Finally, she turned back to me. "This seems like a lot for a young person to handle on her own."

I nodded my head profusely. "Yeah, it is!" She totally understood.

"But I wonder why you are telling me about your friend today?" she said.

I felt pushed into a corner. "Oh, well, I just saw her last night so it's on my mind," I blurted out.

"Okay, that makes sense," said Dr. Arbuckle. "Well, Holly, I know that your own mother died pretty recently. . . ."

I looked away. My dad had told her, just as expected.

"So I wonder how this might be affecting you when your friend tells you this story?" she said.

"I just feel really bad for my friend," I replied.

"Yes, tell me about that," said Dr. Arbuckle.

"Well, I wish there was something I could do to help her."

"Of course. Let's think of what you could do to help her.

But first maybe you can tell me a little bit about your mother and how you're doing with that," she said.

I picked at the seam of the pillow on my lap. "It's been hard," I admitted. "My dad's with this new woman. My aunt."

"Your aunt?" Dr. Arbuckle asked. Interesting that my dad hadn't told her that part of the story.

"Yeah," I said. "My mom's sister. It's weird, this whole thing with her and my dad. My mom couldn't stand her and I guess I can't stand her, either."

"So she and your mother weren't close?"

"No," I said. "My mom tolerated her and tried to make an effort, but there was always a lot of competition between them. See, their mother had a lot of problems."

"In what ways?"

"She had bipolar disorder, just like my mom, actually. Anyway, she gave birth to Claudia and then four years later, she had my mom, but then she got that postpartum thing . . . and never came out of it. . . . She just got worse. . . ."

"Your grandmother?" Dr. Arbuckle asked.

"Yeah, she spent all her time in bed and was just not emotionally available. I guess my mom and my aunt kind of had to raise themselves because their mother was sick and their father was always at work. He ran this big movie studio. Anyway, Claudia blamed my mom for being born. When my mom was a little girl, Claudia would say all this horrible stuff to her."

"Like what?" Dr. Arbuckle asked.

"That she was a bad child, that she was unlovable, and it was her fault that their mom was so sick. And I guess my mom was so young she believed it all. It got, like, ingrained into her."

"That must have been very hard for your mother," said Dr. Arbuckle. "And it must have been hard for your aunt, too. I imagine that she was angry and confused, and her way of making sense of her mother's illness was to blame it on your mother, which of course wasn't fair. But I don't imagine that either of them had an easy childhood."

I nodded slightly. I had never really thought about it that way. I had always just pictured my aunt as this mean woman and my mother as this scared little girl. I guess I hadn't remembered that Claudia had once been a little girl, too.

"So your father . . . he's dating your aunt now?" Dr. Arbuckle asked. "How do you understand that?"

"I don't understand it at all. I think it's insane," I said.

"It does seem surprising, given what you've told me about your mother's relationship with her sister. Did your father know about the history between them?"

"Yeah, he saw that they bickered. But a lot happened a long time ago, and he didn't see that part. And he never got to meet my grandma. She died before he met my mother. He'd tell my mom, 'Of course you didn't destroy your mother. She was depressed before you were even born.' But Claudia had been telling my mom that it was her fault for so long. She never believed my dad that it wasn't her fault, and he never knew how serious the issues were between them. He just thought it was competitive stuff, a rivalry. He'd just wash his hands of it. 'Ladies, if you both keep it up, I'm going to watch TV.'"

"Your dad would say this?" Dr. Arbuckle said.

I nodded. "He would act like they were equally to blame. But it always seemed to me like my aunt was picking on my mom about all kinds of little things, like telling her she should dress sexier or blow out her hair. My dad just didn't understand my mom and Claudia's relationship. He didn't have the patience for it. And I think my mom opened up to me more about it than to him."

"Why do you think she did that?" Dr. Arbuckle asked.

"I guess because she knew that I understood and I'd be empathetic. We were really close, me and my mom. And sometimes with emotional stuff, my dad sucks big-time. I hate him for just brushing things off and acting like everything's okay."

"But in this case, in suggesting that you come to see me, he didn't do that, right? He didn't just act like everything's okay. I spoke with him briefly but I could tell that he was worried about you."

I supposed she had a point. But I wasn't going to admit that my dad was changing in a good way, because he had already changed in a terrible way. He had changed from the man who loved my mom to the man who was practically shacking up with her sister.

Dr. Arbuckle looked like she was trying to read my thoughts. "So I'm curious how you are doing without your mother. How is it affecting you?"

"Well, I miss her. I mean . . ." I could feel my chest tightening. "That makes sense, right? How could I not? We were super close and she really depended on me and . . ." My eyes started to sting. *I let her down. And now I'm letting her down again by not avenging her death quickly enough.* I almost said that part out loud, but at the last second I swallowed my words.

"What's going on with you now?" Dr. Arbuckle asked.

"Nothing." I blinked my eyes, trying to stop myself from crying. I didn't say anything, but deep inside I could feel a huge well of sadness, the place where it was held. It felt like it was smack in the center of my rib cage. Then tears began to run down my face.

Dr. Arbuckle handed me a box of tissues, and we sat there for a minute without talking. Then she broke the silence. "I know. Sometimes there are no words for it."

I nodded my head slowly and wiped my eyes. I blew my nose loudly; it sounded like a tractor. I laughed at myself. Then I started to cry again.

I looked up at Dr. Arbuckle, who was watching me. "If you think I'm crazy you'd tell me, right?" I asked.

"You're not crazy, Holly."

"But maybe I am, huh?" I reached for another Kleenex and blew my nose even more loudly.

Dr. Arbuckle smiled at me. "Holly, you're going through

a hard time. If it wasn't affecting you this way, I'd be surprised. You've lost an incredibly important person in your life. Perhaps the most important person."

"Thanks," I said. It was refreshing to hear she understood me. I quickly wiped my eyes. I felt like a mess of snot and tears. Even though I knew her job was to listen to people's problems, I didn't like breaking down in front of anybody, even trained professionals.

We talked a little longer and she wanted to know more about the other stuff in my life—school and friends and stuff. I was surprised that she seemed genuinely interested in the things I told her about Winchester, my friends there, and Felicia. I even told her a little about Oliver. When it was time to go, Dr. Arbuckle walked over to her desk and picked up her appointment calendar.

"I'd like to see you again," she said, sitting back down in her chair and then opening up the black book.

"Well, I'm heading back to Winchester in, like, two weeks," I said.

"Yes, here's my number." Dr. Arbuckle handed me a business card. I stuck it into my wallet. "Just in case you want to come by again before you go."

I got up from the couch and she walked me to the door. "And in the meantime, stay busy and be good to yourself. Maybe spend some time with your friend Felicia," she said.

"Yes, I will. And I'm sure I'll see my boyfriend, too," I said. I liked hearing the word *boyfriend* in relation to Oliver.

"Great," said Dr. Arbuckle. "Make plans with them. I think being with people who love and care about you can be very healing. Also, one last thing."

I was about to put my hand on the doorknob, but I stopped and turned around.

"About your friend with the ghost," Dr. Arbuckle continued.

"Yeah?"

"Tell her she doesn't have to be alone with something so scary."

As soon as I walked out of the office building, I spotted my dad's silver Porsche parked on a side street. I climbed into the passenger side. I guessed he'd been sitting there the whole time, e-mailing with his BlackBerry.

"How did it go?" he asked, sliding the BlackBerry into his pocket.

"She said I can come back again, but I don't know if I want to make a habit of this shrinky-dink stuff," I said, and leaned my head against the leather headrest. Yeah, I had kind of liked talking to Dr. Arbuckle, but that didn't mean I had to admit it to my dad. I stared straight ahead, but the car wasn't moving.

"Aren't you gonna drive?" I asked.

There was no answer. I looked over at my father. He was pinching the bridge of his nose with his thumb and forefinger. I wondered what was the matter with him. Then I realized that he was crying. I moved around in my seat so I was facing him.

"Dad? What is it?" I asked softly.

"Nothing, I'm sorry." He wiped his face dry. Then he turned on the ignition and pulled into the driving lane.

When we got back to the house, Anna Maria found me right away. She squeezed my arm as I was heading toward the stairs and nodded for me to come with her into the pantry.

"What's the matter?" I asked, following her.

She stopped by the cabinets filled with bags of potato chips and other snacks. Anna Maria shook her head as she looked at me. "Your father came to me this morning. He said he found you in the backyard with a book on Santeria."

Oh no. I felt terrible. I hadn't meant to get Anna Maria in trouble.

"I never use my religion for bad, you understand? That is not what I believe in. I use it only for good," she said.

"My dad ruined it anyway," I said, hoping that would make things better. "He tore the heart out of the ground and messed it all up."

"A *heart*?" Her mouth opened wide. Then she clicked her tongue in disapproval.

"Just a small chicken heart," I said, hoping somehow that would make it better.

"And this is about what? Your mother?"

"Sort of," I admitted. "And Claudia."

"This is serious." Anna Maria shook her head. "I know you don't like your aunt. But you want to hurt her?"

I nodded my head. "In my mom's honor."

"What?" she asked. "What are you talking about, Holly?"

"I'm sorry, Anna Maria, I can't tell you," I said. "I've probably already said too much."

"I won't tell anyone. You know you can trust me. I want to be there for you."

I took a deep breath. Part of me was dying to open up to Anna Maria and divulge everything. My mouth opened to speak, but then I changed my mind. I had made a promise to my mom and I'd stand by it. Still, I felt horrible for upsetting Anna Maria. In the many years I had known her—seventeen, to be exact—I had never seen her this upset with me. And maybe I had even jeopardized her job.

"Was my dad mad at you?" I asked. "Because this has nothing to do with you, and I don't want you to get in trouble."

"No, it's fine. He wasn't angry, just worried."

"I shouldn't have gone behind your back," I said. "I'm really sorry. This is your religion and it wasn't my place to get mixed up in it." I was genuinely starting to glimpse that.

Anna Maria blinked her eyes as she studied my face. "You could have caused a lot of trouble," she said. "You didn't know what you were doing."

"I am truly sorry," I said. "And it'll never happen again."

She seemed to think about it, taking in what I said. "I know this is a hard time for you, but this is not a game. Please."

"I understand." I gave her a quick hug. Then I turned to

leave. "I'll just have to find another way," I said as I walked away. I didn't mean to say it out loud; I just meant to think it. But the words slipped out before I could stop them.

"What?" Anna Maria said.

"Nothing," I said, and then hurried upstairs to my room.

CHRISTMAS

Friday, December 25

Three days later it was Christmas. It was the first one without my mom and I went through the motions like a cheerleading zombie in one of my aunt's movies. My dad, Claudia, and I sat around the Christmas tree in the living room. It was decorated with a mix of our old family ornaments, such as the ones I had made from feathers and Popsicle sticks when I was little and the delicate antique ornaments my mom had spent years collecting, and Claudia's gaudy ones, like rubber skeletons with Santa hats and this ugly little zombie doll that played "Silent Night" when you pressed its stomach. I mean, did she ever hang out at her own place anymore? She seemed to spend all her time here. I wanted to scream, "Hello?! You can go home now for a few nights! Yeah, really! Go on! Get a life!"

As I sat in the oversize sofa chair, I daydreamed that the angel ornament on the top was my mom looking down on us, but I knew that was probably wishful thinking or kooky as all hell, depending on how you looked at it.

My father and Aunt Claudia were all lovey-dovey next to each other on the brown leather couch. I don't remember my dad sitting that cozily with my mother. It seemed like it took him hours to open all the presents that Claudia gave him. Each time he opened up something new, Claudia started chanting, "Fashion show! Fashion show!" and my dad would disappear into the bathroom and then reappear in the latest garment. She also gave him the shiny red box that I recognized from her desk drawer.

"You have to open that present later in private," Claudia told him. "It's a surprise, baby."

I glared at her. *Can someone say "disgusting"?*

My dad presented Claudia with an expensive-looking diamond bracelet and they gave me a card filled with cash, signed from the two of them. He'd always just given me money or gift cards for birthdays and holidays—my mom had been the official shopper in the family. My pops also handed me an IOU for a father-daughter night at the Magic Castle, which was this members-only dinner club for magicians in Los Angeles. It was the kind of place that was so dorky and uncool that it was almost cool.

"My secretary was able to get us a reservation for tomorrow night," he said. "She's dating one of the magicians."

"Thanks," I said. I hadn't actually bought either of them

anything, but just then I had an idea. "This year, instead of buying gifts, I'm donating all the money you guys just gave me to a charity," I said. I would pass on all the cash that was in the envelope to Save the Harbor, the nonprofit Oliver worked for.

"That's so nice. What a great idea, sweetie," my dad said.

"Our little activist," said Claudia.

After all the presents were opened, I had to sit through a Christmas meal with my aunt and dad. Anna Maria and Patty were off for the holiday, so the day before Claudia had made Patty pick up a bunch of dishes from a catering company to store in our fridge. All she had to do then was stick them in the oven. My mom had always made honey-glazed ham on Christmas, but Claudia had ordered duck à l'orange and some fancy vegetable dish that sounded French.

During the meal, my father brought up a news story that one of the guys he played basketball with, an investigative reporter, was covering. Just this past week, eighteen polo horses had been poisoned in Florida.

"Such beautiful animals," my dad said. "And they assume it's intentional because oleander leaves were found in all the horses' stalls."

"Oh, God. Those are extremely toxic," Claudia said. "Especially if they're finely chopped up and mixed in with the animals' food. Even humans can't handle the leaves too much, or they'll get mild poisoning."

And that's when my ears perked up. How interesting that

she knew so much about poison. "Like, what happens to people if they eat the leaves?" I asked.

"It can be terribly uncomfortable. Hot flashes, racing heart, swelling throat."

"Wow," I said, feigning that I was impressed by her intellect. "How do you know so much about poison?"

I swear, it looked like Claudia's fork started shaking in her hand. After she raised a bite of duck to her lips, she took her time chewing.

"Research," she finally said. "For one of my films."

"Oh, right," I said casually. "Which one?"

"*The Clowns of Hell*," she answered.

"That's my favorite," I said.

"You really like it?" Claudia asked hopefully.

"Nope," I said. "Just kidding. But I've seen the poster." I remembered the delirious clown's face staring back at me from the wall of her office.

"Well, it's one of *my* favorites," she said.

Oh, yes. I bet it is, I thought. And I'm sure she found the research she had done on it particularly useful later in life.

As soon as the meal was over, I excused myself and ran up to my room. Oliver called me and asked if I wanted to go to the movies. As much as I wanted to see him, I just couldn't do it. My mom and I had always gone to the movies on Christmas. It was like our little tradition. So I told him that I was full from the duck à l'orange and down for the count.

"Then I guess I have to tell you over the phone," he said. "I'm busting out of dodge. It's a done deal. I told my mom last night. And the room is available as of tomorrow."

"Congrats!" I said. "That is awesome. How'd she take it?"

"She totally lost it at first, but I think she came around. Deep down she knows I need my own space."

"Nice job standing up to her."

"I even told her about us," he said.

"You did not!"

"And that really drove her crazy. She kept saying, 'Don't shit where you eat! You know how much I need this job. If anything happens between the two of you—'"

"I might tell Claudia to fire her. I know the drill," I said. "I wonder what it'll be like when I see her next?"

"It might be awkward, but I had to do this. And now me and you will have a place to be alone. Tons of privacy. Anyway, are you sure you don't want to meet up this evening?" he asked.

"I can't," I said. "But how 'bout tomorrow night?"

"That works."

"Oh, wait!" I said as it suddenly occurred to me. "I have to go to the Magic Castle with my dad, but I could come over afterwards."

"Cool! Come by my new place. I'm gonna start moving stuff over tomorrow afternoon," Oliver said, then he gave me his new address on the Venice Canals. I jotted it down on a lavender Post-it.

"I miss you," I said.

"I miss you, too."

Then we got off the phone. I turned off the light and lay in my bed looking at the shadows on the wall. I wished one of them would come alive and turn into my mother's ghost. That would be the best Christmas present I could get right now. She had said she'd be back, right? I looked at the shadows on the wall for as long as I could, waiting for one of them to move, but nothing happened. And at some point, I fell asleep.

THE MAGIC CASTLE

Saturday, December 26

I should've known my dad was buttering me up for something with this father-daughter night.

We drove up the long, winding driveway that led to the Victorian-style mansion. My dad left his car with the valet and then we walked inside. The hostess, who looked like a twenty-one-year-old Barbie doll, led us through a secret door in the bookcase into the golden-lit bar area. It was filled with the buzz of conversation between men dressed in jackets and button-down shirts and women wearing cocktail dresses.

The hostess took us up the staircase to the second floor. There she seated us at a table outside a door with a sign that read HOUDINI'S SÉANCE ROOM.

She pointed to the door and giggled. "That's where we have

séances and get in touch with the great Houdini. You should hear the things he says."

"Whoa, spooky," my dad said, playing along.

As soon as the hostess walked away, I turned to my dad. "Can you imagine how Houdini must feel if he really does have a ghost? These people at the Magic Castle are conducting forgery of his soul."

My dad opened up the menu and scanned it. "Oh, come on. Everyone knows that ghosts don't exist."

"Really? Everyone knows that?" I asked. "Don't you think it's cocky of human beings to think they know everything about this world?"

"No. It's just reality and common sense," he said. "So what are you thinking for your appetizer?"

"I haven't looked yet."

"Get whatever you want," he said with a smile.

I decided to drop the topic of the paranormal. My dad was too closed-minded to get what I was talking about.

Over the appetizers, he talked about how his office colleagues had started a monthly poker game. Apparently they were going to try to fit one in at our house before the New Year. How exciting. Then he wanted to hear about my classes at Winchester.

"I've been doing well in all of them, despite any distractions," I said, and narrowed my eyes at him. "And I turned in all my college apps, so now I just have to sit and wait."

"Well done. Is Brown still the number one choice?" he asked.

"Yep," I said, nodding my head.

"Great school. I can see you very happy there. So tell me. How are the Wild Bears doing?"

When my dad had gone to Winchester, he was the wide receiver on the school's football team. The Winchester team was called the Wild Bearcats. And every time I came home, he would ask me for an update.

"They're doing better than last year," I said. "We've got a few strong new players." The truth was I wouldn't know much about football in general, except Lulu had a huge crush on number twenty-one and she begged me go with her to most of the games. I guess there are worse ways to spend a weekend afternoon than watching a bunch of cute guys run around in tight pants and navy blue jerseys. During our salad course, my dad relived his glory days. It was while we were eating our steak entrées that he started acting odd, cutting his meat up into a bunch of little pieces.

"Is that filet mignon or chop suey?" I asked.

My dad put down his knife. Then he flashed me a goofy smile. "Holly, I'm really happy to see how you and Claudia have been spending time together. I knew that you'd get along better if you just gave her a chance."

"Yeah, okay. What's your point?" I asked, and then I took a sip of my Diet Coke.

"Claudia and I have been discussing things since the wedding-dress incident in Beverly Hills and . . ."

"What is it?" I asked. I was getting tired of my dad's rambling speeches. They always seemed to precede bad news.

"It's, um . . ." He crossed his hands on the table in front of him. "We want to take the plunge."

"The plunge? You're going swimming?" I asked, not wanting to take him seriously.

"No . . ." he said, fidgeting with a straw wrapper on the table.

"Then what are you talking about?" I said, pulling it out of him. If he was going to ruin my life even more, he might as well own up to it and say it outright.

"Claudia and I are getting engaged. She's been great for me. Very loving and supportive. And she really wants this. I mean, she's never been married before. So she's going to move in officially and we're going to take it from there." He said all of that like he was spitting out a rehearsed speech.

I sat there in silence. I'm glad Dr. Arbuckle thought my dad had changed so much. This sounded like the same weak bullshit to me.

"As it is, she already spends a ton of time at the house," he said. "So this won't really feel that different."

"You can say that again. Believe it or not, I've noticed."

"Honey, what do you make of all this? I know it's a lot to swallow, so let's talk about it."

"What do I *make* of it?" I said. "Well, I'm glad you asked, Dad. What I make of it is that it's sick and disgusting. This is your wife's—my mother's—*sister*. And Mom's hardly been dead six months."

"I'm glad you're saying this, Holly. I want to let it out. I know this is a big shock to you, and honestly, it's pretty shocking to me, too. But as Claudia and I have gotten closer these past months, I've gotten to know a different side of her than the one I've known all of these years. You know, your mother could be pretty hard on her—"

"Mom was hard on *her*? How about how hard she was on Mom? How about what she *did* to Mom?" I almost said it then; I almost told him. But I couldn't. He would never believe me, not now, when he was under Claudia's spell more than ever.

"What are you talking about?" my dad asked. We had both stopped eating; our half-finished steaks sat in front of us getting cold. "What do you mean, what Claudia did to Mom?"

"I, um, just—" I felt my chest tighten. "I need to be excused." I jumped up from the table.

"Holly, wait!" he said, but I was already darting to the ladies' room.

I ran into the bathroom and locked myself in a stall. If Claudia officially moved in and she and my dad tied the knot, it would make it almost impossible to get rid of her. I punched the sidewall and the toilet-paper roll fell to the ground. I watched it roll and unravel across the tiled floor.

Then I leaned my forehead against the door and covered

my face with my hands. I usually don't talk to myself, but I was so frustrated, I started blabbering. Maybe part of me hoped my mom could hear me.

"Why is this happening? I'm messing up. What a failure." I hunched over and tried to catch my breath. "I'm letting you down. I'm so sorry. I'm a bad daughter. I need to do something for you! But are you real? And how do I avenge your death, anyway?"

Just then I heard the sound of a toilet flushing, followed by a stranger's voice.

"Get a grip," the woman said with some attitude. And then, more gently, "It's going to be okay."

Oh my God. I couldn't believe there had been someone else in there with me the whole time. How utterly embarrassing. And she had heard everything that I'd said.

I looked under the stall and saw a woman's brown suede loafers walking toward a sink. There was the sound of running water, followed by silence.

"Do *you* believe in ghosts?" I blurted out while still hidden in my stall.

"I do," the disembodied voice said. And then I heard the quiet sound of the ladies'-room door opening and closing.

I opened the door to my stall quickly, but no one was there. It would've been nice to have more of a conversation with another believer, to hear her stories. Maybe she'd had sightings, too. But now I was all alone.

I splashed water across my face and, as the woman had

suggested, tried to get a grip. When I thought I had my poker face on, I took off back to the table and sat down across from my father.

He was sitting there with the check in front of him. Our steaks had been cleared away. He reached his hand across the table toward me. "I'm sorry. There wasn't an easy way to tell you. I know how much I upset you when I first told you about Claudia when you were away at school, and I didn't want that to happen again. I'm trying to be more open with you. Even when I know it's news that's not easy to hear."

That was more of the changing Dr. Arbuckle had picked up on. It was great that my dad was being more communicative, I guessed, but it would be even better if he just didn't have such bad news to communicate. I'd have loved for him to open up to me about breaking up with Claudia, for instance. But now it seemed like that wasn't going to happen, until I could prove that Claudia had poisoned my mom. That would break her and my dad up for sure. But, of course, I didn't know how to prove it. And I didn't know how to avenge my mom's death. I felt like such a failure.

Then I started wondering if this whole engagement thing was somehow my fault. If I hadn't followed Claudia that day into Beverly Hills, perhaps he wouldn't have known she was trying on wedding gowns, and maybe this wouldn't be happening so quickly.

"So is that why you took me here tonight? Just to tell me this?" I asked.

"No," my dad said. "I thought you'd enjoy having dinner and seeing the magic show."

"Yeah, right. Well, thanks for the Christmas gift; I'm having a lot of fun. Are you having a good time, too?" I asked, putting on an obviously fake smile.

"Please, Holly. Now isn't the time for sarcasm."

"Of course not!" I said. "Because it's time for magic! Are you ready? Let's go see the next show. I can hardly wait."

My dad let out a loud sigh. Then he shook his head as he paid the bill. After signing the check, we hurried downstairs to a large theater called the Palace of Mystery. We grabbed empty seats just as the lights dimmed. Then the magician ran onto the stage and introduced the first act.

"I think this is the magician my secretary is dating," my dad whispered.

"Awesome," I deadpanned. If only my dad would have found a nice lady magician to marry. Anyone would have been better than Claudia. *Anyone.*

"Welcome, ladies and gentlemen! I present to you the Disappearing Girl!" the magician said.

Just then the magician's beautiful assistant, dressed in a bright blue spandex outfit, climbed into a black box.

"We're gonna make her disappear one piece at a time!" the magician yelled as he closed the container's doors. Then he drew a large basic stick figure of a body on the outside of it—like the kind you draw when playing hangman. Suddenly, I noticed my mom's ghost standing in the shadows backstage.

I jolted upright in my seat. She looked at me and raised one finger to her lips as if to say, *Shhh, be quiet.* I turned to look at my dad. I wondered if he could see her, too, but I guessed he couldn't, because he was just smiling as he watched the magician wave his wand in the air like a wild orchestra conductor. I peeked around the audience to see if anyone else noticed the ghost, but the crowd's eyes were glued to center stage. They acted like everything was normal as the magician began erasing the arm of the chalk figure he had drawn. Then he swung open the box and there was his assistant, grinning with one missing arm.

I glanced over at my mother's ghost and she mirrored the magic trick. Her whole body was already slightly translucent anyway, like it had been the first time I saw her, but now her left arm slowly faded until it disappeared completely. A moment later, the magician erased the chalk outline of the other arm, followed by the legs and then the torso. And each time he reopened the box to show his assistant missing a new limb, a little more of my mom's ghost disappeared as well. Eventually all that was left was the assistant's face in the box—and my mom's face floating like a vision off stage left.

My heart started to beat really fast and I feared the next step. If the magician erased the face on the box, all of my mom would completely disappear, too. I cringed as the magician held up his fingers to the chalk drawing.

"Don't do it!" I said under my breath.

My dad looked my way. "It's all right," he said.

I ignored him. He obviously didn't really get what was going on. "Don't, don't, please!" I said more loudly, moving around in my seat. Some people in the audience near us heard; I could feel them staring at me.

My dad reached over and put his hand on my knee. "Shh. It's okay. He's going to make her come back in one piece," he said. "Just wait and see."

"You think so? How do you know?" I asked. But it was a good point. If he brought the assistant back in one piece, maybe my mom's ghost would return, too.

In one big motion, the magician erased the face drawn on the box. I quickly glanced over at the ghost—or what was left of her. She was looking straight at me as the last trace of her disappeared.

"Oh, God," I said, and looked down at my lap. Why did he have to do that? It was just a trick to that magician, but to me it was so much more.

My mom had come back, just like I had hoped she would. But now she was gone without talking to me, although I felt like I knew now what she had been trying to show me without words: the world was erasing her, just like my dad seemed to be erasing the memory of her from his mind a little bit more every day. And if he married Claudia, my mom's memory would be completely airbrushed out of existence. My mother was the disappearing girl. And I had to hurry or it would soon be too late.

I leaned over to my dad. "Do you think he forgets about

her all at once or limb by limb?" I whispered in his ear.

He didn't look at me but kept his eyes on the stage. "You think she's gone, but she's still very much here," he said quietly. I wondered if he really thought I was talking about the magician's assistant, or if he knew whom I was referring to. There was no way to tell.

Just then the crowd started to applaud. I glanced back at the stage. The magician raised a hand up in the air and then dramatically opened the box's doors to reveal his beautiful assistant back in one piece, unharmed and smiling.

I turned and looked back toward stage left, hoping to see my mom's ghost there again. But the space remained empty and bare.

If only it were that easy to bring her back, I thought.

As soon as we got back home, I jumped into my mom's car to drive over to Oliver's, as promised. I brought with me the Christmas cash that I wanted to donate to Save the Harbor, as well as a handmade card and a poem that I had written for him that afternoon.

"Isn't it late to start heading out?" my dad asked before I could shut the door and make my getaway.

"It's only nine o'clock, and I have plans with Oliver," I said. Earlier in the day, I had mentioned to my dad that I was dating Oliver, and he was cool with it. Then, of course, he ran and told Claudia, who told me that Oliver and I made "the most adorable couple in the whole wide world." I guessed there was nothing to hide anymore now that Oliver had told Patty.

"Well, be careful," he said. I could tell he was laying off me because he felt guilty for ruining our night with his stupid engagement news. "And be home my one o'clock."

"Yup, sure," I said. Then I was off.

As I drove south to Venice, I thought about how good it would feel to see Oliver and curl up in his arms and tell him about the bomb my dad had just dropped on me. When I got there, I parked my car on a side street and walked over to the address Oliver had given me, on a road called Court D.

I knocked on the door and Oliver answered. I guessed he could tell by the expression on my face that something was wrong.

"What's the matter?" he asked.

"It happened," I said. "The worst possible thing."

"All right, well, come meet my roommates quick and then we can go up to my room and talk."

Oliver led me inside, where I officially met Spike, whom I had seen in the kitchen at the *Caddyshack* house party, and two other guys, named Chuck and Tommy. They were gathered around the television playing Rock Band. Then Oliver introduced me to his two other roommates, Andy and Big Red, who were playing beer pong in the backyard overlooking the canals. They all seemed super friendly.

"It's nice to finally meet Big O's girl. I've heard a lot about you," said Big Red. He was a tall guy with—you guessed it—bright red hair.

"I hope you've heard all good things," I said.

"Ah, yeah!" Andy said. "That boy's whipped!"

"Shut up," Oliver said, laughing, and then he chucked a Nerf football that had been lying on the grass at Andy's chest. Andy caught it and then spiked it on the ground. "Touchdown!" he screamed.

We all laughed and then Oliver led me by the arm. "This way," he said.

Then he guided me back inside and upstairs, where he gave me a tour of his roommates' four messy bedrooms, a bathroom that looked like it hadn't been cleaned in six months (note to self: put paper on the seat if I ever have to use the toilet), and then his own bedroom. He grabbed a pair of boxers from the floor and tossed them under his bed.

"I love your place," I said. There was a mattress on the floor with a green comforter and an open suitcase with his clothes falling out of it. The space was messy and bare, but it was all his, and that was the best part.

"I still have some unpacking to do," he said, and plopped down on his bed.

"Well, you just got here," I said, sitting down beside him.

"So tell me what's up."

We both laid back together on the bed. Then I went off on my dad and Claudia's engagement. "I can't believe this is happening!" I said, shaking my hands in the air. "Once he marries her, it's gonna be even harder to ever get her out of the house."

"Man, that sucks," Oliver said. "I'm so sorry. I wish there was something I could do."

"I know," I said. I wished there was something I could do, too. There had to be a way; I just wasn't trying hard enough. And when was my mom's ghost going to come back? Maybe she'd give me some advice, or some more information. "Thanks for listening," I said, and then put my head on his chest and lay there. "Your bed is so comfortable. Just being here with you . . ."

"In my own room, away from everybody . . ."

"Makes it a little better. Exactly," I said. Then I thought it was a good time to give him my present. I pulled the cash out of my purse and handed it to him.

"I wanted to donate this to your job."

Oliver looked at all the money and smiled. "Wow. That's super generous of you."

"There's nowhere else I'd rather spend it. And here," I said, giving him the card I had made. I had cut out tiny strips of paper and then carefully taped them on top of each other so the small scraps looked like twigs forming a nest the size of a silver dollar. Then I had drawn two birds on top of the nest. On the first bird I had written the letter *O* and on the second one was an *H*.

"Oh man, this is so beautiful. But now I feel terrible. I didn't get you anything for Christmas. And I didn't make you anything, either," Oliver said.

"I don't want any gifts, and you don't have to make me

anything. You make me happy. That's enough," I said. And it was true. I didn't want gifts this year. It just wasn't Christmas without my mother.

"You might be the coolest girl ever," he said. "Did you know that?"

"Hmm. Sometimes," I teased. "But when I forget, maybe you can remind me."

"I will," Oliver said, and then he kissed me.

He opened up the card and read the poem I had written inside.

> *Doubt that the stars are fire, doubt that the sun moves,*
> *doubt truth to be a liar, but never doubt that I care.*
> *I'm not good at writing verse or iambic pentameter*
> *Mrs. Luten taught me back in ninth grade so that's all*
> *I got.*
> *With every square inch of my heart,*
> *XO,*
> *Holly*

"I love this!" Oliver said. I watched him read the poem a second time. "This is the best thing anyone's ever given me."

I grinned at that. Then we lay back down and I rested my head on his chest again. He turned his body into mine and put my arm over his waist. "When I moved my stuff in today, I had this weird fantasy. . . ."

"Ooh, sounds intriguing," I said. "What about?"

"One night, me and you taking off our clothes and going for a swim in the canals here."

"Like skinny-dipping? Wouldn't people see us?" I asked.

"I don't know, it gets pretty dark out here at night. I don't think anyone would see," said Oliver. "And we could just lie on our backs and float together in the water."

"But is the canal water clean enough to swim in?" I teased.

"It's just an idea."

"And isn't it cold?" I added.

"Maybe it's a bad one. . . ." He ran his fingers through my hair and it made me feel a little bit sleepy.

"So it's almost New Year's Eve," I said. "Do you know what you're doing yet?"

"Hopefully, spending it with you," Oliver said softly.

"You know, I've never had someone to kiss on New Year's Eve before," I admitted.

"Well, this time you will."

DREAMING OF YOU

Sunday, December 27

I didn't get home until three in the morning. I quietly snuck up to my room so my dad wouldn't hear me. He'd told me to be home by one o'clock, but I wasn't exactly in the mood to follow his rules.

In my room, I put on my pink and green plaid pajamas and a tank top. Then I crawled into bed and tried to sleep, but I couldn't. Every time I closed my eyes, I saw an image of Claudia in the wedding dress she'd tried on at the bridal salon. Soon she'd be wearing it again, but this time it would be for real. She was marrying my dad, unless I did something to stop it. But what could I do? I tossed and turned for almost an hour before I decided to get up and get a drink of water.

As I was walking downstairs to the kitchen, I heard a woman's voice. It sounded like she was saying, "Hell, hell."

I followed the noise to the dining room and then I heard the sound again. I froze when I realized it was my mother's voice and she was calling out, "Help! Help!"

I turned around and behind me I saw my mother's ghost wearing a nightgown. She was sitting in a wicker chair. I was so happy to see her again. She'd come back, just like she'd said she would. And now maybe she could give me some help. I took a step toward her and saw that her eyes were glassy, kind of like they used to get when she was depressed. And she looked fainter than the last time she had visited me—now she was nearly see-through. But I was happy to see her all in one piece after she had disappeared limb by limb at the Magic Castle.

"Mom, are you okay?" I asked, walking closer. "I wanted to talk to you earlier. Why didn't you stay longer?"

"You were in a big crowd of people. I had to wait until you were alone."

"I get it. Well, I'm so glad you're here now. And I won't let this world forget you, ever. I promise."

"Thank you, love," my mom said, and she seemed happy to know that I understood her.

"I missed you."

"I missed you, too, sweetheart," she said. Her voice sounded sad. "I can't believe how quickly time has been passing."

I nodded my head. "I know. And soon I'll be back at school."

"Time is running out," she said. "And Claudia's still here."

I couldn't tell if my mom knew about the engagement, but I wasn't going to be the one to tell her.

"I've been trying," I said. "It's just I have so many questions. I'm confused. . . ."

"I know this is overwhelming, Holly. I wish I didn't have to come to you with this. I've already put you through so much. Too much." My mom's ghost smoothed her hands over her nightgown.

"It's okay, Mom," I reassured her. "I can do it. Just help me figure out how."

"It's going to take time. Time and focus. Tell me, how have you been spending your time since you've been home?"

I instantly thought of Oliver, and it was like she could read my mind.

"There's a boy you've been seeing, right?" she asked gently.

"Oliver." As I said his name, I couldn't suppress a smile.

My mom smiled, too. "You like him a lot," she said. "I can tell."

I nodded.

"I'm happy for you, honey. So happy. To love and to be loved is the greatest thing in the world. I had that with your father. For a time . . ." Her smile faded. "But love can be an illusion. It can trick you. I don't want to see you tricked, or hurt. Ever."

"Oliver's not going to hurt me, Mom," I assured her. "He's a good guy. A really good one."

"It's just so hard to tell," she said. "Maybe you should take it slowly with this boy, honey."

I thought about what she was saying. My mother had always given me the best advice when I was younger and had trouble with my friends or problems with teachers. Maybe she was right. Maybe I was rushing things with Oliver. If I spent less time with him, I could spend more time working on getting even with Claudia and getting her out of my dad's life, and my own.

"I don't know, Mom," I said. "Maybe you're right. How am I supposed to avenge your death, though? Just tell me that. Please."

But she was gone. The wicker chair was empty. I heard her say one last thing before she disappeared completely.

"Time is running out for me, my love. Please hurry."

"I will, Mom," I said to the empty chair. "I promise."

HEARTBREAK

I must've gone to sleep, because the next thing I knew, I was in my bed and it was nearly ten o'clock. As soon as I opened my eyes, I knew what I had to do. I went back over to Oliver's new place in Venice. He was surprised to see me again so soon, but he gave me a big hug and told me he wished I had never left last night. It felt so good to be in his arms, but everything my mom's ghost had just said echoed in my head. She was right. Love could be an illusion, and it could fade. Look at what had happened between her and my dad. She knew so much more than I did when it came to stuff like that. I wanted to talk about it with Oliver, to see how he felt about taking things more slowly—maybe he'd think it was a good idea, too—but it was hard to find the right moment because he was playing Rock Band with his roommates and they all wanted me to join in, so I did.

Big Red, Andy, Oliver and I spent hours playing the game. It was totally addictive. When they let me have the microphone, the Clash song "Should I Stay or Should I Go" came up on the screen. I sang an only slightly off-pitch rendition of it. As I belted out the tune, I couldn't help but think about the lyrics while I looked at Oliver's adorable face. It was oddly fitting with my situation. *Do I keep hanging out with Oliver and falling for him? Or do I pull away, protect my heart, and focus on helping out my mom's ghost?* This song was so eighties, but it still fit around my modern life like spandex leggings.

Finally, when Oliver and I went upstairs to his bedroom and were lying across his mattress, I realized I had to bring it up now before we started making out. Because once he started kissing me, I knew I would never want him to stop.

I let out a sigh. "There's some stuff I want to talk about with you."

"What's going on?" he said as he ran a finger up and down my arm.

"This is really difficult for me to say." I paused and looked up at the ceiling. "And I'm not even sure what I want to say, or how I want to say it. . . ."

"Uh-oh, that doesn't sound good." Oliver pulled away from me a little and sat up on the bed.

"I think maybe we should spend less time together." There, I said it. And it felt horrible.

"What? Why? I mean, I don't get it. Everything's been going so cool."

"It has been cool. And I really like you. I mean, more than you know." I reached over to hold his hand, but he pulled it away.

"I feel the same way," Oliver said. "So what's the problem?"

The image of my mom's ghost flashed through my head.

"I'm not saying there is a problem. I'm just saying maybe we should spend less time together, take things more slowly," I said. This had seemed so much easier in my head than it was to actually put it into words. I didn't know how to explain myself. I wished I could just tell Oliver about my talk with my mom, but, of course, I couldn't. "I still want things to be good between us."

"Yeah, this is a great way to make that happen," he said. "I feel so stupid. I thought you really cared about me."

"I do care about you. But this has nothing to do with how much I care. It's something bigger than me. . . . I mean, it's about me, too, but also something else. . . ."

"What? You're not making any sense," he said. "I think I get what Spike means when he says girls are crazy."

"There's something I have to take care of before I can ever really be with you."

"Oh, I get it," Oliver said with an angry look in his eyes that I had never seen before. He got up and walked across the room, as far away from me as he could get. "Is there another guy? Back at Winchester or something?"

"No! It's nothing like that. You have to believe me." I got

up and walked over to him, but he moved away. "It's compli-cated."

"Yeah, it feels pretty complicated. But it's starting to make sense now. Since the beginning, it felt like you've been hiding something. I tried to tell myself it was just in my mind, but now I can see that I was right to be worried," he said.

"Listen to me, this is getting all blown out of proportion. I'm not saying I want to break up. I just need, you know, a little space."

"No," Oliver said. "Listen to me. You either want to be with me or you don't. It shouldn't be so confusing."

I looked down at the floor. I wanted to be with him, but I also wanted to honor what my mom had said. It was the least I could do, wasn't it? I turned to him, but he wouldn't look me in the eye.

"I do want to be with you. . . ." I said. My stomach was tied in a huge knot.

He turned to me. I could see a flicker of hope in his eyes.

"But I need some time to be with myself, too," I said quietly.

"Right." Oliver nodded his head. "Well, then, take all the time you need."

All I wanted to do right then was grab his face and kiss it. I wanted to throw my arms around him and hold him tight. But the ghost of my mom was dancing in my head and she wouldn't go away. In fact, I imagined her nodding with approval, commending me for guarding my heart.

Oliver walked to his bedroom door and opened it. Then he nodded toward it.

"Man, I didn't see this coming," he said. "And to think my mom was worried about *me* breaking *your* heart."

"I'm sorry," I said.

"You should probably go."

"Yeah . . . I guess you're right." But it felt like my feet were rooted to the floor.

We stood there in silence for a moment. Leaving him was the last thing that my heart wanted to do. I took a deep breath and then quickly headed out the door. If I stayed a moment longer, I knew I might try and take it all back.

When I got home, I could hear my dad and a bunch of other men laughing in the den. I poked my head in and saw that they were playing poker. This must be the game my dad had told me about at the Magic Castle. I was definitely not in the mood to see anyone, least of all my dad and his buddies, so I tried to duck out quickly before anyone noticed me.

"Two dames and one on the river!" my dad yelled out excitedly as he scooped up a pile of chips from the pot. Then he looked up and saw me.

"Holly, come say hi," he said, and waved me in.

I reluctantly slid into the room.

My dad introduced me to the crew of fortysomethings in button-down shirts with loosened collars.

"Hi," I said with a small wave.

"Your dad said you had quite a wipeout last week," one of the guys said, and then he took a swig of his beer.

"What?" I asked.

"Honey, I told them about your tumble in Beverly Hills," my dad said.

I felt my cheeks get red. "Great. Thanks, Dad."

"Used to play soccer at UC San Diego," a different guy said. He was bald but he had a bushy red beard. "Had five concussions by the time I graduated. It's part of growing up. Getting knocked in the head and falling on your ass."

I didn't want to show any interest in engaging in this conversation, so I just nodded.

"Shut up, Carter. You sound like an asshole," the first guy said, punching his buddy in the arm. Then he turned back to me. "Trust me. Get banged up as little as possible. You don't want to end up like this guy." He gestured with his thumb at Carter.

"Thanks for the advice," I said, then I left the room. It seemed like these old guys were trying to act hip and cool when talking to me, but they just came across as weirdos.

Patty was hanging out in the hallway. It looked like she was waiting for me, and apparently she was.

"Do you have a minute?" she asked. "Claudia wants to speak with you in her office right now."

"Sounds official," I said.

Patty laughed awkwardly as we walked along the hallway to the stairwell. This was the first time I'd seen her since

Oliver had told her about our relationship, and now, little did she know, it was already over. Or so it seemed. That wasn't what I had meant to happen, but it seemed like somehow it had worked out that way. How had that talk gone so badly? Why was I always messing everything up?

"I don't know if you heard, but Oliver left me," Patty said.

I nodded.

"For Venice Beach," she said. "It's like they say: 'Little children, headache; big children, heartache.'"

I felt bad for her. I could see how hard it was for her to let Oliver go. It was going to be hard for me, too. "Yeah, I know he moved," I said, and started up the stairwell.

Patty took the first few steps up, but then stopped and leaned against the banister. "Holly . . ."

I stopped and looked at her. "Yes?"

"I've never been good with money. Haven't had a lot of it. And I wish I could've provided more for Oliver and Lara." She looked around our lavish hallway, with its French wallpaper and the crystal chandelier on the ceiling. "But the little I have, I want to protect, and . . ."

I knew what she was getting at. "Look, Oliver's been nothing but wonderful to me. And no matter what happens between us, you never have to worry. I wouldn't do anything to hurt your job. And I know that the two of you are fighting now, but he cares about you a ton."

Patty cocked her head to one side. "You know?"

"Yeah, he told me that you had a huge fight."

"Not that," Patty said. "The other thing . . . that he cares."
She looked down at her feet and shuffled her clogs around.

"Oh," I said. "Yes, it's obvious."

Patty let out a sigh. Then she smiled to herself. "That's nice
to hear."

Then we continued walking up the rest of the staircase. I
was struck by how badly Patty needed to hear that. Maybe the
two of them didn't say "I love you" that much to each other.
My mom and I used to say it to each other all the time.

A moment later, we stopped in front of Claudia's office. It
was weird to think of it that way, since it had always been my
mom's office. But I guessed it was Claudia's now. "Patty, give
us ten," Claudia said as soon as she saw me.

"Okeydokey, Pokey," Patty said, and shut the door behind
her.

Claudia stood up from her desk. She moved over to a more
casual meeting area, with a couch and a beautiful antique
chair covered in chocolate-brown velvet. My mom had had
it forever and I'd always liked to curl up in it and watch her
when she worked late.

"Get comfortable." Claudia gestured to the couch.

I wondered what on earth she wanted to talk to me about.
I plopped down on the couch and she sat in the chair. I hated
seeing her in it.

"How ya doing, Holly?" she asked, smiling.

"Fiiine," I said, but of course that was far from the truth.

"So I know when your dad talked to you about our plans, it didn't go over great."

"You mean the *engagement*?" I asked.

"Yes, he mentioned you weren't a fan of the idea so I thought maybe you'd come around if you knew how much I really love him. I would do anything to make him happy, Holly. And I think I do make him happy. In fact, I'm positive that I bring him a lot of joy. You know, he had a cold few years."

"What exactly are you saying?" I asked, leaning forward.

"I'm not sure how well versed you are on the side effects of those antidepressants your mother was on—when she took them, that is—but shall we say, they didn't make her the most affectionate person. She could be so hard to be around, moody and difficult. Your dad couldn't take it anymore and when he asked her for a separation, it was only a few days before she took her life and—"

"He wanted a separation?" I asked, caught off guard.

"I thought you knew that," Claudia said. Her tone dripped with fake concern. "That's why he feels so guilty. Sometimes he blames himself for what happened. But my point is, your dad has gone through a lot, and I just want to make him happy now and be good to him. You're away at school and next year you'll be at college, then after that you'll be off living your life. I'm sure you don't want him to grow old alone. Maybe he and your mom were never really compatible."

"My mom loved my dad the best way that she could. Nothing you do to him can ever take that away," I said, rising to my feet.

"Of course not," said Claudia. "And I wouldn't want to take that special bond away from them. Or you."

"That's great, 'cause you can't," I said, and stormed out the door.

MISSING HIM

Monday, December 28–Wednesday, December 30

The next couple of days were filled with the ache of
missing Oliver. I couldn't stop thinking about him . . .
his smell, lying next to him, feeling his arms around me,
kissing him, laughing together, his smile. I had to live with
these memories of him, and they haunted me like the ghost of
my mom.

Now that she was officially engaged to my dad, Claudia
had wasted no time moving in more of her clothes and belongings. She said she had already put her house on the market
and would start selling her own furniture, because she liked
our stuff much better. I noticed while she was in the kitchen
pouring a glass of white wine one afternoon that there was

a ring on her finger, a giant, tacky rock—four karats, at least. Not at all like my mom's engagement ring, which wasn't exactly small, but was very tasteful. My dad had given it to me after she died, and I thought I'd wear it myself one day, when I was ready to get married.

As an escape on Tuesday, Felicia and I went to grab homemade ice-cream-cookie sandwiches at Diddy Riese in Westwood. It was the best deal in town, and the yummiest. I ate five of them. Literally. Ice cream had always been my favorite comfort food, especially peanut-butter swirl.

As we ate, I told Felicia about what was going on with my dad and Claudia, and then I filled her in on the status of Oliver and me.

"You broke up with him?" Felicia yelled, and hit me on the arm. "I can't believe it. What happened? And why didn't you tell me ASAP?"

I couldn't tell her that my mom's ghost had suggested that I slow things down with Oliver because she was afraid he might hurt me, so instead I tried to describe to her the other feelings going on inside me. "It just happened on Sunday, and I guess I didn't call you right away because I needed to deal with it a little."

"Fair enough," Felicia said as she took a bite of her ice-cream sandwich. "But I still don't get it. Last I left off, you were like a pair of goo-goo lovebirds."

"Yeah, well, I'm still going through stuff with my mom.

And I'm not quite ready to get deeply involved with someone yet. I guess it took me a little while to realize that." A drip of ice cream landed on my sleeve, and I licked it off.

When Felicia heard this, she changed her tone a bit. "Oh yeah, I get that. Sometimes I forget that it hasn't been that long since your mom . . . since what happened to your mom."

We were quiet for a minute. We never talked much about my mom, about what had happened that day. Felicia had been there with me when I got home, when I found out my mom was dead. She had seen me at my absolute worst, my most devastated. It had been super hard for me but it was hard on her, too.

"The thing is, I didn't even mean to break up with him. I just told him I wanted some space, but he took it all wrong," I said.

"Ah," Felicia said knowingly. "The 'I need some space' talk. That's the kiss of death!"

"Thanks, Felish," I said in a flat voice. "I guess I didn't know that. I really did just want to take things more slowly."

"Well, hopefully he'll still be waiting for you when you're ready."

"Do you think he might be?" I asked.

"Yeah! And if he isn't, you'll meet someone else and move on."

It occurred to me that this was a real possibility—that I'd have to meet someone else, that I'd have to move on. I didn't want to meet someone else. And I didn't want Oliver to meet someone else, either. "I've never met a guy it felt so good to be with," I said.

"Yeah, that stuff is hard to find," said Felicia. Then we both finished our ice-cream sandwiches in silence. I wondered if she was having a sweet daydream about what she might be finding for the first time with Devin right now. And I was having a nightmare about what I might be losing.

On Wednesday, to take my mind off Oliver and off Claudia moving in more of her designer wardrobe and horror props— including a fake gorilla head and a pair of machetes—I decided to be productive and go through my mom's stuff that was packed in boxes in the upstairs hallway closet. Maybe I'd find some sort of clue or evidence of what had really happened between Claudia and my mom the day she died. Also, I had to pull out the stuff I wanted to keep before my father donated everything to charity.

When my dad saw me yanking out the boxes, he offered to help me.

"No, I'm fine on my own," I said.

"Are you sure?" he asked. "There's a lot to deal with here."

"I guess you can help me carry the boxes. But I want to go through them in my room."

"Whatever you like, hon," my dad said with a big smile. He was trying to be super nice to me since our talk about Claudia at the Magic Castle. He could pour on all the charm he wanted—it wasn't going to change how I felt about what he was doing or how I felt about Claudia. He helped me bring a bunch of stuff into my bedroom and then he left.

I spent the afternoon going through my mom's things, and at a certain point I recruited Anna Maria to help me. I thought this would be a nice way to move past our argument over the spell I had done behind her back. We sat on the floor of my bedroom, sorting through old clothes and papers. Sampson stopped by to sniff around for a few minutes. He whimpered softly and I wondered if he was picking up my mom's scent. Then he looked around the room for a minute before heading off into the hallway. Maybe the faint smell of my mother brought back the memory of her and he was now hoping to find her somewhere in the house.

In one suitcase I found the same shirt my mom's ghost had worn the night I saw her in the Chinese garden. I tried it on right away.

"What do you think?" I asked.

"It's very nice on you," Anna Maria said. She sighed. "You look so much like your mother."

"I do?" I was pleasantly surprised. No one had ever thought my mom and I looked too much alike in the past, but maybe as I was getting older I was starting to resemble her more. I hoped so.

Then I went through my mom's old jewelry and pulled out a bunch of thin silver chains and beaded necklaces and put several of them on at once. Wearing her things made me feel close to her.

I didn't find any evidence to incriminate Claudia, but I did discover a stack of letters that my dad had written to my mom ages ago. One was written on hotel stationery from the Ritz-Carlton in New York. I guessed he'd been there on a business trip.

> *Kate,*
> *Only five more days, then I get to come home to you.*
> *I miss you more than I can say. You are the best thing*
> *that's ever happened to me. And I will love you forever.*
> *Love,*
> *G*

It was crazy reading a letter from my dad that was so sweet to my mom. I didn't know he had it in him. I mean, I had never seen that side of him. It made me smile for an instant, imagining the two of them happy together as a young couple. I wondered if they had felt the same giddiness that Oliver and I felt when we were together. But as soon as Oliver's face flashed through my mind, I felt the sting of missing him.

For three hours, Anna Maria and I went through my mom's clothes and papers. By the evening, we had divided up the possessions into two piles: To Keep and Not to Keep.

That night, my father did a double take at my outfit as I sat down to dinner with him and Claudia. I was wearing a long skirt of my mom's with a drawstring-waist top and all these cool necklaces and silver bracelets.

"You're wearing your mother's clothes?" my dad asked.

"Yeah," I said. "I love them so much. And they fit perfectly. I kept a bunch in my closet."

"Right," my dad said softly. Then he glanced at Claudia, who was raising one eyebrow slightly.

My aunt cleared her throat and then shrugged her shoulders as if she had no idea what to say. I hoped seeing me dressed in my mom's clothes made them as uncomfortable as seeing them together as a couple made me. I carefully watched Claudia for her reaction. She barely ate anything and didn't talk much. Neither did my dad. Good. They both felt awkward, as well they should. Maybe, just maybe, seeing me dressed like my mom would remind them that she had existed, and that it was totally wrong for them to be getting together now that she was gone.

During that meal, there were only the sounds of the forks and knives cutting the roast chicken and brussels sprouts— and the noise of my mom's bracelets clanking together on my wrist. I made them bang together as loudly as possible. *Clank. Clank. Clank.* Like the sound of a ghost pulling metal chains through an attic. I think I saw that in some movie once. *Someone dead is still alive*, I thought. *And she's not happy.*

RHYLEE AND GINGER

Thursday, December 31

I spent Thursday morning in my room writing in my playwriting journal. I was trying to jot down any bits of dialogue that I could remember from the past few days, especially lines from my breakup talk with Oliver. Thinking about him was painful, but somehow writing about him made me feel a little better. By the afternoon I was feeling pretty claustrophobic, so I decided to get out of the house and take Sampson for a walk. I had told him the night of the attempted chicken-heart burial that I would take him for one of our long hikes together in the canyon, and it was time to make good on my promise.

As I walked Sampson down the street (or rather, as *he* walked *me*—because he was so big and determined, he had never really learned to walk next to the person holding his leash), I noticed a limousine trailing behind me. I felt like I was being followed by the FBI. I walked over to the side of the road to let the limo pass by. But instead of driving on, it cruised beside me. One of the tinted windows lowered and a girl with chestnut brown hair pulled into a side bun like a flamenco dancer's stuck her head out of the car and hollered.

"Hey, pretty girl, you want some bonbons?" Then she let out a loud whistle, like she was a construction worker watching a beautiful woman walk by.

I was kind of freaked out until I realized it was my cousin Rhylee, the twenty-two-year-old world traveler. "Rhylee? What on earth are you doing here?"

Just then a second girl popped up behind Rhylee's shoulder. "And Ginger, too!" she yelled out. Ginger was Rhylee's twenty-year-old sister and partner in crime. She had long, flowing mermaid hair; half of it was pulled up into a twist on top of her head.

"Ginger! I can't believe you're both here," I said. I had always liked Rhylee and Ginger, but we were never great about staying in touch. The last time I saw my cousins had been four years ago when I went with my mom for a weekend visit to San Francisco. They had lived there with their mother, my dad's sister. She was a successful art dealer and had raised her daughters to be free spirits. I remembered thinking it was so cool that they were allowed to wear whatever they wanted all the time, even Halloween costumes in the winter or ski pants in the summer. One time when she was little, Rhylee wore a bathing suit for two weeks straight, even to school, and her mom was totally fine with it.

When my mom passed away, Rhylee and Ginger sent flowers and a nice card, but they didn't fly back for the memorial service because they were living in South America at the time. Maybe they were here now because they hadn't come then.

They jumped out of their limo and hugged me while Sampson ran in circles. I was blasted by the brightness of my cousins' clothes. Rhylee wore a red and yellow floral-print top with a pair of white bell-bottom pants. And Ginger was in a purple spaghetti-strap sundress; her entire left arm was covered in orange beads.

"What's up, cuz?" Ginger asked, playfully tugging at my hair. "We've missed you like hotcakes."

"It's so good to see you!" Rhylee said. "We landed over two hours ago and we would've been here sooner if Ginger wasn't such a huge flirt." She teasingly scowled at her sister.

"I met five cute Australian guys by the luggage carousel," Ginger said. "I love those accents."

"So what are you guys doing in L.A.?" I asked. "Last I left off, you were shaking your booties at some tango club in Buenos Aires."

"That's so old news, Holly," Rhylee said, playing with the long strand of green beads she wore around her neck. "Ginger decided to take time off from Vassar, so we moved to Chile, where we've been teaching dance to children with special needs."

"It's been awesome," Ginger said. "Teaching children with special needs is so meaningful to me." She talked fast and moved her hands a lot as she spoke.

"I can't believe your mom let you run all around the world," I said. "I'm jealous."

"You know what an intellectual bohemian freak our mom is. She says the planet is the school of life," said Rhylee.

"Besides," Ginger said, pulling a loose hair out of the bottom of her long blond mane, "we might as well have fun before we become old ladies and get J-O-B-S."

"Next we're stopping by our mom's place up north for a week before heading off to go backpacking—"

Ginger cut her sister off. "You mean *partying*, through Thailand. Holly, you should come with."

"Thanks, but I'm going back to school pretty soon. And in the meantime, there's stuff I have to take care of at this prison."

Ginger gasped. "Prison? What are you talking about? Your family's place is bangin'."

"It used to be," I said.

"Listen, Holly-bolly. We're really sorry about your mom," Rhylee said. "When we heard—"

"I could barely breathe," said Ginger. "I cried all night."

"We felt really bad," Rhylee said. "How ya holding up?"

"As well as can be expected, considering my dad's new roommate," I said. "Or should I say, his new *fiancée*."

"Oh man," said Rhylee. "We heard your dad and your aunt got together. That's pretty wild! But I didn't know they were engaged."

"Yup, that's the story, hot off the presses." I pulled on Sampson's leash to bring him closer to me; he was trying to wander off down the road. I guessed he wasn't happy that our walk had been interrupted.

"In America, it's wild," Ginger said. "But in other countries that stuff happens all the time."

Rhylee hit Ginger on the arm. "No, it doesn't, Gingie."

"It's true!" said Ginger. "The Europeans are much more loosey-goosey with love affairs. But don't get me wrong, it's still very weird!"

"Weird. Twisted. Wrong. Crazy. Call it what you will. But hey, what brought you both to Cali?"

"We missed you, that's all." Rhylee smiled warmly.

"We thought you could use a happy surprise," said Ginger. "This must be a really hard time of year for you, the holidays, without your mom."

I was touched.

"Hop in! And ride back with us to the house," Rhylee said.

"But I have the dog," I said, patting Sampson's head.

"He can come, too!" Ginger said.

"Are you sure?" I asked.

"Totes!"

We all got into the limo and Sampson ran back and forth inside it as we drove back to my house.

Once we arrived, the chauffeur opened the limo door and then grabbed my cousins' two matching bright green suitcases out of the trunk. Then Rhylee, Ginger, Sampson, and I headed inside.

There we found Claudia and my dad sitting on the white leather sofas, drinking afternoon cocktails as if waiting for our arrival. Wait, had they known about this little holiday visit?

"Rhylee and Ginger? Oh my God. What on earth are you doing here?" Claudia said with what seemed to be a measure of fake surprise. She jumped up from the couch and warmly hugged both of the girls. "It's great to see you beauties. How are you both?"

Claudia had met my cousins only a few times over the years, but she was acting like she knew them so well.

"I'm as blue as a night in Cuba. I have vines and stars in my hair," Ginger said. She took one hand and waved her fingertips through her hair.

My dad and Claudia looked at Ginger as if she was speaking another language. Rhylee explained, "Ever since we visited Pablo Neruda's house in Chile, she quotes his poetry."

"He had the most amazing butterfly collection. Did you know in Egypt butterflies were the symbols of immortality? The tour guide at Neruda's house taught me that."

"Oh, I didn't, how fascinating. I wish I could've seen it. Gardner, you'll have to take me to South America one of these days, won't you? You said you were always interested in butterflies as a kid." Claudia tickled the back of his neck with her fingers.

He was? I didn't know that. And since when was my dad talking to Claudia about butterflies and his youth?

My dad smiled and reached back to hold her hand. "I'll work on it. In the meantime, I hope one night in Palm Springs will do. It may not be below the equator, but it's south of Sunset Boulevard."

Claudia laughed, then turned to my cousins. "He surprised me. Tonight, for New Year's Eve, he booked us a suite at La Quinta Resort and we have an evening of massages planned."

I thought then of how Oliver and I had talked about New Year's Eve. Now we wouldn't be together; we wouldn't have a New Year's kiss. And what had I even done in the past few days to help my mom? I was supposed to be using my extra time to help her, but once again I had done nothing. I felt like the worst daughter in the world.

I realized everyone was looking at me.

"Did you hear me say your father and I will be out tonight, Holly? We're going to a resort for massages."

"Yup," I said. "Gross."

"What?" Claudia asked.

"Nothing," I said.

Claudia smiled at Ginger and Rhylee. "Such bad timing.

We have to leave the three of you alone tonight. But we'll be back tomorrow for New Year's Day. In fact, we're planning a barbeque in the evening and we invited over a few of my friends."

"Like who?" I asked.

"Tomoko and his wife, Annie," my dad said.

"You met them at the party," Claudia reminded me. I remembered. *The Dead Bachelorette.* And they had brought her the rhinestone tiara.

"Anyway, I hope you'll stay for a while so we can catch up properly," Claudia said to Rhylee and Ginger.

"Oh, we're not running anywhere. We'd love to!" Rhylee said.

"Perfecto," said Claudia.

Then my aunt put her arms around Rhylee and Ginger. "Come on, let me show you to the guest quarters." I noticed Claudia wink at Rhylee as they walked toward the stairs.

That night while my dad and Claudia were rendezvousing in their suite at Palm Springs, Rhylee and Ginger and I had the house all to ourselves. We lounged outside by the pool and caught up. It was good to see them again, even if I didn't fully trust their motives for being here.

But I couldn't stop thinking about Oliver. How was he doing? *What* was he doing? Was he with another girl? No, it would be too soon for him to have found someone else. Right? Finally, I couldn't help myself; I texted him.

To: Oliver

Dec. 31, 7:08 pm

How are you doing? I really miss you.

He had always responded to my calls and texts right away, but he didn't tonight. Rhylee noticed me checking my phone incessantly, so I explained the situation to her.

"You can't dump a guy and expect him to text you back," Rhylee said, and rolled her eyes.

"I didn't dump him," I said. "We're taking time off."

"Sounds like a dump to me," Ginger said. She slid her shoes off and put her feet into the pool.

"Boys have fragile egos," Rhylee explained. She was lying down across from Ginger on the other side of the pool. "If you break up with one, don't expect him to talk to you ever again."

I prayed that wasn't true. Besides, Oliver wasn't like every other guy.

My cousins and I decided to order in a ton of food from Mr. Chow's, a fancy Chinese restaurant in Beverly Hills. As we waited for the food to arrive, I touched base with Felicia on the phone. She had plans with her new guy and a few other people from the Groundlings, but she said they'd all come by later. I wanted her to meet my cousins.

As Rhylee, Ginger, and I enjoyed our dinner inside, I decided to grill them about the real reason behind their "surprise" visit.

"Look, I'm not dumb. I know my dad and Claudia probably sent for you," I said as I doused my egg roll in duck sauce.

"Why would they ever do that?" Ginger said casually. She
stuck a piece of General Tso's chicken in her mouth.

"I have no idea. Gosh," I said sarcastically.

"Listen, I don't want to lie to you," Rhylee said. "I mean,
we're cousins and there's blood between us. They did invite
us here, but only because they're worried about you. And I
guess they think it'll be easier for you to talk to us because
we're closer to your age."

I finished chewing and leaned back on the couch. "Look,
guys, the last six months have been so hard. And then just
when I thought it couldn't get any worse, my dad shacks
up with my crazy aunt. It's made me kind of stop seeing the
world the same way I did before all this bad stuff happened."

They looked at me like they were waiting for me to say
more.

"Like, you know in school we're taught that humans are
civilized and evolved? The king of all animals?"

"It's 'cause humans have logic, reason, and souls," Rhylee
said.

"Yeah, but lately I feel like our entire species might be
completely overrated. And—" Rhylee started giggling and
nudging Ginger's arm. "What's so funny?" I asked.

"Zip. Zero," said Rhylee.

"Zilch," Ginger said.

"What are you laughing at?" I narrowed my eyes. "I

thought you guys were here to listen to me talk. Well, I'm talking."

"It's just if you're not a fan of humans right now, you probably won't like the Aussies we met at the airport," Ginger said.

"What?"

"Look outside." Rhylee pointed at the window and kept laughing.

I turned around and spotted a green Jeep pulling up in front of the house.

"Who are they?" I asked.

"The guys I met at the airport." Ginger started listing a bunch of names. "Angus, Josh, Roach, Flynn, and Carson."

"They're Australian filmmakers passing through L.A. on their way to Alaska. They're gonna shoot a documentary on glacier surfing," Rhylee said. "Isn't that hot?"

"They had a one-night stopover in L.A. and I told them if they wanted to party for New Year's Eve, they should come by your place. I didn't really think they would, though," Ginger said.

"I told her not to do it," said Rhylee. "But Ginger has a crush on Mr. Ringlets."

"Oh, no!" I said. "Ginger, this is perfect." I loved the idea of messing up my dad's plans. Instead of having a heart-to-heart with my cousins, I'd party with some Aussies.

Ginger gave me a big hug. "You're the best cousin ever!" she said. Then she ran to the front door and swung it open.

There was the sound of reggae music blasting from the Aussies' Jeep, and loud honking.

I raced outside to join them and watched as five guys wearing worn-in T-shirts, hemp necklaces, and ripped jeans jumped out of the car.

We ran over and helped with their large duffel bags and camera equipment. Ginger threw her arms around a tall guy with corkscrew blond curls and gave him a hug around his waist.

"This place is ripper!" one of the guys yelled.

Right away I loved their adorable accents. "Welcome to the city of angels!" I said.

"Happy New Year!" another guy said. "Are you ready to rage?"

"Bring it on! Let the party begin!" I hollered. And we all headed into the house.

A BUNCH OF AUSSIES

As soon as we got inside, I invited the Aussies to eat whatever they wanted from the well-stocked kitchen and pantry.

"We have everything from potato chips to foie gras! Dig in!" I said.

The guys' faces lit up as I opened up all the cupboards. Normally I wouldn't want the house I had grown up in to be trashed, but lately, with Claudia's stuff everywhere, this place was starting to feel less and less like my home.

"I love all this American food," Angus said, rubbing his big belly. He was the shortest and heaviest of the crew.

The Aussies grabbed Cheetos, an Entenmann's cake, extra Russian caviar from the Christmas Spectacular, and our leftover cartons of Chinese food. Then we moved outside to the pool. I snuck a few cases of beer and some bottles of champagne from my dad's cellar, as well. I hoped they were the most expensive ones, but it was hard to tell. Rhylee said she wanted to play DJ, so she hooked up her iPod to the living-room stereo and blasted all this international dance music she had discovered while living in South America. Most of the songs sounded like salsa music infused with a techno beat.

Rhylee, Ginger, and I changed into bathing suits and the three of us went swimming while the guys kept chugging back beers and eating everything in sight. They were really messy, throwing cans and empty bags of potato chips all over the place. One time when I was swimming from the deep end to the shallow end, I passed a floating Chinese takeout container. And when I somersaulted off the diving board during a cannonball contest, I opened my eyes underwater and saw an egg roll on the bottom of the pool. I dove down to get it and when I got back up to the surface, I raised it up in the air.

"Did someone lose an egg roll?"

Flynn splashed over to me and grabbed it out of my hand. "That's where that went," he said, and then took a big bite of it. The egg roll was soggy and falling apart all over his face, but Flynn didn't seem to care one bit.

Then around eleven thirty Felicia showed up with Devin and three of their friends from the Groundlings. When Felicia walked in, she was holding Devin's hand with a smile plastered all over her face. It was so nice to see her happy with a guy, but when I saw her with Devin, it made me think of Oliver. I wondered what he was doing right that second and if he was missing me, too. He still hadn't texted back.

"Since when do you throw house parties?" Felicia said, jabbing me in the arm. Devin had wandered off to talk to the Aussies.

"Now that Claudia's taking this place over, I can do whatever I want here," I said. "I mean, if my dad can marry his sister-in-law, there's no more rules in *this* house."

"Well, good job, lady. You deserve to have fun," she said. "Who are all these dudes, though?"

I explained the situation to her and we all made introductions.

At ten seconds to midnight, it was time for the countdown. When the clock hit twelve, everyone started screaming, "Happy New Year!" Felicia kissed Devin, Ginger made out with her favorite Aussie, Carson, and Rhylee even pecked Flynn on the cheek, and when I turned to my left there was this cute guy from the Groundlings standing next to me. He had taken his shirt off to go swimming and I noticed that he had a perfect, chiseled chest. He leaned in and tried to plant his wet lips on mine, but I moved away.

"Sorry," I said. If I wasn't going to kiss Oliver this New Year's Eve, I wasn't going to kiss anyone.

"That's cool. No worries." He quickly turned around and started making out with the girl he had come with instead.

I rolled my eyes. *Wow, he seemed really disappointed,* I

thought. Then I got up and checked my phone again. Still no reply from Oliver.

As the party kept trucking, Josh got an expensive-looking video camera from his luggage and brought it out to the pool. I sat next to him and watched as he panned around the make-shift soiree. I leaned in so I could see what was on the preview screen. Josh filmed Flynn shaking up a can of beer and then opening it so the liquid sprayed all over his face. Then he scanned over to Rhylee giving Roach dancing lessons. I laughed as she tried to make Roach spin her in a circle and he looked at her cluelessly and then put one finger on the top of his head and twirled around like a ballerina.

"Was that *Swan Lake*?" I joked.

"Roach needs to work on his moves," Josh said.

Then Josh panned his camera over to Ginger in her polka-dot bikini flirting with Carson in the shallow end of the pool. She giggled as they leaned their foreheads together, and then they started seriously kissing. I mean, it looked like they were swallowing each other's tongues.

I turned away. Just then Angus walked over smoking a cigar.

"Is that one of my dad's?" I asked.

Angus blushed. "Um, maybe? I found it inside."

"Cool. Enjoy!" I said. I liked the feeling of taking this place over, making it mine again, and leaving my mark.

"Really? Your dad's Romeo y Julietas are beauties," he said, passing the cigar to Josh.

"They've got the moolah," Josh said, and then took a puff.

"Take some for the road," I offered.

Angus and Josh thanked me and told me this was the best New Year's party they had ever been to.

"So isn't it gonna be dangerous filming out there in the middle of glaciers?" I asked.

"We're surfies, not shark biscuits," Angus said. "See, when the weather changes, it makes a rock fall into the ocean, which causes bonzer waves."

"And when a chunk of icy pole falls, I'm gonna ride it like this!" Angus got up and started running toward the pool. He jumped in and made a huge splash. When he came up for air, he had wet snot running out of his nose.

"Dag! You've got a bush oyster!" Josh yelled, gesturing to Angus's nostrils.

"Holey doley, thanks, mate." Angus wiped his nose clean with the back of his wrist.

Josh turned back to me. "Carson drives a boat and pulls Angus like a water-skier, then Angus rides the wave."

"So it's gonna be, like, an extreme-sports video?" I asked.

"But there's more. We want people to watch the surfies in our doco, but get knocked in the head when they see the movie's about global warming, too. The earth's heating up and I reckon all of us might be bloody fucked soon 'cause the sun's melting these glaciers."

"It sounds intensely Gorian," I said.

"Gorian?" Josh asked.

"You know, earthy like Al Gore, our former vice prez." I didn't know how much he knew about U.S. politics.

Josh nodded in agreement. "We're a bunch of true-blue greenies. We want these images to hook into people's minds. We need to wake up the hoons and the drongos and get them in touch with some monumental guilt."

I leaned over to Josh and nodded at his handheld video camera. "Hey, do you mind if I give it a try?"

"Be gentle. It's a prezzy from my mom." Josh handed the video camera to me. I picked it up carefully and looked through the lens, and just then an idea hit me.

"I need to make one," I said aloud.

"What?" Josh asked.

I talked in a quiet, intense voice. "A movie. Right now."

"But we're raging and it's one in the morning." Josh picked up his beer can and took a swig.

"Think of it as fair trade for room and board," I said. "Grab two of your buddies; I need actors. And don't let Rhylee and Ginger know."

"Why can't your cousins be in on it?" Josh asked.

"I have my reasons. Now, let's go." I jumped up. I paced back and forth as I watched Josh grab Angus and Flynn. The three guys walked back over to me.

"Follow me, quickly," I said as I led them back into the house, holding the video camera tightly. I looked back at Felicia. She was cuddling up with Devin on a chaise longue.

I could've used her help, too, but I didn't want to interrupt the romance.

Up in the master bedroom, Josh set the camera on a tripod he had grabbed from their luggage on the way upstairs and put a fresh DVD into it.

"Hang out one sec while I grab the costumes," I said.

A few minutes later, I handed Josh a pair of my dad's pajamas. Then I gave Flynn one of my mother's bohemian tops and scarves and Angus the same long red dress Claudia had worn to the Christmas Spectacular.

"Dang! She's dressing us up like girls!" said Flynn.

"I'm gonna be prettier than you!" Angus said, teasing his friend.

Angus forced the dress down over his wide frame and shoved his arms through it. There was the sound of a rip as he tried. "Uh-oh, I'm too chubs."

"No worries," I said. "It's trash. We'll just throw it away when we're done." I smiled when I saw the way the dress stretched across Angus's hairy chest. Then I got focused again.

"Okay, get under the blanket," I told Flynn. "Go on. Hurry up. Now, Angus, you walk in there. I want you to make Flynn drink this cup and pretend it's filled with poison. Then, Flynn, you need to do your best job of pretending to convulse and die. Got it?"

"Can I foam at the mouth and drool?" Flynn asked, getting into his part.

"Do whatever you want," I said. "Just get the point across. You're dead, and Angus killed you."

Angus took his place by the doorway, holding a cup and saucer.

I looked at the clock. It was already 1:22 A.M. I wanted to do this as fast as possible. "Come on, quickly," I said. "All right, Josh, is the camera ready?"

"Yeah, mate."

"Places!" I yelled out.

"We're rolling," Josh said.

"And action!"

I stayed up almost all night listening to music while I edited the night's footage on my laptop. I had taken a film-editing class at Winchester during sophomore year, so I knew how to use iMovie. The movie I had made of Lulu and two other girls from our dorm sledding on cafeteria trays down a big hill on campus, had earned me an A.

Felicia stopped by my room to say good-bye at one point. "Dudette, you've been MIA," she said.

"I know," I said, closing the screen on my computer. "I got sidetracked. So how are things with Devin?" I asked, trying to change the subject. I didn't have time to explain the whole thing to her now. I had to finish editing this video before my dad and Claudia got back, since I was planning to show it at their New Year's barbecue.

"He is so cool!" Felicia said. "Don't tell anyone, but we

hooked up yesterday at his house and we did an improv comedy in his bed."

"Sounds kinky," I said.

"We pretended he was a fireman and I was a housewife cleaning shirts on his washboard abs."

"You're too much." I smirked. I looked back toward my computer, hoping she'd take the hint that I was busy.

"So how are you doing without Oliver?" she asked.

"Horrible. How often is a baby born?"

"Every second."

"That's how often I think about him."

"Maybe you should call him?" she suggested.

"I texted him," I admitted. "But he didn't write back."

"He's just hurt," said Felicia. Then we heard a guy's voice calling out her name in the hallway. "That's Dev," she said, jumping toward the door.

"I'm coming!" she yelled, and then turned back to me. "Love ya like a sister."

"You too!" I said.

Then she took off and I finished creating the movie. The sun was practically rising as I dragged the last clip into the iMovie viewer screen. Finally, I burned the final DVD and got into bed. I felt like I had slept for about five minutes when I heard a loud knock on my door.

"The guys are leaving," Rhylee said as she opened the door and stuck her head into my room. "Come down if you want to say good-bye. They have an early flight."

I crawled out of bed and headed downstairs. I wanted to be sure to say thanks to Josh, Angus, and Flynn for all their help with filming last night.

When I got to the first floor, the Aussies were already packing up the Jeep. I walked over to Josh, who was sitting in the driver's seat, and we bumped fists.

"Thanks a million for your skills last night," I said. "I'll never forget it."

"No prob," he said. "Hope it came out wicked."

"I think it did." I walked away from the car and looked over at Ginger and Carson, who were holding hands sweetly.

"As soon as I have a few acorns stowed away, I'll be on your doorstep," Carson told Ginger.

"You promise?" Ginger looked up at him with star-dazed eyes.

Carson nodded and then kissed her on the cheek—a much tamer kiss than last night's, I noticed. He climbed into the shotgun seat. Angus, Roach, and Flynn piled into the back.

As the car sped away, Josh hit the horn and then Angus leaned his head out and hollered back at us. "Ladies! Get yaselves to Perth!"

Ginger watched as the Jeep disappeared out of sight. Then she let out a sigh and turned to Rhylee. "I really like him. Do you think he'll ever call me?"

"I really don't know," Rhylee said. "In my opinion, they all seemed like a bunch of players."

NEW YEAR'S DAY

Friday, January 1

The house was a bona fide pigsty, a war zone of beer cans, plates, and glasses. Someone had left a ripped T-shirt and a visor hat by the pool. Ginger claimed the visor as her own and plopped it down on her head.

"I think this was Carson's," she said. "A souvenir of our love affair."

"Don't you mean *fling*?" Rhylee said.

"Shut up, Rhy!" said Ginger.

Then we all went silent as we took in the mess in the backyard by the pool.

"Where do we even begin?" I said.

"I don't know, but we have to clean this place up ASAP.

Claudia and your dad are gonna be back this afternoon," said Rhylee.

It would have been kind of funny to see my dad and Claudia's reactions if we left the mess, but if we didn't clean it up ourselves, the job would go to Anna Maria and that wouldn't be fair. Plus, I wanted the mood to be just right when I showed them the movie, and starting the day with a fight over the state of the house and yard didn't seem like the best way to accomplish that.

"Okay, let's get to work," I said, and hurried to the kitchen to grab garbage bags.

When I returned to the pool, Rhylee gathered me and Ginger around her. "Also, I vote we keep the Aussies and the party a secret," she said. "If Claudia found out—"

"She'd take back our gift certificates," Ginger said.

"What?" I asked.

"Ginger, you have the biggest mouth." Rhylee punched her sister's arm.

"Oops," Ginger said, and put one hand up to her mouth.

"What gift certificates?" I asked.

Rhylee let out a sigh and shrugged her shoulders. "The ones she gave us before they left for Palm Springs. Three hundred dollars each to Prada."

I shook my head. "So she bribed you guys to hang out with me?" I asked, offended.

"No way!" Rhylee said. "Listen, Holly. We wanted to come

hang out with you. The gift certificates were just a Christmas bonus."

"I just don't want you guys running to her and telling her everything I say. Whatever I tell you guys is just between us. Promise?"

"Promise!" they both said at the same time.

I wanted to trust them, but just in case, I wasn't going to say a word to either of them about anything I didn't want Claudia to know. They were on the enemy's payroll.

"I agree about the party, though," I said. "Let's keep last night quiet. Pinky swear." I stuck out my hand.

Rhylee, Ginger, and I interlocked our fingers just like we used to do when we were little, squeezing our pinkies together.

"My lips are sealed," Rhylee said.

"Mine, too," I said.

"Mine, three," said Ginger.

That afternoon when Claudia and my dad got home from Palm Springs, the place looked spotless. Anna Maria was off work for the holiday, but Patty was there helping Claudia get the place ready for the barbecue. I figured she got paid extra for having to work on New Year's Day.

When I saw Patty she gave me a big smile, and I wondered if she still hadn't heard that Oliver and I had broken up. I couldn't help but make an attempt to feel her out. Maybe she knew how he was doing, or what he was up to, or if he was hanging out with anyone else—like another girl.

As Patty was setting the patio table with fresh flowers and place mats, I went outside to talk to her.

"The orchids look great," I said, admiring the vase of purple and white blooms.

"They've always been my favorite," Patty said.

I fiddled with the edge of one of the place mats. "Sooo," I began, "what's Oliver up to today?"

"I thought you'd know."

I bit my lip and shook my head.

"Claudia said I could invite him over for the barbecue, but when I mentioned it to him, he said he had other plans," she said.

"Oh, that's right, I remember now," I said, playing like I was in the know. "He's going to that thing with his friends."

"Oliver wasn't really in the mood to talk when I called. He said he hadn't been sleeping well and he'd call me tomorrow," said Patty. "I really hope it wasn't a mistake to let him move out on his own. . . . How can I be sure he's taking care of himself?"

"I don't think you should worry," I said. "Oliver's pretty responsible. I'm sure he's fine."

Honestly, I wasn't so sure. And he clearly didn't want to come over tonight and see me. I couldn't blame him, of course. I'd told him I needed space, so he was giving me space. And so far, I had to admit, it had paid off. Maybe if I'd been with

Oliver last night instead of with the Aussies, that great movie idea wouldn't have come to me.

"Can I help you? I could finish setting the table," I said, putting on a cheery voice.

"Oh, dear, thanks for asking!" Patty said. "That would be so nice! Claudia gave me a list a mile long of things to do. And all this running around is killing me. I just got a new pair of clogs and they're too tight."

"Ouch, time for some Band-Aids," I said. "Well, cross the table off your list. I got it covered."

That night, my aunt, my dad, Rhylee, Ginger, Patty, and I hung out on the back patio eating barbecued free-range chicken breasts and rib-eye steaks. Tomoko and his wife, Annie, were there, as well. I loved that Claudia was having some friends over. The more the merrier to witness my feature presentation.

I decided to wait until dessert to announce my big surprise. My leg was shaking up and down under the table as Patty brought out the chocolate cake and ice cream.

Annie couldn't stop talking about Claudia's engagement.

"Have you set a date yet? Do you want to get married in California? Tomoko and I got married in Malibu overlooking the ocean and it was so beautiful."

Then she and Tomoko wanted to toast the happy couple. I noticed my dad looking at me to see how I would take it, but I just gave him the biggest smile I could in return.

"We wish you both a lifetime of happiness and love," Annie began.

I nearly gagged on my ice-cream spoon as I looked at Claudia. She was smiling, basking in all the attention.

Then Tomoko put his arm around Annie. "I know here in the U.S. you say, 'Cheers!' But in Japan, we like to say, '*Kampai*.'"

Everyone raised their glasses and shouted, "*Kampai!*"

Then I stood up and busted in. "And I would like to take this moment to say that I have an engagement present for the two of you," I said as sweetly as possible. I pulled out the DVD that I had been storing in my purple bag and held it out to Claudia.

"What's this?" she said, licking chocolate icing off her fork.

"I made a movie."

"A movie? I didn't know you could do that," said my dad.

"Surprise! Let's watch it," I said. "Now."

"That is so sweet, but we'll watch it later," Claudia said. She smiled and looked around at her guests.

"But come on, *Aunt* Claudia," I said, emphasizing the word so that her friends would remember that the happy couple they were toasting was made up of a man and his dead wife's sister. "Everybody likes presents. What would Elizabeth Taylor do?"

She took a bite of cake and chewed it slowly. She knew I had won.

"Okay," she said with a smile. "Sure, Holly. If it would

make you happy, let's watch the movie now." She wiped her lips gently with her napkin.

"It will definitely make me happy," I said. "You all stay here! I'll set up the projector so we can watch it outside. Nobody even has to move."

"Yay, movie time!" Ginger said, clapping her hands. Rhylee was smiling like she thought it was going to be fun, too. Little did they know . . .

I ran inside and got my laptop and a projector that we had stored in a closet in the den. I carried them outside and set up the projector so the movie would be shown on the side of the house.

Did anyone know what was coming? I couldn't tell. My dad was trying to play it off like this was the best surprise ever.

"What a thoughtful gift, Holly," he said. Then to Annie and Tomoko he said, "She's always been such a generous girl. She even donated her Christmas money to charity."

Tomoko and Annie both thought that was wonderful. I wondered what they'd think of me—and of their friend Claudia—after they saw my movie.

As I hit the Play button on my computer, Patty was talking about her new shoes to Claudia.

"I've got a blister on my big toe," she told my aunt, and then she kicked off her clogs. "Hope you don't mind if I go au naturel."

"Do whatever you want," Claudia said; her tone sounded annoyed. She never took off her stiletto heels once she'd put them on in the morning. For all I knew, she slept in them.

"Come on, it's starting!" I said. "Quiet, please."

"Sorry," Patty said, then she gestured like she was closing an imaginary zipper across her lips.

I stood off to the side where I could discreetly watch Claudia's face the whole time the movie played. I couldn't wait to see how the images on the screen affected her. I hoped they really drove her crazy with guilt.

I could barely breathe as the movie began to play.

On the screen, we saw the outside of our estate at night, the beautiful orange trees and rosebushes.

"How pretty," Claudia said. "The house looks great. You could have used some better lighting, though."

"It really does look nice," my dad agreed. "The ivy is coming in nicely."

Just then the camera focused on Flynn's face with lipstick and rouge on his cheeks.

"Oh, look. How funny!" my dad said. "That boy's in drag."

Flynn, playing the role of my mom, combed his hair while smiling peacefully at his image in the mirror.

"Look at his lipstick," Claudia said. "This is great! Maybe we could use this guy in *Dead Bachelorette*. What do you think, Tomoko?" She turned around to look at Annie and Tomoko, who were laughing at the screen.

Tomoko nodded. "Sure, good idea. He might make a really good zombie."

"Where'd you find these actors, Holly?" my dad asked.

"Just some new friends," I said, and then glanced quickly at Ginger and Rhylee. Both of my cousins were looking at me, furrowing their eyebrows. Rhylee raised up her hands as if to say, *When on earth did you make this?*

I shrugged my shoulders innocently: *Oh, I don't know. It just kinda happened.*

Then the camera panned out to show Flynn dressed in my mom's clothes, walking into the master bedroom. I watched as Claudia cocked her head to one side.

"What is he doing now?" she asked; her tone had an edge to it.

"That's our bedroom! You filmed in there?" my dad exclaimed. He turned around and gave me a stern look.

"Keep watching. It gets better!" I said cheerfully.

My dad swung back around to look at the screen as Flynn climbed onto their king-size foam mattress.

"I can't believe that boy is in my bed!" Claudia said. *Her* bed? Until six months ago it had been my mom's bed. I guess Claudia chose not to think about that. Well, starting pretty soon, not thinking about it was going to get harder.

"He's not alone," I said. "Look!"

Just then Josh, who was dressed in a pair of my dad's pajamas, got under the covers and canoodled in a comical way with Flynn. They brushed their noses back and forth, making loud, fake kissing sounds.

I could see my dad's shoulders stiffen. He must've recognized his pajamas, but I wondered if he noticed my mom's clothes, too.

"Good morning, my dear," Josh said in an extra deep voice. "Off to work. I love you."

"I love you, too," Flynn said in a high voice.

Suddenly, Tomoko let out a loud laugh. He was, like, doubling over because he was cracking up so hard. I turned to him and smiled.

"Can I get a copy of this? I want to watch it again when I get home," he said, laughing some more. Annie shook her head, smiling, and patted him on the back.

I have to say, they were a great audience.

Back on the screen, Josh took off, leaving Flynn alone in the bed, eating a bowl of cereal from a breakfast tray.

I rubbed my sweaty palms together as I waited for the grand entrance. *Ba-ba-da-dum!* And then it happened: Angus appeared on the screen with Claudia's red gown squeezed down over his short, heavy body.

I heard Claudia gasp. *"What?* Why is that fat thing in my dress?" she said, glaring at me.

Tomoko started laughing again. I could hear Rhylee and Ginger giggling, as well. Claudia turned and looked at Tomoko.

"He's so fat and hairy." Tomoko cracked up even harder.

My aunt bit her lip and then gave him a forced smile. "Yes, isn't he?" she said.

Then she turned back to look at the movie as Angus walked into the room and handed a coffee cup to Flynn.

"Just stopped by to say hello," Angus said in a woman's voice. "I brought you some morning coffee."

"That is so sweet," Flynn said and reached out from the bed to take the mug.

The movie pulled in for a close-up of Flynn's mouth sipping from the coffee cup. Then it zoomed out and there was Flynn grabbing his stomach and rolling around in the bed.

My focus was on Claudia while this played out. I watched her eyes get wide as she raised one hand to cover her mouth, like she was looking at something truly shocking. My dad turned back again and gave me a dirty look. Wonderful. This meant they were getting my intended meaning.

Then Flynn suddenly started convulsing and drooling—this had been his favorite part of playing that role. I think he loved having an excuse to drool excessively in public.

"He needs a baby bib," Tomoko said, laughing more. Clearly, he had an offbeat sense of humor.

"Shush." Annie kissed his cheek.

Claudia clenched her fists tightly; the veins in her hands looked like they were about to pop out of her skin. Then, just as the movie was ending with Flynn as my mom lying lifelessly in the bed as though he was dead, Claudia jumped up out of her seat. "I need a drink!" she said, and then she hurried into the house.

My dad stood up and stared after her. Then he looked back at me and I swear he tried to burn holes through my skin with his glare.

"Excuse me," he said to Tomoko and Annie, and then hurried after my aunt.

Yes! I proved it! She's guilty! I thought to myself, jumping up from my chair. The movie clearly had gotten to her.

Rhylee and Ginger both got up and walked over to me. "Oh my God. That was crazy. When did you make it?" Rhylee said.

"While everyone was partying." I glanced toward the house. I could see my dad and Claudia in the kitchen. Claudia was moving her arms around a lot and it looked like she was yelling.

"That was classic! Angus looked so cute in that dress," Ginger said.

"Ooh, Claudia seemed pissed, though!" said Rhylee.

"Yeah, I loved every minute of it," I said.

"What?" Rhylee asked.

But before I could answer, Tomoko came over to me, grinning. "I loved that movie. You've got talent! I could see a future for you behind the camera in Hollywood."

"Thanks. I'm glad you dug it," I said. "I'll be right back. Everyone have fun and eat cake!"

I hurried inside to see how my aunt was doing. As soon as I got close, I heard her conversation with my dad.

"I'm past my breaking point," she said. "You have to do something about her. That movie was insulting and suggestive—"

"I don't know what she was thinking," my dad said.

"And in front of my friends! She embarrassed me. I've tried to be patient, Gardner, but this is beyond what I can be expected to put up with. She has no sense of respect and—"

When Claudia saw me, and her face blew up like a red balloon.

"What the hell was that? How dare you go through my things!"

"It was just a little horror movie. I thought you'd like it," I said.

"Horror movie, my ass!" she said.

"I thought it'd be right up your alley! What didn't you like about it? Did it hit a nerve?" As I talked, I flung my hands all over the place and accidentally knocked over a full wineglass that was sitting on the counter.

"Watch out!" my dad yelled as the glass fell to the floor. Red wine splattered all over his pants as the glass shattered.

"Shit!" he said as he looked down at his stained jeans.

Just then Patty, still barefoot, walked into the room from outside. "Be careful!" my dad called to her, but it was too late. She was already stepping into the trail of broken glass.

"Ow!" Patty screamed. She grimaced in pain as she lifted

her left leg up to look at the bottom of her foot. We could all see that she had just stepped on one of the larger chunks of glass. The sole of her foot was slashed open and bleeding.

Claudia grabbed a chair and ran it over to Patty. "Here, sit down," she said. "Let me see. Are you okay?"

"It stings! It stings!" Patty said as she held her foot up.

"Is there still glass in it?" my dad asked, hurrying over to take a look.

I stood there watching the blood streaming out of Patty's foot. It was my fault she was hurt—I did knock over the glass, after all—but I was annoyed that she was taking Claudia's attention away from the movie. This was it, my chance to confront Claudia in front of my dad, to get her to admit that the reason the movie had upset her so much was because the scene it depicted had actually happened. But now Patty was causing such a commotion that it was impossible to get back to the matter at hand.

"I'm going to bleed to death," she said. "I can tell. This is the end." *Oh, please.* She'd just cut her foot and she was acting like she was starring in a Greek tragedy.

"You're going to be fine," my dad said. "But I do see a chunk of glass. Hold still."

"Owwww!" Patty hollered in agony.

"Almost got it," said my dad.

"Heavens to Betsy!" she yelled even louder.

"One more second," he said.

"He's almost done," Claudia said, resting one hand on Patty's arm.

Then finally my dad cried triumphantly, "I got it!" I saw him lift out a piece of glass the size of my thumbnail.

"That was in my flesh?" Patty said, and then put one hand up to her forehead.

I ran and grabbed a clean towel from a kitchen drawer and handed it to my dad. He took it and held it tightly around Patty's foot.

"Now, hold that there," he said to Claudia.

"Got it," my aunt said, taking over where his fingers were on the cloth.

"Keep it nice and tight until the bleeding slows down," he said.

"I can handle this. You go deal with *her*." Claudia glared my way.

Tomoko and Annie poked their heads into the kitchen. I could see Ginger and Rhylee peering into the window from outside. "Did someone get their head chopped off?" Tomoko asked. "We heard screaming."

"My assistant cut herself. Be careful," Claudia said, nodding to the glass on the floor.

"Oh no," said Annie. "Are you okay?" she asked Patty. Patty nodded, but I could tell she still thought she was going to die.

"It's late. We should be getting home anyway," Tomoko said.

"No, you don't have to go. Please," Claudia begged them.

I didn't find out what happened next because my dad came over and grabbed me by the shoulder. "Holly, you're coming with me upstairs."

I glared at him without moving.

"Now!" he demanded.

THE BEDROOM

As soon as we got into the master bedroom, my dad got out of his wine-stained jeans and threw them on the floor. "Holly, you've deeply upset Claudia," he said.

"And she has deeply upset me," I answered.

"Cut the crap, I'm not in the mood for one of your games," he said. "What's the matter with you? What was the meaning of that movie?"

It was hard to take him seriously while he was scolding me in only his shirt and boxers. The last thing I wanted to see was my dad's pale, hairy legs.

"Figure it out. It doesn't take a genius."

"Don't talk to me like that. I'm your father," he said, slipping into a pair of gray slacks.

"Yeah, my father by blood. The rest of you is Claudia's

plaything," I said. "You used to share this room with Mom. You don't feel guilty sleeping in the same bed with her sister?"

My dad shook his head as he paced around the room. "Sit down, Holly, and let's have this out already."

"Yeah. Bring it on." I stared him right in the eye as I plopped down on the edge of the bed. "Claudia told me you asked Mom for a separation right before she died."

"What? She told you that?"

"Yeah, she did," I said. "Are you saying it's not true? Are you calling your *fiancée* a liar?"

My dad sat down on the edge of the bed next to me. He put his head in his hands. "Holly, I never meant to hurt you or your mother . . . but I wasn't happy."

I just looked at him, waiting for him to say more.

"Your mom and I had a lot of good years together, but sometimes, it was hard. . . . I really tried to make things work."

"You could have tried harder to help her get better," I said. Before I spoke the words, I hadn't realized I blamed my dad for not trying hard enough. First I had thought my mom's death was my fault, then I thought it was Claudia's. But maybe I had held my dad partially responsible, too.

"I tried, Holly, I really did. But your mother was a grown woman. I wanted her to take her medication; I begged her to take it. But sometimes she wouldn't. That was her choice. You have to face it. What happened to her wasn't my fault. She took her own life, all by herself."

"Or maybe not," I said. I could feel the truth rising up inside me. I couldn't keep it a secret anymore.

"What do you mean?" my dad asked. "She was all alone that day, Holly."

"No, she wasn't," I said. "Claudia was with her. Claudia poisoned her. That's what happened."

"What are you talking about?" My father jumped up like he'd been burned. "Is that what you think? Is that why you made that movie?"

"Yes," I said. It felt so good to be able to finally tell him. "Claudia poisoned Mom. She didn't kill herself. That's the truth. And did you see how Claudia responded to my movie? She was freaking out because she's *guilty*. I know it. And now you do, too."

"I know there's no love lost between you and Claudia, but do you know how serious it is to accuse someone of murder?" My father was really fuming now. "Where the hell are you getting this from?"

I couldn't figure out what to say. It was one thing to tell my dad that Claudia had killed my mother, but it was another to admit how I knew.

"Holly, listen to me." My dad sat back down and took my hands in his. "What you're saying, this isn't true. It just isn't. I don't know where you got this idea, but I'm telling you as your father, that's not what happened that day."

"Then what happened?" I asked.

He turned to me and let out a sigh. "It's hard to talk to

you about this. But you're growing up, and you're not a kid anymore. . . . It was hard to realize that we couldn't make it work after so many years together. . . . It had to get to this point. Your mom said *she* wasn't happy with *me*."

"She told you that?" I asked, studying his face.

"Yes. It happened after you went back to school at the end of last summer. She said she needed time on her own, 'to heal'—I think that's how she put it. She's the one who asked me for the separation."

I looked at my dad and tried to figure out if I could believe him. Claudia had told me one thing, my mom's ghost had told me something else, and now my dad was saying something altogether different.

"Why would Claudia say the separation was your idea?" I asked.

"I don't know." He sighed. "Maybe she thought it would be easier for you to take that way."

I thought about that for a minute. Was it easier that way, to think the split had been my dad's idea and not my mom's? I couldn't tell.

"We had been growing apart for a long time," my dad said. "I guess it was hard for you to see because you were away at school."

Thinking back on it, I *had* noticed when I was home for breaks and vacations that they spent less time together than they had when I was little. My dad was working even more at the office. And when he came home, my mom would already be asleep in bed. They didn't get dressed up and go to movie premieres or industry events anymore. When my mom had to go, she usually went alone. And there were a couple of times those last few years that I remembered her turning to me and saying, "If only I could just walk away." But I had never thought she would actually do it. Or that she really meant it. Because there were other times when I'd see them laughing together as if everything was fine. I guess I had just wanted to believe they were still in love with each other. And that I still had the perfect family.

But now I was starting to realize how much more complicated it was. My dad wasn't perfect, for sure, but maybe my mom hadn't been perfect, either.

He and I just sat there for a few minutes. I felt exhausted. The combination of getting no sleep the night before and taking in everything my dad had just said left me completely wiped out. But there was one more thing I had to say.

"All the stuff you're saying doesn't change how I feel. I still think Claudia killed Mom. I think she was with her the day she died," I said softly.

I looked over at my dad. He looked tired, too, and older than I remembered.

"Holly, that's just not true. She didn't kill your mother. She wasn't with her that day."

"But how are you so sure where Claudia was?" I asked. And the second the words were out of my mouth, I knew the answer before my father could reply.

"Because she was with me."

THE GUILTY TRUTH

Saturday, January 2

My dad tried to get me to stay and talk to him, but I couldn't. I ran to my room and threw myself on my bed. I couldn't believe it. He had told me things didn't develop with Claudia until after my mom died, and that was bad enough. But now it turned out that he had been cheating on my mom with her own sister all along. He was even running around with her the very minute my mom passed away.

I just wished that wherever my mom's ghost was now, she didn't know this. I wished I didn't know it myself. And I wondered why the ghost had told me Claudia had poisoned her if it wasn't really true. I was so confused. Nothing made any sense.

I cried myself to sleep and woke up the next morning

feeling like I'd been hit by a bus. Everything hurt, especially my back, from falling on it in the bridal shop. It was like I hadn't slept at all. I must have tossed and turned all night, tormented by dreams about my father and Claudia and their secret affair.

I turned to look at the clock and saw that it was almost noon. My dad would be home soon from his basketball game. I wished I'd set the alarm super early so I could be up and out without having to see him or, worse, Claudia. But now it was too late. I could hear her clicking around downstairs in her stilettos. I'd climb out my window before I'd face her. There was no solace in knowing that my aunt wasn't a murderer after all. She was still an adulterer, and I hated her just as much as I had before.

While I was lying there trying to plan my escape from the house, there was a knock at my door.

"Holly?" Damn, it was my dad. I decided not to respond, so he'd think I wasn't there.

He knocked again. "Holly, are you in there? I know you don't want to talk to me right now, but there's more I have to say."

I didn't say anything.

"Okay, then," my dad said. "I'm coming in."

I wished then that I had a lock on my door, but my mom hadn't believed in having locks on any doors in the house. She said a family didn't need to lock each other out. I guess she hadn't known our family well enough when she'd said that.

My dad was all sweaty from his basketball game, and he was still wearing his T-shirt and shorts. Usually he showered at the gym, but apparently he'd decided to rush right home today to continue our talk from last night. Wonderful.

I hid my head under the covers and rolled away from him to face the wall.

I felt my dad sit down on the bed.

"Holly, honey, I know last night was really hard on you. You had to hear things that a daughter shouldn't have to hear about her parents. But now that you know some of the story, I have to tell you the whole thing."

"Please spare me the details of your sordid affair with Claudia, Dad. I don't think I can take any more," I said to the wall, through my blanket.

"Holly, I told you that I was faithful to your mother during our marriage, and that's true. Nothing romantic ever happened between Claudia and me while Mom was alive."

"Yeah, right. I'm supposed to believe that?"

"Yes, because it's the truth. I told you last night that Mom asked for a separation after you went back to Winchester for your junior year. That was a very hard time for me. I didn't know what to do, who to turn to. I didn't want to lose your mother, but I didn't know how to help her anymore, or how to help myself. I went to talk to Claudia, to see if she could give me some insight."

"Great idea, Dad, given how close she and Mom were. I'm sure she was about to give you lots of *insight*."

My dad ignored my snide comment and continued.

"Claudia was empathetic, and she tried to help me understand what she and your mom had gone through when they
were children."

I was about to say, "You mean what Claudia *put* Mom
through," but then I thought of what Dr. Arbuckle had said,
how their childhood had been hard on both of them. Maybe
that was a little bit true, but I was still pretty sure my mom
had had the harder time.

"We began to talk more, Claudia and I. She was a big
support for me that year. I know you see this one side of
Claudia, how she looks on the outside, how she can be brash,
but she has a really good heart on the inside, Holly. She
does."

I wasn't quite ready to hear about how great Claudia was.

"The day your mother died," my dad began. Then he
stopped and took a deep breath. I was still under my blanket,
but I could feel him shifting around on my bed. "That day
I was supposed to be at work, but I'll admit it, I took the
day off to spend it with Claudia. We drove up the coast, we
stopped for lunch. We talked and talked about your mom,
about how I was feeling, about what would be best for her,
and for me. At the end of the day, I dropped Claudia off at
her house and went home. That's when I found your mother.
She was in bed—I thought she was asleep. There were
pill bottles on the nightstand and I was pleased because I
thought she was taking her medication again. But then I got

closer and realized just how many pill bottles there were on the nightstand, and that they were all empty. She had been stockpiling her pills for years, Holly. Each time a doctor wrote her a prescription she took just a few pills, then she kept the rest."

I knew she hadn't always finished her prescriptions, of course, but I had assumed she had thrown the old pills out. I hadn't imagined that she had kept them.

"She died of an overdose, Holly," my dad said. I could feel his hand on my hip through the blanket. Then he started to cry.

"I couldn't save her. But I really tried. I tried as hard as I could."

Now my dad was completely sobbing. I'd never heard him cry so hard, even right after my mom died.

I rolled over toward him and lifted the blanket off my face. I sat up and hugged him, and we both cried.

"It's not your fault," I said into my dad's sweaty T-shirt, which was now wet with my tears. And it wasn't my fault, either. It wasn't even Claudia's fault, as much as I had wanted to blame her.

After my dad left my room, I tried calling Felicia, but she didn't pick up. Maybe she was getting ready for her shift at Geisha House, or she was out with Devin. Then I decided to take a big chance and call Oliver. I just needed to hear his voice. I looked at his name in my contacts list for a long time before I actually pressed the button. My heart beat fast and as the phone rang I was worried he wouldn't pick up. But then, finally, he did.

"Oliver," was all I could say. It felt so good just to say his name.

"What's up?" he said, but his voice sounded cold and distant.

"Nothing," I said. But I meant: *Everything.* "What about you?"

"I'm going out to meet my mom and sister for lunch. Lara flew down to visit. I think she felt bad about Mom's bloody foot—she had to get stitches, you know, and now she can't really walk on it for a while."

"How's your mom doing?" I asked.

"Whatever, she'll be fine."

"I know things are really weird between us right now and I know it's my fault, but there's something really crazy going on here and—"

"Look, I'm not really in a mood to talk," he said, cutting me off. "I haven't been sleeping much and, I don't know . . . I gotta go."

"Wait," I said. "It's gonna be okay for us."

"You don't really know that, do you?" Oliver said. "I mean, of all people to say that. Everything hasn't worked out okay for you in this world."

"That's true," I said. "I'm sorry."

"I don't feel like operating on false hope," he said. "When I first met you, I didn't always get what you meant when you said some of those philosophical things you rant about, but I get it now."

I thought I heard sniffling on the other side of the phone. "Are you crying?" I asked.

"No, hell no," he said defensively. "I gotta go."

"Wait . . ." My voice trailed off. "I'm leaving soon to go back to Winchester."

"Okay," Oliver said. "Why are you telling me this? We're not together anymore. You broke up with me. You can do whatever you want and go wherever you have to go."

"But—"

"See ya," he said, and then hung up the phone.

I couldn't blame him for being so upset. This was my fault. I must've hurt him a lot. Why did it have to be so complicated? I had always thought love should be like in the movies, walking off into the sunset, or drinking milk shakes like in a Norman Rockwell painting. But maybe that kind of perfection can exist only in art or film, because it's just a moment, and then the moment passes and there's another moment and another one. But in the real world time keeps moving. And it doesn't ever stop.

Talking to Oliver hadn't exactly made me feel better, and Felicia still wasn't picking up her phone. I didn't know who to call, but I knew I had to talk to someone about everything my dad had told me or my head was going to explode. I got up, got dressed, and paced around my room. And then it occurred to me. There *was* someone I wanted to talk to. I called her and she agreed to see me in two hours.

I listened closely to the noise in the house, trying to tell if anyone was around. I still didn't want to face Claudia, and I didn't feel like seeing my dad again yet, either. I didn't hear a sound, so I tiptoed downstairs. On the kitchen counter I found a note from my dad. He wrote that Rhylee and Ginger had decided to cut their trip short—I guessed it hadn't gone quite like he and Claudia had hoped—so they were flying up to San Francisco to see their mother today. He and Claudia were driving them to the airport. Then there was a note from my cousins in girly handwriting with flowers drawn all over it.

> *Hey, Cuz!*
> *It was bangin' to see you.*
> *We love ya!*
> *Come visit us in South America anytime.*
> *Or maybe we can all visit our new friends down*
> *under* ☺*.*
> *Luv ya,*
> *R & G*

I still had some time before my appointment but I didn't want to wait around the house for my dad and Claudia to come back, so I got into my car and decided just to drive around and kill time. I was aimlessly driving from street to street without any destination in mind, but when I took one last turn, I realized that I had driven to Memorial Park in Westwood, where my mom was buried. Maybe her ghost had guided me here. And maybe this would give me a chance to ask her why she had told me Claudia had poisoned her if that wasn't really true.

As I entered the graveyard, I saw a woman with frizzy hair and too much blush selling pamphlets by the entrance.

"Eight dollars for a star map," she said, and then she stepped right in front me, blocking my way.

On Sunset Boulevard, people sold star maps of celebrities' houses. I guessed this was something similar, but this map would point you in the direction of a whole different type of celebrity home—the permanent kind, six feet under.

"No, thanks," I said.

I tried to keep walking, but the woman stepped in my path again. "My map will show you where everyone's buried! Eva Gabor! Merv Griffin! Billy Wilder! Who you looking for, cutie?"

I wasn't about to tell her that I was looking for my own mother.

"I can point you to Frank Zappa! Truman Capote! Marilyn Monroe!"

"I'm not looking for them," I said, and moved past her.

"Wait! I'll sell the map for five dollars! Bargain city!" the woman yelled, lowering the price in one last attempt.

"Next time!" I kept walking away.

"But what you see here today might not be here tomorrow."

"I'll have to take my chances," I said, and then hurried farther away from her into the cemetery park.

I spotted my mom's grave from about ten feet away. I recognized the flowers, now crinkly and brown, that I had left last time I was there, at the end of the summer, before I went back to school. That seemed like such a long time ago now. I sat down next to my mom's grave and I felt this powerful wave come over me. My skin tingled. Did this mean her ghost was near? I hoped so. I needed to see her now more than I ever had.

"Please come back," I said. I looked around the cemetery. There was a gardener in the distance carrying a shovel. But otherwise the place was empty.

"Mom, please, I have so much I need to ask you," I continued. "I need to see you."

I looked around again. I saw chirping birds and the bright roses someone had left on the grave across from my mom's. Sunlight shone down on the freshly mowed grass. But there was no sight of her. I thought it might help if I started to talk to her in my mind, so I closed my eyes and tried to put together all of my questions. What really happened between you and Claudia when you were little? Were things hard for her, too? What was going on between you and Dad? Did you really ask for a separation? Why didn't you tell me? Why did you ask me to avenge your death if you took your own life after all? Why did you come back to visit me? Why did you leave me in the first place?

Question after question streamed through my mind. I kept waiting to hear my mom's voice gently answering them. I kept waiting to feel her ghostly presence. I thought for sure she'd come back to see me, just this one last time. I waited and waited. But she never came. And I had to wonder: Had she ever really come back at all?

I sat on the edge of the couch in Dr. Arbuckle's office. She watched me from her chair and smiled. It seemed like she was happy to see me again. And I don't think it was just about making more money. "It wasn't my friend," I admitted. "I was the one seeing the ghost."

Dr. Arbuckle didn't look surprised.

"It was my mom. I saw her three times before and I wanted to see her again today. I needed to see her again. But she didn't come. And now I'm afraid I might be crazy."

"You're not crazy," she said. Then she smiled, but it was kind of a sad smile. "You're lucky."

"Lucky?" I asked. That was the last word I would have used to describe my situation.

"When we lose someone we love, especially when we lose that person suddenly, like you did, we experience a lot of trauma."

I nodded. I definitely felt traumatized.

"Our minds can't take all of the sadness we're feeling, so they come up with ways to ease our pain. Some people take drugs, some people harm others, some people hurt themselves. Some people see ghosts," Dr. Arbuckle said. "Those are the lucky ones."

"So are you saying the ghost wasn't real? It was just my mind's way of helping me?" I asked.

"Yes, that's what I think. I wonder if coming home and seeing your father with your aunt was just too much for you to take? So you subconsciously came up with this ghost of your mother to help you through."

"She seemed so real, though," I said. What Dr. Arbuckle was saying made sense, but I wasn't ready to let go of the idea that my mom had really been there with me.

"I'm sure she did," Dr. Arbuckle said. "That's because she was real—to you. And she'll always be real to you, even though she's not here anymore."

I looked down at my hands. "But she said all this stuff to me when she came back. She told me there were things she needed me to do."

Dr. Arbuckle nodded as if she was saying, *Go on.*

"If she didn't really want me to do those things, who did?" I asked.

"What do you think?" Dr. Arbuckle said, and she leaned in like she was really curious to hear what I would say.

"Me?" I asked in a soft voice.

Dr. Arbuckle nodded.

Could that be true? Was I the one who wanted to get revenge on Claudia? Was I the one who wanted to take a step away from Oliver so my heart wouldn't get broken?

"But she asked me to do things for her so she could rest in peace," I explained.

Dr. Arbuckle was quiet for a minute. Then she spoke again. "Maybe that was about *you* looking for peace, not your mom. Do you feel at peace right now, Holly?"

"No."

"But you told me that you wanted to see the ghost again today and she didn't come. Maybe you're getting closer to peace than you were before. Maybe you need the ghost less than you once did."

I thought about that. Hearing what my dad had told me certainly didn't make me feel good, but I guess it had answered some questions. Did that mean I was closer to peace?

"But I don't know," I said. "I think I still need her. How will I get through certain things in life without talking to my mom?"

"You'll never stop needing her, but you'll find other ways to work through that need," Dr. Arbuckle said. "But your mom will always be with you; she'll always be inside of you. That will never change. And in your life, you'll meet people who remind you of her. As you grow up, maybe you'll even remind yourself of her." I thought of Anna Maria telling me I looked like my mom when I had tried on her old clothes the other day. Maybe I'd grow to look even more like her. Maybe I'd be like her in certain ways.

"But I still hate it that my dad's with my aunt," I said.

"I understand that," Dr. Arbuckle said.

"And I'm still angry at him for some stuff he told me last night," I said. I was thinking of the time he had spent with Claudia before my mother died.

"Or course," she said. And I liked that she didn't pry or try to find out what I meant specifically. I wasn't ready to talk about that yet. "You have lots of time to work through things with your father. It doesn't have to happen overnight. You and I can keep working together on this, if you'd like."

"I think I would," I said. It felt kind of good to know I'd have help.

"We can have phone sessions when you're back at school," Dr. Arbuckle said. "You're going back soon, right?"

I nodded and I think I smiled just a little, thinking about Christine and Lulu and getting away from all of this. Maybe the ground would be covered with snow in Connecticut. Maybe we'd go sledding on cafeteria trays again.

"Perhaps you're getting ready to feel joy again. Our time on this earth is so precious and short. Your mother would want that for you."

"You're right," I said. And suddenly, I knew what I wanted to do next.

THE CANALS

As soon as I left the psychiatrist's office, I drove south toward Venice Beach. After I found a parking spot on a side street, I walked along the inlets that lined the houses. I hurried over one of the pedestrian bridges and looked down the length of a canal. There I spotted the familiar backyard with the beer-pong table and empty cups thrown across it.

I knocked on the front door. Big Red opened it. He had sunglasses plopped down on top of his red hair.

"Hey, I was looking for Oliver," I said. "Is he here?"

"Yeah, but . . ." Big Red hesitated.

"What is it?" I asked. I figured Big Red was going to say Oliver didn't want to see me.

"I think he has a visitor," he said quietly.

My heart sank. Had Oliver already moved on from me so fast? Was he with another girl already?

"Oh, really?" I said.

"Yeah, I heard them both upstairs. So it might not be a good time. Sorry." His tone sounded sincerely apologetic.

Just then I heard footsteps and looked toward the landing. A girl appeared on the top step. It was Lara, Oliver's sister. And I remembered my phone conversation with Oliver earlier in the day.

"Hello, Holly," she said in a chilly tone.

"Oh man," Big Red said. "You know each other? Is there gonna be a catfight?"

"Yuck!" Lara said. "I am Ollie's sister."

"Whoops, sorry," Big Red said. "We've never met."

"I'm on my way out," Lara said, coming down the stairs. "Could we have a moment?" she asked Red.

"Oh, yeah, sure," he said, and then took off toward the kitchen.

"Hey, Lara. I know this is awkward 'cause you're his sister and everything," I said. "But these last few days have been completely insane; you have no idea. And I really miss him. I was wrong about wanting space. I don't want space. I just want—"

"Shh." She raised one hand to shut me up.

She leaned in toward me intently. "Break his heart again and you'll have me to deal with."

I nodded my head; I got it. Then she gave me a smile and headed out the door.

☠ ☠ ☠

The door to Oliver's room was only partially open. I knocked and waited for his voice.

"Yeah, what's up?" he said.

Then I slowly pushed the door open. Oliver looked over and saw me. The room was dark and I noticed he still hadn't unpacked all of his things. In fact, the place looked messier than the last time I had seen it. His clothes were in piles on the floor, and takeout bags and wrappers were all over the place.

"What are you doing here?" he asked. There were dark circles under his eyes, and the T-shirt he was wearing was stained.

"I needed to see you," I said, and took a few steps in.

"What for?" He ran his hand through his hair. It was sticking up a bit in the back and looked a little greasy, like he hadn't washed it in a few days.

I think he suddenly became self-conscious about his messy room, because he started to make his bed and straighten the pillows.

It was hard to see him like this. "Oh God, I don't know how to begin to tell you. . . . I'm so sorry I did this to you. . . . If I hurt you in any way . . . and I have to fix it . . ." I rambled.

"It's too late. I don't want to go back and forth. You must've known what you were doing when you broke up with me," Oliver said.

"I never wanted to end things."

"Oh yeah, that's right. You wanted 'space.'" He made little air quotes around the last word.

"Oliver, look," I said, and sat down on the edge of his mattress. He scooted away from me, toward the other end. "These last few months, especially since I've been home, I've had to deal with some heavy stuff," I said.

"I know you've had a lot going on. And I tried to be there for you."

"You did and that was awesome," I said. "But I guess I needed this time to deal on my own with everything that has happened this year. . . . And now I see so clearly that . . . I want to be with you."

"How do you know that?" Oliver asked. "What's changed?"

"I see so much more about life, and about the world, that I didn't know before . . . the complexities of being part of it. And I want to feel it all, and be open to it . . . with you. The pain, but also the joy and the love that I feel, because that's all we have, really."

Oliver nodded his head a little, like he was taking in everything I was saying. I reached over and put my hand on his arm.

"Hey, I need you to come with me now," I said.

"Where?"

"Please follow me," I said.

"Where are you taking me?" he asked.

"Come outside."

"Why?"

Despite all his questions, I managed to get him up off the bed. And that seemed like a good sign, like maybe he was willing to trust me again, if even just a little bit. We walked out of the house into the backyard, overlooking the canals. Then I led him down the bank to the edge of the water.

"It's not too cold out, is it?" I asked. I unzipped my jeans and yanked them off.

"What are you doing?" Oliver asked me. I thought I had managed to get a smile out of him.

I was standing before him in just a T-shirt, cotton under-wear, and a bra. "Come on. Let's go for a swim," I said.

"But what about my roommates and the neighbors? People might see," he said.

"I don't care."

"And the water might not be clean," he said.

"I'm ready now," I said. "For anything."

Oliver took off his jeans and T-shirt; he was wearing only his boxers, which had a starfish pattern on them. Then we both waded into the canal together. We started to swim, pad-dling with our hands. After a moment, Oliver lay on his back so he was floating in the water. I did the same, floating on my back beside him. Then I reached out in the water and took his hand.

ACKNOWLEDGMENTS

I would like to thank my amazing editors, Joy Peskin and Kendra Levin, for giving so much of their spirit and energy to this project. We went on this adventure together and you stood by me the whole way. In addition, a big thank-you to my wise publisher, Regina Hayes. Much gratitude to the fabulous team at Viking Children's Books and Penguin Young Readers. Also Leila Sales for her creative input, my skillful copyeditor, Kym Surridge, and innovative book designer Sam Kim.

Thank you, Tina Wexler and Josie Freedman, my fabulous agents at ICM, for their notes and encouragement. Also to Stephanie Lehmann, for her smart insights and belief in me.

I am grateful to Joseph Melendez for sharing with me

his stories of family ritual; to Irfan Mughal, Shakespearean Scholar and Oxford and Cambridge alum; also, to glamorous Barbara Andreadis for cheering this project along. The theatre is a temple.

Much appreciation to the Playwrights and Directors Workshop at the Actors Studio in New York moderated by Carlin Glynn and Carol Hall. I developed scenes from this book in the unit and value all the members' keen insights, especially those of the generous and brilliant director, Robert Haufrecht and festival producer, Jason Furlani. Thank you to the talented actors who helped me develop my scenes from the book: Megan Tusing, Christina Bennett Lind, Robert Mobley, David Holmes, Bo Corre, Aneglica Torn, Stella Pulo, Carla Brandberg, Suzanne Didonna, Annalyse McCoy, Paula Pizzi, Kris Kling, Ilana Becker, Alexandra Phillips, Kristen Cerelli, Nathan Spiteri, Costa Nicolas, Daniel Genalo, Lars Engstrom, Kaitlin Colombo, Tim Kubert, and Connor Fox.

Thank you to the baristas who took such good care of me as I wrote for hours, weeks, and months at my favorite café. You know who you are.

Thank you to my brother, who thanks to the change in time zones, I could call at two in the morning for a good laugh before sleeptime, and to Steve Bello for reading my many drafts and providing a writing retreat between a pond with swans and sandy dunes.

And to my mom, I love you. Thank you for the valuable

advice you always give me. And for reading to me as a kid every night before I went to sleep. Also, for all the journals, paint pens, and books you gave me. And thank you for allowing me to run around free when I was a child, barefoot in pigtails, my head filled with daydreams.